4140

£ 3
p3

A.N. Wilson was born in 1950 and educated at Rugby and New College, Oxford. A Fellow of the Royal Society of Literature, he has held a prominent position in the world of letters and has been Literary Editor of both the *Evening Standard* and *The Spectator*. As a writer his award-winning novels include *The Sweets of Pimlico* (John Llewellyn Rhys Prize), *The Healing Art* (Somerset Maugham Award), *Wise Virgin* (W.H. Smith Literary Award) and *Incline our Hearts* (E.M. Forster Prize). The last of these was the first of his celebrated sequence of novels, *The Lampitt Papers*. He is also a distinguished biographer. His non-fiction ranges from lives of Tolstoy (Whitbread Biography Award) and Hilaire Belloc to studies of both Jesus and St Paul. He lives in London.

'Excellent'   *Mail on Sunday*

'A hypnotic storyteller who leaves in his wake a trail of curiosity and unease'   *Anita Brookner*

'Absorbing . . . The suspense is admirably long, the ending a ricochet of surprises . . . beautifully observed'   *New Statesman*

'Carried along by acrid social comment – which is often mordantly funny – and a literary and intellectual liveliness, the narrative grips with a scaly claw'   *TLS*

D1081070

Other novels by A.N. Wilson

The Sweets of Pimlico (1977)
Unguarded Hours (1978)
Kindly Light (1979)
The Healing Art (1980)
Who was Oswald Fish? (1981)
Wise Virgin (1982)
Scandal (1983)
Gentlemen in England (1985)
Love Unknown (1986)
Stray (1987)
The Vicar of Sorrows (1993)
and

THE LAMPITT PAPERS
Incline Our Hearts (1988)
A Bottle in the Smoke (1990)
Daughters of Albion (1991)
Hearing Voices (1995)
A Watch in the Night (1996)

Dream Children

A.N. WILSON

An *Abacus* Book

First published in Great Britain by
John Murray (Publishers) Ltd 1998
This edition published by Abacus 1999

Copyright © A.N. Wilson 1998

The moral right of the author has been asserted.

All characters in this publication are fictitious and any resemblance to real persons, living or dead, is purely coincidental.

All rights reserved.
No part of this publication may be reproduced, stored in a retrieval system, or transmitted, in any form or by any means, without the prior permission in writing of the publisher, nor be otherwise circulated in any form of binding or cover other than that in which it is published and without a similar condition including this condition being imposed on the subsequent purchaser.

A CIP catalogue for this book is available from the British Library.

ISBN 0 349 11125 1

Typeset in Berling by M Rules
Printed and bound in Great Britain by
Clays Ltd, St Ives plc

Abacus
A Division of
Little, Brown and Company (UK)
Brettenham House
Lancaster Place
London WC2E 7EN

Dream Children

'He forced me, I'm telling you . . .'

'And you waited thirty-five years before you thought of telling anyone?'

'I have been hurting for thirty-five years . . . I have been in deep pain for thirty-five years. It was only my therapist who helped me recover so many of those memories which had been lost. So much was buried . . .'

In the tiny courtroom, the air-conditioning whirred. The figure slumped in a chair at the witness stand became silent, so that the air-conditioning and some awkward shuffles were all you heard.

'Are you okay?' asked the judge, a middle-aged woman of Chinese ancestry who had been widely praised for her firm, sympathetic handling of the case.

'I'm okay,' came the barely audible response.

'So,' persisted counsel. 'So much was buried that you forgot it for thirty-five years. Or could one put it another way: that it never in fact happened? That these memories

1

of yours are false memories? That these sexual encounters you supposedly had at the age of six, seven, eight years old . . .'

'Are you calling me a liar?'

'I am not calling anybody anything. But I put it to you again –'

'I am not a liar, I am not . . .'

'But you haven't told us how you can distinguish, have you, between things which happened in reality, and things which you believe to have happened because they have been suggested to you by your therapist –'

'Objection!'

'Objection sustained. Miss de Bono, you have established your point. Everybody now knows that there are difficulties in the way of making up our minds on this issue. But is it really necessary to put the plaintiff through quite such a relentless and repetitious cross-examination? In this trial, we have heard your client defending himself. We have heard character witnesses. We have heard both sides of the question debated by expert witnesses, experts in the field of psychotherapy and the recovery of memory after trauma. Are we really supposed to believe that the cause of truth is served by your baiting the plaintiff like this?'

'Your Honour, I am not deliberately baiting anyone. My client stands charged with repeated rape and molestation of the plaintiff when she was a child. If convicted, he stands to suffer whatever penalty is exacted of him; but he has already suffered the collapse of a professional reputation, and the destruction of his peace of mind. It is my duty to establish the truth. I shall do all in my power, your Honour, to do that, and to show that the submissions of the plaintiff have been founded on psychological theories which would have been considered arcane by voodoo witch-doctors or old shamans.'

'Objection!'

'Objection sustained, Mr Braithwaite.'

'Your Honour, I am not attempting to cause pain to this witness; I am attempting to arrive at the truth. That is what my client expects of me.'

'Very well, Miss de Bono. You may proceed.'

Only those who ever penetrated the courtroom itself during the trial were able to observe the extraordinary contrast between its smallness, its intimacy, and the huge audience who followed the deliberations there. Judge Chang, Christopher Braithwaite (for the plaintiff) and Deborah de Bono had, thanks to Court TV, become like figures in a soap opera.

The case raised many interesting legal points about the nature of evidence. Could a person be charged for a crime which might not have taken place? It was on this legal quibble that the magnificent de Bono had spent ten days before the trial. But on this point, the plaintiff's lawyers had won the day. It was deemed legitimate by the no less magnificent Chang that the nature of the alleged crimes was sufficiently serious for it to be proper to proceed on the basis of a hypothesis.

It was one of those cases which divided the nation. Those of a conservative disposition felt that the plaintiff was hysterical, probably deluded, certainly, which amounted to something pretty similar, female. Those of a more radical turn of mind saw the dignity and high standing of the defendant as all the more reason to investigate this thing thoroughly, to give the shaking, quivering plaintiff the benefit of the doubt.

All over the states of the Union, the drama in that tiny courtroom was relayed. This was not a case, like the William Kennedy Smith rape trial, or the Bork hearings, which satisfied a public appetite for seeing the famous brought low. No one had ever heard of any of the individuals involved in this drama. But it had the intrusiveness of Oprah. Clever articles in the *New Yorker* made the point that good liberal highbrows, who would switch off dating shows or fictionalized soap operas when they came on to the TV screen, were all held by this little story.

'So,' said de Bono, 'you tell us that you have never been able, in adult life, to form a sexual relationship with anyone?'

'That is correct.'

'Miss de Bono, we have dealt with this material many times.'

'I am aware of that, your Honour. But I would assure your Honour that there are elements here which I am not satisfied have been cleared up.'

'Proceed.'

'You see, everything in this case hangs on interpretation, doesn't it?'

'Are you calling me a liar?' This again from the witness stand. How often the question had been thrown back at de Bono in the previous week of cross-examination.

'I am not calling you a liar. Would you agree with me, however, that there might be many reasons – or no reasons at all – why a person finds it difficult to make sexual partners?'

De Bono paused for the cameras, and closed those moist lips. It was one of her favourite facial gestures. No one in the United States had supposed for an instant that this particular difficulty was one she had experienced herself.

'You look around you, and you haven't got a husband, got a boyfriend.'

'I'm telling you . . . it's because . . .'

'Go on.'

'It's because that man raped me when I was six years old. He forced me . . .'

The man sat, as he did throughout the trial, with his head bowed. All the TV viewers remarked on the curious physical transformation which overcame the plaintiff when she made these outbursts and denunciations. She seemed, then, less like a woman of forty-three than a child of six.

Chapter One

It was Bobs who broke the news to the three of them, to her mother, her grandmother, and to Catharine Cuffe: to the quorum, one might say. Others would hear eventually. The news spread – throughout the circle of Oliver's admirers; beyond London. It even found its way into the newspapers.

(Absurdly, as Janet said later to Catharine Cuffe, 'My first thought – my very first thought – was *who* is going to tell Margot Reisz?')

But to be quite certain that this was not one of the ridiculous shared jokes which Oliver and Bobs evidently enjoyed, Janet asked her grandchild to repeat herself.

'What did you say?'

'Ollie's getting married.'

'But he can't,' said Catharine Cuffe.

'Let her finish,' said Bobs's mother, Michal.

'He's been trying to tell us for weeks, but we wouldn't listen.'

'That,' said Janet Rose, 'is nonsense. We all knew about this friendship.'

'What friendship?' said Michal. 'I didn't even know of a friendship.'

Janet said, 'We had noticed his absences. He's missed several suppers with Margot.'

Catharine Cuffe said, 'A failure to have supper with Margot hardly constitutes the announcement of an engagement.'

'Only we didn't listen,' said Bobs O'Hara. She allowed the word 'listen' to shatter into syllables, particled by laughter.

There was a strong family resemblance between the grandmother, the mother and the child. But the face of Bobs, at ten years old, gave no clue whether it would develop into Janet's handsomeness, which increased with the years; or whether she would come to resemble her parents – a dull-looking fellow called Terence O'Hara, who had long ago remarried and of whom they saw little these days, or Michal, who in most lights was inescapably plain. It was a paradox that Michal should 'look like' Janet, since the features which looked so appealing on the one face did not immediately please on the other. They were features which might have struck the unsympathetic observer as failing to put themselves to good use. 'Michal doesn't make the best of herself' – advice, or more likely an *ex cathedra* pronouncement, from Margot Reisz (herself no oil painting) which seemed, like many cruel clichés, to be true.

The face which they all had in common was basically

oval. A complexion which in the mother was clear – the sort of thick-skinned face which always responded well to a little sunburn – in the daughter seemed merely sallow. Janet looked like an animated, highly intelligent gypsy. Her brown eyes were glossy. Her once black hair was now a white bob. Michal, who had begun to grow her hair out, had tresses which were too heavy, and which frequently looked unwashed even when they had only recently emerged from the shampoo.

Young Bobs had much of this gypsy look. Her fine little nose could grow into her grandmother's clever-bird beak, or grow to the point where people said, as they did of Michal, that she was 'beaky'. (Perhaps it would develop quite differently, this nose, and follow the O'Hara genes.) It was all too early to say. Bobs stood on the threshold of things. Her hair, almost black, had been lately cut, showing off the unformed beauty of her neck's nape and the purity of her throat. Adolescence had cast no blemish on her chin, which was as firm as her granny's but which could never (unlike Michal's) be described as jutting.

The lips of Bobs always curled in a smile which suggested a joke which few would be asked to share. Usually it was a joke between herself and Oliver Gold. They were all pretty used, the three of them, to the larks, japes and pranks of Bobs and Ol. This alone would have been enough to explain the silence, the agonized and palpable shock on their faces, when Bobs gigglingly broke the news of his engagement.

'Camilla, of course,' said Bobs mercilessly. 'In case you thought it was going to be someone else.'

'We haven't so much as met her,' said Janet.

'He says they are tremendously in love, and they can't wait to be married.'

Bobs's mother asked, 'You've known about this for some time, haven't you?' in accusatory tones.

Bobs coquettishly lowered her head and nibbled a piece of her hair. She stood there, in her white blouse and her grey pleated skirt. A school blazer hung from her shoulders like a cape, perpetually looking as if it was about to fall off. One of her knee-length white socks had fallen to the ankle of her spindly legs.

'Oh, this is serious,' said Catharine Cuffe, impatient with the teasing tone by which the news came out piecemeal. 'Why didn't you say?'

Bobs smiled, with inscrutable frivolity, and ignored their direct questions.

'She's got pots of money,' she said. 'She's just bought Ol a sports car.'

'I don't believe you,' said Janet. 'In all the time he has lived in this house, Oliver has ridden a bicycle. The sight of him free-wheeling down Muswell Hill in that little helmet – well, it's one of the sights of London.'

Her breeziness suggested a determination not to be broken by her grandchild's tease, rather than a failure to take seriously news which threatened to undermine all their lives.

'They say they're buying a country house, and that I can come and stay whenever I like,' said Bobs. 'But it won't really be the same as having him in the house, will it?'

At last, it seemed that she had caught the mood of desolation which engulfed the others, sympathized with it. She was neither an insensitive nor an unkind person, and she could not fail to know that Oliver Gold's marriage (an unlooked-for and unexpected development) would cause suffering to all her three hearers.

Janet Rose had made Oliver into something more than a son. His presence in her house elevated her existence; it made her more than a widow living in North London, and established her place in some intellectual scheme of things. Appearances were deceptive. Though Janet looked intelligent, she wasn't – or not intelligent in the way that she and her late husband would have chosen. Nature seemed to have drawn her for a part. Her high-cheek-boned and still beautiful face could easily have been that of a poetess who dined with the Sitwells, or a minor Bloomsbury who had flirted with Virginia Woolf. Even without her late husband's social and literary aspirations, she might, without such an appearance, have felt constrained to struggle against the humdrum, and to declare herself something rather more bohemian and interesting. The presence in her house of a genuine intellectual had been something which did more than enhance her standing in the eyes of neighbours like Margot Reisz. It had quite simply given her something to live for. There are women in oriental cultures to whom is entrusted the nurture of the next enlightened one or avatar before his public emergence as a saviour. The noise of Oliver Gold's portable typewriter rattling in her attic rooms had given Janet Rose a comparable feeling of weighty vocation. She did not need the repeated assurances of Catharine Cuffe that Oliver Gold was a remarkable writer – one who, given the time and the nurture, would flower as a genius. His first published books were only apprentice work, which told nothing of the fire which Janet knew to smoulder within him.

Like the other two women, Janet was aware that it was more than a purely intellectual fascination which bound her to Oliver Gold. She did not hope to marry him herself, although, at sixty-two, she was barely ten years his senior. But she found every detail of his physical appearance obsessively interesting and took as much delight in (for example) his clothes, as might a mistress or a wife.

Catharine Cuffe, a pallid and very thin redhead of thirty-five, had been responsible for introducing Oliver Gold into this house. He had been her tutor at the university. She had been 'attached' to him, almost from the very first hour which she had spent in his college rooms. Remarkably early in their relationship, considering his well-known distaste for intimacy or commitment, he had accepted Miss Cuffe as someone who would occupy a special role in his life. He had, for instance, spent Christmas with her family in the Midlands, and accompanied them on their summer holidays in Wales. This arrangement had continued until Miss Cuffe had moved into Janet Rose's house.

Following in his footsteps, Cuffe had written a Ph.D. thesis (on the Idealists) and eventually secured a teaching post at one of the London colleges. It was at this time that she had befriended Michal O'Hara (who was in the middle of a painful process of divorce and was slowly reverting to being Michal Rose). An early infatuation between the two women soon became a thing of all-pervading obsessional intensity. Catharine Cuffe had moved into 12 Wagner Rise.

But ever since she had known him, Oliver had been Cuffe's chief intellectual passion, and she had judged all her own achievements by the sole criterion of whether they matched, or were worthy of, his standards. Even when they did not see one another, they would correspond: long, calligraphed letters on the college writing paper from him, typed affairs on copy paper from her. In these letters, even more than in their conversations, they appeared to share and to understand all that mattered in life. There was undoubtedly an element of self-consciousness in their correspondence – as though they wrote, if not for publication, then for an audience not themselves. She used her letters to sound out ideas; what was so flattering, he did the same, and she was convinced that some of his letters to her contained undeveloped thoughts of an unrivalled importance. In the course of this deep sharing, she had come to feel that she knew Oliver Gold better than anyone ever had, or ever could. This confidence allowed her to accept, without rancour, the fact that Oliver was twittered over by so many adoring disciples. 'The Vestals', Cuffe called them, though they were by no means all virgins. Even Janet and Michal had shown an element of silliness from time to time in a slavish desire to be Oliver's best-loved disciple. And the sycophancy of Margot Reisz was something embarrassing to behold. Cuffe could cope. None of the others had what she had.

There were matters which were not discussed between them – of course there were. They were not, she had reasoned, college kids, swapping intimacies over mugs of instant coffee. He had never asked her, for example, why she had chosen to move in with Michal. The emotional explanations did not need to be made: the situation was obvious enough. Garish bedroom confidences would not have been welcome, even had Cuffe been the sort of person who wanted to unburden herself of such matters to her old tutor.

And this was what he always was, and always would be, her old tutor; a fact, perhaps, which strengthened her wish to assume that he was either a celibate, or one who chose to satisfy 'that side of life' with those of his own sex. Had there not, even when he was still at the college, been 'forays' to London? She had guessed so, but never considered for a moment that they could interrupt his intellectual union with herself. It had never crossed her mind that he would wish to involve himself with any woman, apart from herself, in that way. When she had been on the point of suggesting such things in the old days, an unspoken but palpable feeling had forced her to hold back, so sure had she been that this was not something he wished for. The risk of destroying what they had, their uniquely intense intellectual friendship, was not worth making.

'Camilla is quite a countrywoman,' Bobs had resumed. 'Daddy hunts.'

At 12 Wagner Rise, there was something almost insulting about this piece of information. They were not the sort to indulge in such activities themselves, and the newspapers which were to be found draped over the backs of Janet's kitchen chairs, or put down to catch Hector's droppings, on the whole disapproved of field sports, as of the class who indulged in them.

'And there's pots and pots of money.'

'You already said that,' said Miss Cuffe.

Janet said, 'Oliver does not need money.' This had become an article of faith for her, in rather the same way that Cuffe had chosen to deny his need for sexual fulfilment. 'I've provided him –' Janet checked herself, lest this should suggest something too proprietorial. She switched to the royal, or papal, plural. 'We've given him all he needs: two rooms at the top of the house. Complete privacy and calm. He has more than once told me that it is the fulfilment of a dream.'

Oliver had known them, in the way that so many people knew Janet and Hensleigh Rose, for nearly twenty years. As a young don, he had been to Hensleigh's parties, in those days of crowd and noise. The cavernous Arts and Crafts house, with its gabled attics, its spacious landings, its large parquet floor, and its drawing-room looking towards Alexandra Palace had often filled with poets, journalists, editors of small magazines, politicians and novelists. True, perhaps, the crowds had always chiefly consisted of those, like Margot Reisz, who did not belong to any of these categories themselves, but who liked to drink wine with them. But silence and emptiness had begun to possess 12 Wagner Rise, even before Hensleigh had his heart attack. The ochre and green hessian on the walls, and the slatted sauna-style cupboard doors, so daring when installed, had begun to look outmoded even before his cremation at Golders Green. And the Heal's furniture, all bought new for their marriage, had begun to look scuffed.

It was not morbidity which made Janet, in those early months of widowhood, consciously allow silence and emptiness to repossess that big house. She needed to take stock, and to discover that a newer, quieter phase of life had been reached. And sure enough, in time, the house had come into its own. Michal had returned when Bobs was still a baby. Lotte, the Austrian nanny, was installed in the attic, in a room with its own bathroom. Janet, who understood the need for personal space, sold the Heal's dining table and chairs, and converted the dining-room into her own spacious bedsit. With Michal and Bobs occupying the first floor, that still left the two rooms on the second floor unoccupied.

They had all liked Cuffe, even Lotte. Bobs could not

remember the time when Cuffe and Michal did not live together. Cuffe occupied what had been Hensleigh's study – a large room on the first floor, next to Michal's bedroom. There were all those empty shelves, after Hensleigh's library had been sold, and they had seemed to await – so Janet said – the arrival of this philosopher's voluminous, if austere, library.

'Your books are not as pretty as Hensleigh's, but I'm sure they're much cleverer,' had been Janet's observation as she watched the many paperbacks and imprints of academic presses take the place of those nineteen-thirties poets (many of them signed), the Hogarth Press first editions, the Victorian sets, and the unbound, greyish-white volumes picked up on visits to Paris, of Colette, Montherlant, Proust, Camus, Gide, Sartre. (Hensleigh, Janet often said if she felt she was losing out in any conversational contest, was *just* too late to have met Proust. She spoke as if in different circumstances – had he only taken care of himself and lived to see old age – the great novelist would often have been seen at 12 Wagner Rise, eating cubes of cheese from a cocktail stick and drinking coarse red wine, in those high old days of the Roses' early married life.)

Cuffe had brought companionship, sometimes a rather stormy companionship, for Michal. More than that, she had converted the atmosphere in the house. After her arrival, the place no longer felt dominated by the baby; by Michal's guilty feelings of inadequacy as a mother; by Lotte's whimsy; by Janet's own need to show herself a good grandmother. The first two years of Cuffe, however, had been but a preparation for the arrival of Oliver Gold. It would seem as though they were like the biblical pair, Cuffe and Oliver: that where she went, he went; that his gods (if existent) were hers; and now, her people, his. The introduction of Oliver Gold into 12 Wagner Rise had been precisely what was necessary – they all saw that now; and it had happened at just the right moment, when relations between Michal and Cuffe had been frayed to the point of dissolution. From Janet's point of view, Oliver brought something which she had hardly dreamed she would have again after Hensleigh's death: a clever man under her own roof. It did not matter that she was not herself a clever woman: she throve on the company of the clever, which was why, at the height of Hensleigh's success (and there had been dinners, as well as the 'little drinks', at Number 12), she had been an almost happy woman. There was no witticism or *aperçu* falling from clever lips in their living-room, of which she would have been capable herself; but this did not prevent her from keenly appreciating such talk. (Terrible old rogue as he was, Claudio Lewis made her *roar* – and he was almost the only 'name' from those days who bothered to keep up.)

While having an untrained mind, Janet could understand the intellectual's restlessness in the social scene. She knew that when Oliver came to live with her, he did not come because he wanted a succession of 'little drinks' or dinners. He was paying her a deeper compliment than that. He wanted solitude, long days in which to think; he wanted relief from the college round, or the need to earn his living as a writer. She had learnt to empathize with his overpowering and communicated sense of life's seriousness. She knew that as an inspired teacher and (in his young manhood) a sought-after dinner-table wit, Oliver Gold could easily talk away his fifth decade, just as he had talked away the previous four. And she discerned what emptiness and desolation would result if he had gone on as before. He wanted, in short, a room of one's own: and she was able to provide him with two – an attic bedroom and a sitting-room. Far from expecting her to furnish them, Oliver had requested that she take most of the furniture out. He had kept the bed – a large bed which had belonged to Hensleigh's parents. Each room had a writing table and a few upright chairs. When he wished to repose he lay on the bed, so there was no other upholstered furniture, no pictures (she had offered him the Topolski drawing of Hensleigh but he'd turned it down) and remarkably few books.

To avoid the embarrassment of Lotte's being obliged to share his bathroom, they had moved the Austrian girl down to the first floor, next to Bobs's room. At a slightly later stage, Bobs kept this room as her menagerie, and moved in to sleep in the small box-room next to Oliver's study.

His needs were modest. Since all three women, Janet, Michal and Cuffe, shared a tactile obsession with Oliver, his hair, his beard, his skin, they delighted in buying him clothes, each fashioning him in some image which she had of his excellence. From Cuffe had come the dark-blue linen suit from Liberty's; from Janet, the Panama for those days when he would read in the garden; from Michal, the Peruvian slipper socks and the shoulder bag. Janet's table provided the food. He paid no rent, made no contribution to electricity or telephone bills. For the first few years, he had subsisted on the small trickle earned by his books, and by payment for the broadcasts he still gave on the wireless; but since his inheritance, a legacy which came to him by surprise about a year ago, he had been able to live without paid work.

To be told now by the grinning Bobs that Oliver had a fiancée with 'pots of money' was not merely shocking, but somehow demeaning. What would their secular saint need with such pots?

'He's taking me for a ride in the sports car,' said Bobs.

'What about Hector?' asked her mother.

'He's all right there.'

'He's not – he'll nibble the telephone wires.'

'Oh, give him to Lotte!' she exclaimed. And for the first time since her grandchild had come out with the news, Janet wondered whether Bobs was truly delighted by Oliver's engagement, or whether she too, in her very different way, viewed it with the same dismay as the rest of them.

Chapter Two

The silence which followed the child's departure, broken only by the improbable sound of the sports car revving up outside and careering off in the direction of Queen's Wood, was one of shock. Even Hector, a large, pink-eyed white rabbit, looked out of countenance, and sat on the stripy Heal's zebra rug, quivering.

This quite unlooked-for, unexpected and unwelcome news threatened a blank, if not a dissolution. All three of them, seven years before, had passed through a period of darkness and twisted unhappiness which the arrival of Oliver Gold in the attic had helped to resolve. Because Oliver was that rare being, a good man, his presence in the household had made them all aspire to a harmony, both within and among themselves, which made them feel ashamed when they recalled the raw tempests of the earlier phase.

Janet's early widowhood had been bitter, dark and raw. Friends, it would seem, had not really been friends, and few of those who came to Hensleigh's funeral had bothered to keep up with her. She had sold the library on impulse, not because, at that stage, she really needed the money. A man from an auction house had been to see if Hensleigh's 'archive' were saleable to an American university. They had kept all the correspondence from the little magazine, and there were letters from several 'names'. The preparation of this material for the valuer had revealed to Janet a Hensleigh of whom she had been scarcely aware. She'd known about the long-standing affair with Poison Ivy. But the others? The letters which she had forked into many a garden bonfire forced the humiliating question – how many people knew of these infidelities? How many of those who came for the 'little drinks' knew how far things had gone with Jean, his secretary at the little magazine? And Vera – whom Janet had always considered a friend. And Dorothy; and Lucy and Molly. By the time their letters had been destroyed, there was not much left of the 'archive', and she was so angry with Hensleigh that she almost believed it served him right, to be deemed too small a fish for the American librarians to fry. This too, though, was a difficult lesson to learn. For if Hensleigh had been rather less in the scheme of things than she had always imagined, where did that leave her? She had seriously supposed in their 'heyday' that he might be the sort of man of whom a subsequent generation would require a biography. All that was saleable – little more than business letters from Walter de la Mare, T.S. Eliot, F.R. Leavis and

Lady Rhondda – had fitted into the auctioneer's quite small attaché case.

Oliver's arrival did more than assuage the broken heart of a wronged wife. Since Oliver, she had been able to canonize the man she now referred to as 'my darling husband'. She could overlook the affairs, and her marriage began to seem, at first in conversational recollection and then in memory itself, an intellectual partnership. She actually forgot that no one wanted to buy Hensleigh's books and papers. It began to seem as though the little magazine, and a short spell as the literary editor of *Punch*, had been rather 'important'; and as though the dinners and the 'little drinks' had a place in the history of letters. Those who had graced the Roses' living-room became muddled in recollection with those who had not, so that it was not exactly a lie to remember Olivia Manning and Ernest Raymond and Stephen Spender and Cyril Connolly holding out their glasses for more Chianti as the *bons mots* fell from their lips. Some of them had been there; but some of the remembered *mots* had really been read by Janet in library books. It was with complete seriousness that she spoke of Hensleigh's reviews, the magazine itself, his hours at the bar of the Savage Club, and his rather slavish cultivation of the more sociable litterateurs of his day as a 'contribution'. Oliver said nothing to contradict her when she remembered some improbable combination of friends quaffing in her drawing-room. (H.G. Wells, whom she remembered coming to dinner, had been dead before she and Hensleigh moved into the house.) They were names seized out of the air; but Oliver would appear to agree with her that the standards of literary life had declined terribly since beloved Hensleigh corrected the punctuation of Muriel Spark, or capped one of the wittier sayings of Kingsley Amis.

The actual quality of life with Hensleigh, either as it had first been lived – that long disillusioning marriage which they had filled with other people and alcohol for fear of finding it empty or dead, descending into regrets and illness, and ending in his death – or as it had been reinter-preted when she had discovered his Soho luncheons with Vera or Molly, when she had had to substitute in her mind the sexless wit of a semi-invalid for the priapic capers of a brutal erotomaniac, 'at it' to the end – had given place to much more comforting pictures, in which she herself, the Mrs Carlyle or Beatrice Webb of Wagner Rise, could be seen as an essential ingredient in a partnership of which posterity would have an awestruck view. Oliver's patience, his capacity to listen and not to belittle her, gave her a sense of self-worth which had never been hers since the 'heyday'.

Oliver's presence, moreover, stopped Janet quarrelling with her daughter, a person whom she had always found disappointing and irritating. There was an insuperable absence of sympathy between the two women, based less on a failure of understanding than on a mutual ability to understand too well.

Michal knew that she disappointed her mother's hopes.

Janet knew that in Michal's scale of values, they were not hopes which a sane person would nurture. There had never been a time when anyone in her parents' circle (not counting the licensed jesters such as Claudio Lewis) had been anything but leftist. But beyond writing about it, or talking about it, few of Hensleigh's friends (unless one counted the occasional MP) had done much to bring human betterment to pass. Janet and Hensleigh's function had, apparently, been to create a climate. Michal could not see how the 'little drinks', or the holidays in the Dordogne, the raised voices in Soho restaurants or the hurried completion of book reviews furthered the socialist position. She had, in any case, a temperament which undermined pleasure by being able to focus more on the negative possibilities of any course of action or social possibility than its positive. To Janet's question, 'Why don't you ask X or Y back to the house?', questions which had been insistently made since Michal's first term at Gospel Oak Primary School, the truthful answers would either have been, 'Because they bore me,' or, 'Because it would embarrass me if they met you.'

Sometimes Michal had hinted at these answers, but she had learned that this truth was more kindly and opaquely conveyed by a truculent shrug of the shoulders. The pointless grind of school and college, coinciding with a period of life (from infancy to young womanhood) when, as far as Michal could see, one was bound to be low spirited, gave place, eventually, to the grown-up things – marriage, a career.

Terence had been chosen for his incompatibility with Janet and Hensleigh. Michal had evidently been so attracted by this that she had overlooked his incompatibility with herself. He was one of the first persons she had met who amused her. His dismissive view of her work – helping a lot of layabouts who deserved a clip round the ear – had been the sort of breezy insensitive idea which in the early days had made her laugh. It was hard to bear the discovery that it was her, and not her work, which he failed to take seriously.

For that reason, she had begun to find a dogged fulfilment in some of the work which she had undertaken since moving back to 12 Wagner Rise. Work with young truants appealed to her own sense that school was a waste of time. Their preference for vandalizing telephone kiosks to 'projects' in which they imagined what it was like to be a Chartist, required, in Michal's mind, no explanation. The fact that such boys came from dislocated backgrounds did not always make them attractive individuals. But Michal could not lose her sense of the injustice of life, and this consciousness increased when her own daughter grew close in age to that of her 'cases'. No wonder Bobs tripped off happily to school – at first strapped into the child's seat on the back of Oliver's bike – and no wonder that there had been complaints from that very primary school where she herself had been as a girl. Bobs's problems were classic manifestations of the child of a broken marriage – an inability at times to concentrate on her work, a slowness to make friends, even, briefly, a tendency to kleptomania. They were nothing, when compared with the problems of the boys whom Michal met in the course of her work. Bobs was never going to get into trouble, as Michal's boys so regularly got into trouble. She lived in a large comfortable house where her grandmother complained about bills but where there was no shortage of money. The fact that there really was, and continued to be, poverty in London was something of which Janet seemed only notionally aware.

There had been rows in the old days about it. She had questioned her mother's right to call herself a socialist. The intolerance and ignorance of comfortable people, however enlightened their supposed views, enraged one who actually saw the inside of council flats, probation officers' rooms, magistrates' courts. Oliver Gold's coming calmed such quarrels. (Michal had attributed it to an instinctive sense, felt by all the women, that he did not view women as objects of sexual desire.) He took her seriously. He listened to what she said. He questioned her, sympathetically and intelligently, not merely about her work, but about her views. Michal regretted, during her early conversations with Oliver, that she had read Social Sciences rather than philosophy at university. His ability to discuss the technicalities of this subject with Cuffe was like a private language between them. But though Cuffe liked excluding Michal from such talk, Oliver wanted to know Michal's views about everything – about music, sexual morality (though not their own), crime, punishment, art, theatre, politics.

This was in the days before he retreated altogether from the world, and she found it flattering that he used her as a vehicle to rehearse discussions which would sometimes form part of his colloquies on the wireless.

The first few years of her association with Cuffe had been stormy. Still bitterly aggrieved at Terence's departure, Michal had brought much 'unfinished business' into her new relationship. There had been not merely verbal exchanges but actual fights between the two friends, terrible quarrels about what, on recollection, seemed to have been nothing at all. Cuffe's discipleship had been an early bone of contention. Michal had been furiously jealous of Oliver, and hated him before she met him. In spite of all Cuffe's protestations, Michal assumed that the tutor and the beautiful redhead had been lovers, or wished to become lovers.

Even before Oliver abandoned his college fellowship, and gave himself up to the life of a scholarly recluse in Janet's attic, Michal had fallen in love with him. The obsessive fear that he loved Cuffe, or that Cuffe loved him, had tricked her into supposing that she hated him. Only after an evening when he had supped in Janet's kitchen and accidentally left behind a woollen jersey, did the strange truth surprise her. She came upon this object, a chunky, navy-blue sweater, while the others were kissing him in the hall, and impulsively ran upstairs with it to her bedroom. Burying her nose into it, and savouring his smell, she had known that overwhelming, mystical joy which was always the accompaniment of falling in love. Seeing her tears, half an hour later, Cuffe had been peremptory.

'Michal, you must fight this jealousy. It's not worthy of you. Oliver's not a threat. He's not. Do you understand that?'

She had known from the first that there was no hope of Oliver feeling this way about her; it would have led to total rupture with Cuffe, and that – after all the pain of her divorce – was something which Michal could not contemplate. It was safer that they should suppose she was still jealous of Oliver. Her love was her secret, and she knew that if she never spoke of it, she could at least have the exquisite delight of his living in the same house, eating at the same table, and sharing every day with her. Once he had moved in, she sensed that he must be aware of the way she felt; in time, her love evolved. It really was possible to sublimate it for the general good, so long as he was there, so long as she could sometimes have conversations with him *à deux*, and could sometimes help Lotte make his bed. By now, seven years on, he had become part of the fabric of everyday existence. Life with Cuffe, Janet and Bobs was immeasurably enriched by the presence of this very special friend. And there was the added bonus (since Michal recognized that she had inherited from Janet a lack of maternal sympathy) that he was so very good with Bobs. It would have been less than satisfactory if the child's only companion had been Lotte, who for all her virtues was a little simple. As it was, Michal sometimes thought she did not need to send Bobs to school, since friendship with Oliver was the best possible education which any parent could hope for.

Fearful of the effects of the divorce on her child, Michal had developed, over the years, a calm sense that, even though Bobs had lost a father, she had gained someone so much more interesting and sympathetic. Oliver was an uncle, a brother, a godfather, and a friend to Bobs. He had also taken over from Lotte many of the functions of a nurse or governess, collecting the child from school, preparing high tea, taking her to Brownies. He had enabled Michal to resume her career full-time, and she had found profound satisfaction in the discovery that she was good at her job, work whose virtue she could not question and whose practical benefits were palpable. And this made her easier to live with, and happier with Cuffe.

Catharine Cuffe, not the sort of person who enjoyed shouting, had been emotionally battered by her first eighteen months with Michal. Once the quiet regime had been established at 12 Wagner Rise, she found yet new reasons to love and revere Oliver Gold. A line from a childhood hymn, *Thou hast made all things well,* fitted the case. Cuffe's relationship with Michal had been, to start with, of the most painful. Love made it impossible to imagine giving it up; but the further they went together, the more, as well as loving, they hated one another; they fought, they stormed, they rowed. She now saw that many of these early difficulties had really been of a practical character. Michal had constantly accused the unmarried and childless Cuffe of uncharity and lack of sympathy. Cuffe just did not see – Michal accused – that a mother needed to spend some time with a child. Cuffe saw it all too well, but resented every second Michal spent with Bobs, changing her nappies, drooling over her, reading to her. Every kiss planted on Bobs's head was a kiss which could have been given to her. By the time Oliver arrived, Bobs was a demanding three-year-old, capable of charging into her mother's bed in the middle of the night, yelling or whimpering for attention, wetting herself, banging, screaming, and in all ways spoiling things. None of them had predicted that Oliver would take over so much of the work which should perhaps have been done by Lotte and Michal. But his genius as a child-minder left Cuffe and Michal time for one another, time to develop those tender and sympathetic ties which were the beginnings of their real love. The first few years had been a prelude; neither woman wanted to go back to that; now they could sleep long nights together, and go out together, without any feeling of anxiety that the child was being neglected. Cuffe even managed quite long periods when she was able to forget her resentment of Bobs, though she had never been able to like the child, and had managed so to order things that she had hardly ever been alone in a room with her.

She knew that her destructive feelings of envy and anger against the child were unworthy – and here was another way in which Oliver's presence came to their help. For at a profound level, Cuffe always wanted to be on her best behaviour with Oliver, and she would never have been able to own the petty jealousy she felt of Bobs. Little-minded squabbles and jealousies detracted from the Good Life, which it was surely their aim to pursue, and from those pure intellectual endeavours which, as an under-graduate, she had learnt from him were the highest goals. Since Oliver's arrival in the attic seven years before, Catharine Cuffe had discovered not only that she was a much nicer person to live with, but also that she had new reserves of intellectual energy. Her mind, in her thirties, was more absorbent, pliable, inventive, than it had been in her twenties. The thesis on T.H. Green had, on rereading, seemed to her so limited; she had completely rewritten it before it was published by one of the university presses. Another philosophical work, highly derivative of conver-sations with Oliver himself, was planned. This time, she had in mind a general, not an academic, audience. Oliver had given her the idea of working through J.S. Mill's *The Subjection of Women* and asking how many of the great Victorian's precepts were helped or hindered by modern legislation, by working conditions, by attitudes deemed 'feminist', and in general by the Way We Live Now. Dryness which in her twenties had been merely dry, devel-oped, in her thirties, a bloom of wit. The lectures in which Cuffe tried to work out some of her ideas had been crowded. There was the distinct likelihood (her striking appearance was no drawback) that she would herself become a cult. Oliver had introduced her to another pupil of his who was a producer of serious arts and discussion programmes, and Cuffe had made several television appearances.

It was all this, the fabric of life itself, which was threatened by the news that Oliver Gold was engaged to be married to someone called Camilla.

When the roar of the sports car died away, the three women sat in a silence broken only by Cuffe striking a match and holding a quivering flame to the end of her mild Silk Cut. Each contemplated the painfulness of life before Oliver, and dreaded a return to its uncertainties and tempests. Each wondered whether the past seven years had been no more than a period of truce and felt a little like African generals, watching the departure of UN peacekeeping troops over their dusty borders, conscious that it was only a matter of time before tribal hostilities resumed.

Even the thought that they now had a common enemy, the unknown Camilla, brought small consolation, since each of them had sufficient experience to know that such an alliance could easily awaken rivalries and jealousies best left unspoken. For – this was the most dangerous question of all – why had they each, distinctly and without discussion, decided so firmly long ago that Oliver was not of the marrying kind?

Unable, quite, to lead a frontal assault on the fiancée

whom none of them had even met, Janet allowed herself to come out with, 'It seems so very unlike Oliver to care about money.'

'It was Bobs,' said Michal. 'Bobs said "pots of money".'

'It was Oliver, we trust, rather than Bobs, who has just driven away in a sports car.'

'There was a time' – Cuffe establishing by this remark that she had known Oliver well before his arrival at Wagner Rise – 'when he drove a little open car. We spoke of it often when we were undergraduates.'

Such an utterance, news to Janet and Michal, immediately created the sense that Cuffe was staking out some kind of claim.

There was brittleness in Michal's, 'No one minds Oliver driving a car. That's hardly the point.'

'No, it isn't,' stated her mother. With her long olive-coloured hands on which the veins stood up like wrinkly earthworms crawling beneath the surface of a tight glove, Janet patted her exquisitely combed white hair. Her brows were naturally black, and these dark arches lent extra brilliance to her eyes. She wore a scarlet Indian kaftan. 'Do you know, Catharine, I think I could smoke one of your cigarettes.'

Janet was one of those who smoked occasionally, normally only at parties, always taking from others. It was not, therefore, unheard-of that she should be lighting up, but the gesture signalled something unusual.

'That bloody rabbit,' said Cuffe.

Hector had begun lolloping towards the telephone flex, which he had a nervous compulsion to nibble.

'I'll find Lotte,' said Janet.

'No,' said Michal, scooping the animal up. 'I'll put him in the hutch.'

They watched her through the window, going down to the hutch at the end of the garden.

'We're all becoming slaves to that child's animals,' said Cuffe, with a bitter exhalation of smoke.

When Michal came back, she said, 'We have got to assume that Oliver has simply fallen in love.'

'Is there any need to state the obvious?' asked her mother.

'Sometimes,' said Cuffe.

'Scoring points will get us nowhere,' said Janet.

'But recognizing the truth can help us come to terms with it,' said Michal in a tone which suggested her friend needed defence from unprovoked assault. 'Admitting the truth might prepare us for what is to happen next. We all *know* Oliver. We all know he isn't the man who would . . .'

She had wanted to say that Oliver was not a man who would let them down, or behave dishonourably, but there were so many things which they had assumed he would never do that any statement of them would seem lame.

'We thought we knew him,' said Cuffe. 'That is why this news is a shock.'

'If it had been some scholar, we could have understood,' said Janet. 'But somebody from a sale-room! It seems hardly his world.'

'Bobs might have got that wrong,' said Cuffe.

'She said it most distinctly,' said Michal, who, having defended her lover against Janet, now felt the need to defend her daughter against Cuffe. 'A child wouldn't even have heard of those grand auction houses.'

'Those air-headed girls with rich fathers often work in the auction houses as a way of finding some empty-headed braying husband in a tweed suit,' said Cuffe.

'That's what I meant,' said Janet. 'Hunting! Bobs said her father hunted.'

'It's hard to see Ol on a horse,' said Michal – but her attempt at levity only deepened the atmosphere of gloom.

'We've always let him come and go as he pleased,' said Janet.

'He's not one of Bobs's animals,' snapped Cuffe.

'Of course not, that's not what I meant. But if he wanted to go away and stay with friends, we made nothing of it. He can go out in the evenings. Of course he did, sometimes, and not just to Margot Reisz's weekly supper. But I mean, we never thought . . .'

'What did we think?' asked Michal. The others hoped she would not say, but words were blurting out, and there was no stopping her. 'Did we think he was going to concerts on his own? Or did we think he was on the prowl, and that we'd rather not ask? Didn't we all guess that there was *something*? That he was in the parks, or hovering outside railway stations, or wherever chaps go?'

'Is Oliver a chap?' asked Cuffe.

'For the purposes of this discussion, evidently,' fired back Michal.

'We never thought about it,' said Cuffe, 'because we never needed to think about it.'

'Oh, that isn't true,' said Michal. 'And you know it isn't true. We all thought there was *something*. Maybe we were all frightened, when he went out, that he would come back and say he had been stopped by the police.'

'By the police!' exclaimed Janet. 'I never heard anything so preposterous.'

'Cottaging,' said Michal.

'You know nothing about that side of life,' said Cuffe. 'Absolutely nothing.'

'That's because it suits us to know nothing,' said Michal. 'Okay, I'm not saying he was breaking the law. He might have gone to bars for all I knew or cared. I didn't want to know – and all the time, we were *blind*. He was looking for a *woman*. A woman, for Christ's sake.'

The knowledge that Oliver, for the last six months or more, had been wooing a young woman of good family, rather than enjoying the emotional neutrality of bachelor escapades, was undoubtedly one explanation for their sense of let-down. It was questionable whether Janet or Cuffe wanted it so prosaically explained. In common with nearly all the residents of Wagner Rise, they associated country life with stupidity. The sports car, the pots of money and the hunters, so artlessly described by Bobs, appeared to be a betrayal of intellect as well as trust.

'I have brought him down,' said Lotte, entering the room with Cuthbert the Cockerel, a noisy and struggling presence in her arms. 'The rat is in his cage, and that I can endure. But the cock in the bedroom – Bobs said she would put him back in the run before she goes out.'

Chapter Three

The trees were coming into leaf, so that Bobs could lean back, as the Mazda gathered speed, and watch a flitting kaleidoscope of pale green and pale blue, and the puffy white clouds over Hampstead. Though she sometimes let her eyes drop, she did not turn to see his face, but watched the rapid and efficient movement of large brown brogues on the car pedals. It was like the time he had taken her into a church and shown her how to play the organ. She had not known that you played with your feet.

The engine noise, louder than any organ, made talk impossible and that was what they both needed: no talk, but the open air, and the beginnings of May, and the small car enclosing them both and conveying them away, away.

They drove for an hour, perhaps, sometimes stuck in traffic, but more usually whizzing along. There was a bit of motorway, then suburban trees again, then down into the bursting buds of Hampstead Heath. It was a funny, trance-like experience for her, this experience of speed. It had always been just the two of them, for as long as she remembered. The knowledge that it was all to end sharpened the sense of togetherness, made it poignant. She was not thinking, exactly. There was no sequence to the tableaux of the previous six months which flitted into consciousness. The secret teas with Camilla, who was so much more friendly than Cuffe. At first it had been a collusion; now Bobs wondered if she had been bought, 'had'. To accompany Oliver to the Fountain Restaurant at Fortnum and Mason, when the others, if they gave it a thought, supposed them to be flying a kite on the Heath, had felt like a game at first. He defined everything in terms of games; and this new lady had seemed like another piece of playfulness, like their private language for things, their teases. Only the real games they liked to play – Snakes and Ladders, Ludo, Spit, Snap, Rummy, two-handed whist, Monopoly, chess, tennis – were acknowledged and spoken about to the others. There had been others of which they did not speak, and Camilla had, it would seem, been such as these. Games are only fun if you stick to the rules. That was one of his (their) sayings. Bobs had so entered into his secret devotion to Camilla that she had felt, on occasion, a crush on the lady herself. The world represented by Camilla was jollier than Michal's. There were larks and laughs over the ice-cream sodas. There had even been the promise that they would go to the pet department at Harrods to buy a longed-for dog.

It had even seemed something of a lark when he had made the curious decision to use Bobs as the messenger by which the news of the engagement should be conveyed to the others. Bobs had initially considered it funny, in the sense both of weird and of laughable, but this was because (she could not say why) laughter had become almost her only way of expressing emotion, so that except in extreme cases, when she found herself sobbing – at nothing, mean school-mates averred – she appeared, as she did to Michal and Granny, to be an uncaring and satirical little person.

He had not meant to be unkind, making her tell them the news. He never meant to be unkind, even when, as happened, he hurt her. Some of the hurtful things flitted into her kaleidoscope of mental tableaux. But most of the things remembered – holding hands at the great fireworks display on Primrose Hill, and watching those explosions and cascades of light in the November sky; rowing in broiling weather on the Serpentine, and making paper hats out of a newspaper to keep off the glare; swimming at the Lido in Parliament Hill Fields; afternoon visits to the cinema; dancing in his room when he played *Swan Lake* on the turntable; visiting the Planetarium; choosing their books for the holiday in the Welsh cottage; listening to him reading aloud – Andrew Lang, *Vice Versa*, Gillian Avery, Noel Streatfield; bathing in the sea; picnics in the snow; sweet dreams on his pyjama'd shoulders – most of the things, were all joy.

There was no need for any other friendship. She kept him abreast of what was going on at school: the incredible ignorance of the other girls, who rotted their minds with pop music and computers; their fallings-out and reconcili-ations; the lengths to which Carol Davidson would go to torment Miss Mack; the strange fact that Sarah dominated the pack, in spite of wearing a tooth brace, whereas Madeline Stirling had been consistently mocked for doing so; Jeannette's dishonesty, Mandy's precocity with boys. All this was a pantomime played out for his amusement. That was why she went out to school, while he stayed behind in the attic, thinking his strange thoughts and writ-ing his incomprehensible books. She was collecting things to amuse him, not having experiences. She was learning to be the most detached and non-participatory observer of the human scene.

She did not envy girls with parents. It was necessary, of course, to conceal from them all the true state of things at 12 Wagner Rise. The very last thing she wished to do was to expose herself as a butt for their curiosity or ridicule. She sometimes had even referred to Oliver as 'my Dad', when they had seen him waiting at the school gate; though all the girls knew he was not her biological father, they had been given to understand that he 'lived with' Michal. Plenty of the girls had mothers who lived with a man. None of them had ever been to the house, so there had never been the need to apprise them of Cuffe's existence. They could not avoid knowing about Granny, since she insisted on coming to those many school events in which Bobs avoided playing much part – such as the annual drama; but she had done her best to keep her in the background. The very worst manifestation of Granny's visits to the school had come like a bolt from the blue one day in the middle of English.

'Perhaps you'd like to read this one, Roberta?' had been Miss Mooney's question. A silly, bright expression had enlivened the woman's face as she had confided to the twenty other girls in the class, 'Roberta's family were very good friends with the man who wrote this poem. Isn't that right, Roberta?'

It was the poem about the Traveller arriving at an empty house, and no reply coming when he knocked at the door, even though there were 'listeners' inside. They kept having that poem. Bobs was not aware that its author was a friend of anyone at home. Granny did not really have any friends, except old Margot Reisz, Oliver, a few neighbours, and the awful people who came to 'drinks' now and then. It was possible that the poet was one of these, but Bobs was silent on the matter, like the Listeners themselves, and she had somehow managed to get out of reading the poem aloud.

'Is your grandfather famous?' had been Madeline Stirling's intrusive question after the lesson.

'He's dead.' Bobs had been able to adopt the expression which might plausibly presage tears. That had been the end of that.

All the other girls found their mothers really annoying; but it was her granny who occasionally made Bobs squirm. Of Michal, she often felt protective, particularly if the Cuffe said cutting or dismissive remarks to her, or if Daddy wrote one of his unkind letters. But her relationship with

Michal was distant, less close, really, than her feelings for Lotte, who had brought her up while Michal, in one of those phrases she liked, was 'sorting out her life', or out, doing good.

Life was never so good when Oliver was away. Sometimes he had gone back to his old college for a week to work in libraries, and the seven days had lasted a year. Bobs never thought she would get to the end of the fortnight this last January when he had visited a Swiss university. That he had done so was the truth; that he had only spent two days at Zurich, giving a lecture, and twelve days with Camilla in a hotel, was information which Bobs kept to herself. She did not need to be told, after that, that a storm was brewing.

Life during these absences was not life at all. She took refuge in the animals. Hector was very sweet; so was Josh, the rat. And when Granny had said she could not have Cuthbert indoors, Bobs had broken into one of her rare fits of grief – crying as she could just remember crying as a very young child, with strange jerks and yelps over which she had no control.

'You'll have to let her keep Cuthbert indoors just this once.' This from Michal.

'But it's so unhygienic. It has fleas – it will go poo-poo' – Granny.

'Oh, for Christ's sake let the sprog keep it if it'll keep her quiet' – Cuffe.

Granny had been right to say that allowing Cuthbert

indoors once would establish a precedent. He often came in now. Bobs had reared him from a chick, and had hopes of getting a hen. Fresh eggs would be lovely. When Oliver had returned from Switzerland, everything was all right again. The three women learned to control their hysterical intolerance of the animals, and Cuffe kept to herself her thoughts about the smells emanating from the menagerie.

'It's interesting,' Oliver had once said when this subject had come up, 'as with all branches of aesthetics, how we classify "nice" and "nasty" smells. Clearly some pongs – let's say, pig swill – are nauseous. Our stomachs make up our minds for us whether we find this smell "nice". But there are other smells which are debatable. I find all after-shave lotions quite disgusting; but if my view were universal, no one would try to make money by selling them. Cuffe says that the smell in the menagerie is disgusting, but to my nostrils it is really rather a delightful smell – it is a mingling of straw – all right, perhaps a little excrement but these are small animals we are talking about, and for the most part what they pass is either odourless, like Hector's, or harmless like Josh's and Christopher's.' Christopher was a budgerigar. 'I think that in certain contexts, this warm, straw-filled smell would strike even Cuffe as agreeable . . .'

It was lovely, the way he stuck up for her against the Cuffe. The primary sense, as all these impressions played in her head, and the car sped along, was the bleak one: life without Oliver at 12 Wagner Rise was a series of discontents.

When he withdrew for ever, would the discontents be all she had left?

When the car stopped, Bobs wrestled with what to say. Instinct told her that to say too much, even to come down from the level of jokes, would be to risk frightening the bird away. She dreaded his anger – that she had seen: had the others, ever? – and it was worse than anything. And yet, if she said nothing, or continued to behave as if she was delighted for Oliver and Camilla, might he not come to believe it? She surely should tell him he was breaking her heart? Or was that the one thing she would never be able to tell him – since he plainly did not want to know it? But what if he did? What if he genuinely understood, this wise man who knew everything? What if a word from her would make him forget this Camilla nonsense?

Having parked the car, they walked a little way into the bushier parts of the Heath. It was possible to hear birdsong in the thickets, though the groan of traffic, straining in a queue up East Heath Road, was never out of earshot. It was she who decided to sit down on the grass, and when he had come to join her, she said, 'Do "One Man Went to Mow".'

This was a real appeal to early childhood, and to all the shared perceptions of the world which they had developed since. When she was three or four, Bobs had been happy to join in the repetitions – '*Five men, four men, three men, two men, one man and his dog – and a bottle of Pop – went to mow a meadow.*' The ditty had lost some of its interest, particularly for Oliver, by the time she was five or six. He had

46

begun to vary it, and turn it into a guessing-game. The game consisted in an enumeration of personal qualities by which it should have been possible to guess the identity of a shared acquaintance. At first, they only had four acquaintances in common – Lotte, Janet, Michal and Cuffe. With the years, they became able to add Margot Reisz, and various teachers and school fellows of Bobs.

It was a long time since they'd played, or sung, the game. It was really a choric form of gossip, since you could not doubt, once he had started, '*One man went to France, went to buy some sausage,*' that Margot Reisz was in question. (All the men who went to mow were women, as it happened.) '*In the dear Dordogne, such delightful pâté . . . Sausage, cigarettes, cheap white wine . . . Went to mow a meadow.*'

It was obvious that it was Margot, but she hugged her knees and grinned, and did not declare that she knew.

'More, more!' she said. Her skirt had fallen to her lap, and her legs were bare.

When she had giggled enough about Margot Reisz, she 'guessed' her identity, and asked for another.

'No, you do one.'

'You're better.'

'No, you.'

'*One man went to mow . . .*' She always started off, either being Miss Mack, or Cuffe. Today, clearly enough, was Cuffe . . . '*Went to eat some fibre!*' (this line was almost too funny to sing). Her usual quotations from the Irish philosopher held him in formulaic bafflement until she had got them off her chest: '*Schoolgirl maths is just common sense . . . Went to mow a meadow.*'

The Icelandic skalds developed verse-narratives that were so allusive that few, if any, could have understood them without knowing beforehand the extended traditions to which they referred. 'One Man Went to Mow' was a little like this – the line about schoolgirl maths was an allusion to a refusal to help her with homework, and a lofty dismissal of Michal's suggestion that Bobs *needed* help. (Of course she wanted help – else why had she asked for it? Huffy Cuffy.)

It was unkind of him, when it was his turn, to send Granny off to mow. With her chin on her bare knees, Bobs concentrated with a mixture of seriousness and delight as the catalogue of Janet's foibles was unfolded.

'It's *mean*,' Bobs laughed, but she did not want the song curtailed. The one about her mother was even worse, and she pretended not to be able to 'get' it until each prosaic and unfortunate detail had unfolded. Michal had only joined the *dramatis personae* of the mowing song at quite a late stage. Perhaps they had drawn the line at the mutual admission that Bobs's own mother was a bore. They concentrated upon very mild characteristics, like Michal's dunking her biscuits while reading the Jill Tweedie column, rather than anything which could be said to be positively damaging.

Then, as they sat on the grass holding hands, he sent another man off to mow. His voice was a fluty tenor, not unlike the pre-war crooners on Granny's 78 records, which they sometimes played on the old wind-up gramophone.

'*One man went to mow – looking very pretty.*'

'Camilla,' said Bobs at once. She had allowed the other examples to run on and on, even when the identity of the mowing man was perfectly obvious. She did not want to discuss Camilla, even in this obliquely choric form.

'How did you know? It might have been you going to mow.'

'Only it wasn't.'

'You are very pretty.'

'I've never gone to mow. Nor have you. We don't go to mow. It's only the others.'

'You are still very pretty. I hadn't decided who it would be. I was going to make it up as I went along.'

This attempted retreat from embarrassment was itself embarrassing.

'So is that the end of our games for today?' she asked, taking her hand from his, and placing it on the blue corduroy leg which stretched out beside her own bare, spindly limbs.

With no further words, he got up, and they walked back to the car. There was a line in her head which, ever since he had let her into the secret of Camilla, she had been wanting to say. And as they sat there on the grass, she had very nearly been brave enough to say it. *You know, you did once say that you wanted to marry me.* Fiddling with her seat-belt in the car, she had one last chance to say it, this line which might just change everything. But he turned the key of the ignition, and the roar of the Mazda made all further speech inaudible.

Bobs, who had once spent a week in County Wicklow with her father learning to fish, knew about letting the line go loose in order to secure your catch. This had been her decided 'policy' since Camilla had been part of the story. But there was a difference between teasing the fish and letting it go altogether, and she felt that some outright statement should have been made. There was too much ambiguity in her gesture, merely allowing her hand to rest on the blue corduroy leg as the Mazda roared back to Muswell Hill.

Chapter Four

It was the voice which occasioned surprise.

'Bobs gave us all such a very wild impression,' said Janet, as she passed a cup and saucer to Camilla Baynes.

Impeccably mannered, Camilla, who examined ceramics professionally each working day, received her tea with no discernible curiosity about the factory, or year of manufacture, of the blue Spode 'Italian' ware. She could not have hoped that they would not have been discussing her before her arrival, but she might have wished that Mrs Rose would not make this so disconcertingly obvious.

'Oh, really?'

This quietly spoken interrogative had been her response to nearly all Janet's observations, and she knew that there was a danger, if nerves made her say it once more, that instead of an expression of interest, it would become one of distance, if not indifference. There had seemed so little else to say to Janet's jumble of assertions – that you never heard traffic in the back garden, that the cigarette burn on the hall carpet had been made by W.H. Auden, that if Camilla had seen the house in Hensleigh's day, it would have been bursting with books, that the climate in this part of London was quite different from that of Kensington – you really *noticed* being this high up – that Bobs was going to North London Collegiate, like her mother before her, and that the tea bags had been purchased at Tesco.

'Oh, really?'

'Really, Bobs! We'd thought from what you said that Camilla came from the hunting set.'

'Excuse me?' asked the baffled visitor.

'I never said set,' said the child, who appeared to think everything funny.

Though it was supposed to be a tea-party, there was an element of the job interview about this occasion – an impression increased by the fact that they had seated Camilla at the head of the kitchen table, with Oliver at her side, while they – Janet and Michal – sat at the other end or – Miss Cuffe and the child – stood at different points of the kitchen.

'But you did say that Camilla's Daddy went hunting,' said Janet, 'and that rather implies a set.'

'Oh, but he does,' said Camilla, wide eyed. 'Or he has. Or, okay, he sometimes has, sometimes does. But does this cause problems to you folks? I know there are those who have problems with this.'

Cuffe, who had enfolded her cup with both hands, did

not look directly at Camilla as she spoke. She seemed someone, this very beautiful and red-haired Irishwoman, who was hugging to herself some joke which was slightly too sophisticated to be shared.

'I think we all imagined, from what Bobs told us, that you were English,' she said.

'Well, I hope *that's* not a problem.' And there was perhaps more indignation than mock indignation in Camilla's response. 'They do hunt foxes in Virginia.'

There was no questioning this. And Cuffe the philosopher was the first to concede that they had leapt to some very false conclusions. Just because you were called Camilla, the daughter of a hunting man with pots of money, did not necessarily signify an upbringing within an hour's ride of the dukeries. Afterwards, when they would chide Bobs for her failure to convey the primary information that Camilla Baynes was an American, the child would be cagey; hopping between the positions of saying that she had thought she had mentioned it, and that it was not worth mentioning. The concealment of vital information was itself a weapon.

When Camilla spoke, it was not with the accent of Virginia. None of them had a fine enough ear to 'place' her in the United States – she just sounded American – and they were to learn piecemeal that Camilla had been raised in Detroit (where the 'pots of money' were presumably accumulated), educated at Vassar, and subsequently employed by one of the swankier auction houses in New

York. (It was some rather remote family connection which took the Bayneses to Virginia in the hunting season.)

When Janet advanced upon her with a teapot for the umpteenth time, she looked at the untasted liquid in her blue and white cup and said, 'I'm fine. Really.'

Bobs thought this self-assessment by the visitor questionable. Camilla was wriggling in her seat, and her startled expression (how weird love was – did he *really* think she was pretty?) recalled Hector's when Cuthbert flapped his wings and squawked.

The atmosphere in the house for the previous week had been terrible. Michal, whose long sallow face looked rather fine this afternoon, had been in one of her heavy sulks, and had reverted to the subject whenever Oliver was out of the room. She had, to Bobs's intense embarrassment, chosen to put into words feelings which were obvious to all but which did not improve on expression. Could Michal really be expected to get on with her work without Oliver there as back-up? Oh, she knew there was Lotte who would always willingly 'mind' Bobs, but a child needed more than a minder, and Oliver was simply the best thing that had happened. She had recalled the miserable year when Bobs was born, and the three of them, Terence O'Hara, Michal and the baby, were marooned in Kennington in that dreadful flat. Nor had it merely been the practical arrangements which Michal had been tactless enough to rehearse. Without Oliver there, might not she and Cuffe rediscover all the fragilities of their relationship? Was it possible that she needed to have a man about the place, as well as a woman?

Catharine Cuffe herself had comparable fears, but she kept most of them to herself. Though we have described Michal as appearing 'rather fine' at the tea-party, a visual disillusionment had occurred in the imagination of her lover. Since Bobs broke the dreadful news, Cuffe disturbingly found Michal less alluring. Of course, her beauty was chiefly to be observed when she was naked; her marvellous shoulders and back were still definitions of perfection. But her face, which had seemed to Miss Cuffe when she first fell in love with it, to be that of a chiselled Aztec, uncompromisingly and fascinatingly unhappy, now looked simply truculent. It seemed sweaty rather than 'passionately intense' – which had been the epithets drawn for it with the impressions of love. The faint down on the upper lip, which added delight to slow kisses, now seemed a symptom of Michal's sluttishness, a failure to make an effort to please.

Cuffe had reverted, quite simply, since hearing the cataclysmic news, to being Oliver Gold's student. Emotional competitiveness took over. There was no helping herself. Unlike Cuffe, none of these people knew what was going on inside this extraordinary man's *brain*. And he was hers, not theirs. And it was she who had introduced him to Wagner Rise.

She remembered a cruel thing he had once said – not, as it happened, about Janet, but the remark was applicable.

'These London women! That's the *trouble* with London.
It is what distinguishes it from all other towns, even this' –
he had been speaking in his college rooms to a Cuffe aged
twenty-two, and his words had seemed the height of
sophistication to one who knew almost no one. 'Too many
chances for tuft hunting. An eager woman like that only has
to move into a house in North London and look up and
down the street. Maybe not her own street, but the one
half a mile up the road. She'll find someone there whom
she can get her teeth into, someone who's written an article or composed some music or appeared on the television.
That will be enough to get her going. London is full of
aspiring *salonnières* – and God, they waste our time.'

She had not questioned his unspoken claim to wear a
tuft. It had been an intimate moment – she and he
together, warding off the intrusive collectors of human
specimens. She thought of it now at the tea-party, as she
watched Janet in action. She could see the knowing little
sprog, with the squirming embarrassment which ties of
kinship enforce, noticing the clumsy way in which the
grandmother forced the visitor through this clumsy quiz.
There was a paradox, as it seemed to Cuffe, in Janet's reaction. Was there not some sense of let-down that Camilla
was not a well-born Englishwoman of the shires? Of
course, they all professed to despise that kind of thing, but
would there not also have been some element of excitement had Oliver bagged the daughter of a lord? Janet was
surely one of those who revere the English upper class in

the same measure that they despise it? An American, however, required a little adjustment of view.

Bobs watched Oliver staring very hard at a digestive bis-
cuit as Janet said, 'I don't suppose you knew Robert
Lowell? Hensleigh liked to see him when he came over
here.'

'Oh, really?'

These words were being stretched to breaking point,
and the more Camilla Baynes seemed, with her gentle
smile, to imply a respectful willingness to hear more, the
more the interrogative tone implied the opposite.

'But,' added Janet with no attempt at consequence, 'you
are at Christie's now.'

Camilla corrected her, not for the first time.

'It's how they met,' explained Bobs. 'When Ollie got left
all that loot.' Now why was that funny? 'You remember,
books, china, everything, and he didn't want any of it.'

Janet, understandably perhaps, preferred to hasten over
the legacy which had come to Oliver Gold. It had appeared
to make so little impact at the time – to have been pre-
sented, indeed, merely as a set of practical inconveniences:
having to go down and clear Arnold Maar's rooms, and to
dispose of the treasures – the three Ingres drawings, the
Turkey rugs, the highly polished but, as it transpired, largely
worthless Viennese furniture, the china. The money had
obviously changed him, and perhaps they all knew it would,
even as they had made their airy jokes (not meant at the
time) about his having no time for them, now that he was

rich; no need to live in an attic! The extent to which he had been obliged to her for his sustenance was not a matter on which Janet allowed her mind to dwell, either before or after the death of Arnold Maar. It was so much pleasanter to believe that Oliver lived in the attic because he wanted to do so, rather than because he had to. He had never suggested, when he learned the contents of the old man's will, that he would now look about for a place of his own. He had told Janet that he was Arnold's sole beneficiary, but he had never disclosed how much the old fellow had been worth.

It was a mistake to pretend that anyone remained unaffected by money, its possession or its lack. Janet knew that. What stung at the moment was that, at some point after Arnold's death a year before, Oliver must have met Camilla Baynes. It must have been quite shortly after Arnold's death, since the college, with a degree of callous expedition, had wanted to clear the rooms in readiness for another fellow, who had had his eye on them for years. So, for nearly a year – it made her feel such a fool – Oliver Gold, Janet's pet hermit, her beloved intellectual, had been seeing this – she tried to find in her vocabulary an apt word for Miss Baynes, and settled on *this person*.

Camilla Baynes did not regard the matter as a secret. That much was evident; for, in answer to Bobs's prompting, she had begun to tell the others her story.

'If he hadn't been left all that china, we'd never have met . . . And you were so shy, weren't you?' She reached a hand towards his cheek and stroked it – a gesture, no doubt, intended affectionately, but which made its own uncompromising point to the witnesses. He was Camilla's now. Goof spoke to goof, and his response seemed to have a glow which suggested the mating season at the zoo; but rather than allow themselves to admit that the greatest thinker of the late twentieth century was in love with this girl, they looked away, or failed to concentrate.

'A lot depended on the Coalport,' he said.

'Don't forget the Sung bowls,' she said.

The love story was entwined in a sale-room saga. To those such as Cuffe who lived on a higher plane, there could be little interest in such a commingling of sentimentality and commerce. It was the Coalport which, in three sizeable crates, Oliver had arranged to be delivered to the sale-room. He had not so much as troubled to go there himself, and it had only been a letter from Miss Baynes which had alerted him to the fact that, among the countless painted cups and plates, had been nine bowls of a completely different calibre. These celadon-glazed Chinese objects, eight hundred years older than the painted English china which formed the bulk of Maar's collection, had perhaps escaped Mr Gold's notice? So Miss Baynes had inquired. It had been the most casual decision on Oliver's part to take a bus down to Bond Street to view his inheritance. His memory of Maar's rooms in college had stored only the most casual impression of 'clutter', though he had spent so many hours stretched out in talk with the most interesting and lovable of the fellows.

Only upon seeing the bowls in a different setting had their simple perfection caught his heart, and he had recognized that there was something a little bleak about having no tangible objects by which to remember his dear friend.

'Of course they were more valuable than all the Coalport put together,' pursued the ceramicist. 'But wasn't it just so beautiful that he wanted to keep them – just because they *were* beautiful? Do you know, I asked him out on a date, there and then?'

'They are lovely bowls,' said Janet. No one could tell whether she was deliberately missing the point.

'There was bound to be something special about a man who did not want to be parted from this lovely Sung. He couldn't care tuppence about boring stuff like *money*.'

Camilla screwed her face up into monkey-irony. Her new friends considered her a plain little thing; not merely mouse-coloured but mouse-resembling. Her smallness, too, had been such a surprise. Now they had had an hour to take account of the paradox, there was no sign of ostentation in the loafers, the jeans, the beige jumper, the absence of jewels. This did not seem like a woman who would splash out on a sports car for her paramour. Her face was small featured. A small skull was punctured by a small mouth, almost colourless lips, a small nose and small though startled eyes. The only features in rebellion against this general smallness were the upper teeth, slightly too large for the mouth and adding to that 'goofiness' of which, at a later date, Janet was to complain.

Almost more surprising than Camilla's appearance was
the normally reticent Oliver's preparedness to let her prat-
tle of the progress of their love.

'Do you know – on our very first date when I took him
to a Schubert piano recital at the Wigmore Hall – I said to
him, "You are a man I could marry"?'

Unable perhaps to hear too much in one go, Cuffe inter-
vened with: 'So have plans been made? A date fixed?
Where will you live?'

'We thought my flat for a little while – didn't we?' said
Camilla, looking at Oliver, but speaking with speed and
certainty. 'It's too small for him to work there – it's only
two rooms; it's in Knightsbridge. But we can look around.'

'You'll be married from this house, of course?' said Janet.
'Oliver's mother is dead.'

'Mine's not,' said Camilla brightly.

'I just thought, since Oliver does not have much contact
with his family, and since you are alone in England,' said Janet,
'that you would both like to have the wedding party here.'

'That's very kind, but . . .' Camilla tried to finish her sentence.

Janet did so for her, with, 'That's settled then. Michal
had her wedding party here, didn't you, darling?'

'I don't think that is a very auspicious recommendation,'
said Cuffe.

'I could be a bridesmaid!' Bobs spoke as if it was the fun-
niest suggestion imaginable, as if the whole marriage was
still being planned as a practical joke.

'It is more usual for the woman to be married from home,' said Oliver quietly.

'Oh, but if your flat is so small . . .' said Janet.

'My parents' house in Detroit isn't small,' said Camilla Baynes quietly, and she looked round Janet's large kitchen with momentary disdain, as though 12 Wagner Rise was a mean little place by comparison with the home of childhood memories.

'It would be very exciting to come to America to be a bridesmaid,' said Bobs, still laughing.

The next question posed itself naturally; it had to be asked, and the silence seemed by some arbitrary process to be selecting which of them would be strong enough to pose it. Bobs was not the one. It was hard to know (and afterwards Cuffe and Michal debated it at length) whether Bobs even sensed the need to ask it. The tremulous tone was the right one as Cuffe was brave enough to come out with, 'You're not thinking of *living* in America?'

There was something morally weak in Oliver's shrug.

Camilla Baynes turned a goofy interrogative glance in his direction, as if asking for permission to continue; then she said, in a matter-of-fact tone, 'I've been offered promotion. A post in the ceramics department in our New York office. It's a big job, it'd be more money.'

'Fantastic,' said Bobs with automatic politeness. 'Isn't that wonderful?'

Chapter Five

'Well, my lover, have we left behind us three broken-hearted women, or did it not go too badly?'

He had never seen Camilla in such a state of excitement. Her understatedness, of appearance and manner, had always sat oddly beside her darts of boldness. He would not, in any previous circumstance, have been tempted to go out on a date with a woman he had just met. When he did so, however, it had been to discover someone shy and demure, who kept back her secret and who now, nine months later, retained it yet. She had been very frightened of meeting the women of 12 Wagner Rise. The tea-party had not allowed them to show open hostility, but she could hardly mistake their feelings, as they had all sat there, or stood there, inquisitors.

'What did you think of it?' he asked.

'I've only just met them. They are your friends. You'll have to judge for me.'

'Then, I should say that both your suggestions are true. It did not go badly, but, yes, we left some heartbreak.'

'Bobs was wonderful.'

'Yes, she was.'

'She's such a nice little kid. When they were all staring at me as if I'd just landed from the moon, she made me feel at home. Wasn't it funny she hadn't told them I was from the United States?'

'I suppose it was.'

'All that stuff about hunting. She must have remembered the time I told her about Daddy going hunting once in Virginia. I'd forgotten I even told her. She remembered it all. Kind of made me real to herself.'

'I suppose.'

'Oliver, does it worry you that they were all so sad – Michal, and Catharine and Janet?'

'They weren't *that* sad.'

'They were too. Is it any wonder they love you?'

And she stood on tip-toe to kiss his ear.

The words were spoken in the crush bar at the opera before they went into the auditorium. When they had taken their seats for *Rigoletto*, she nuzzled his shoulder, happy to have passed this difficult, much prepared-for, much-rehearsed hurdle. When the overture began, she continued to nuzzle him, and he wondered why she had only mentioned the sadness of the three grown-ups. The puzzling thing was the brightness of Bobs, not the sorrow of the three women. As he responded, with a gentle stroke of the shoulder, to her affectionate demonstration, and as she squeezed and unsqueezed his fingers, it was of Bobs that he thought.

When he had given up his college fellowship and moved into the house of Janet Rose, Oliver had been in a state of profound depression and mental exhaustion. He was forty-three years old, and the promises of an extraordinary career, and the expectations of many admirers, remained unfulfilled. His lectures, conversations, private teaching hours and wireless broadcasts had made him into a figure to whom many looked as to a guru. His genius – such was the belief in him that it made sense to use this strange word – stretched across the disciplines. He was widely considered one of the great prose stylists of the day and there was a rumour (alive in the university, but without any foundation in fact) that he might be writing a great novel, not your common tale which wins favour for a season and is then forgotten, but a master work which would immediately take its place beside Mann, Proust, Dostoyevsky. How a man could have developed such a reputation when he had never penned a single line of fiction, it was difficult to say, but Oliver had almost come to believe in it himself; he had even wrestled with his conscience when a former pupil, now a London publisher, offered him an absurd sum to write 'the Nobel prize-winning novel'.

Oliver Gold had read Classics for his first degree, and become a barrister. He had made an early success at the

Chancery Bar, but he missed the academic life, and would return to his old college once a week to teach law. In time, this lecturership in Law was upgraded to a fellowship, and he became the law tutor, while continuing his practice, and membership of his chambers.

What he actually wanted, however, was to be a philosopher, and every available bit of spare reading time was devoted to this subject. Analytical philosophy, and questions about the theory of knowledge, did not interest him as much as they appeared to obsess some of his colleagues. He enjoyed exploring those areas of applied thought where political theory, ethics and law all came into play. His first short book was in fact about Plato's *Laws*. It was published by the university press, and it was a signal to his colleagues that he was, from now on, something rather more than 'the law don'.

He always liked to quote Wittgenstein's distaste for academic philosophy, and to remind himself that Wittgenstein had urged his pupils, if they wanted to 'do philosophy', not to teach the stuff. When the philosophy tutor at Oliver's college left to take up a readership, and Oliver was appointed to his job, he quickly learned what Wittgenstein had meant. He found himself, willy-nilly, giving a 'crash course' in the History of Thought to his pupils every term, taking them through the movement of Western philosophy from Aristotle to Ayer with a superficiality which almost made him resign at once and go back to the law. But he slogged on, and in the first two years of his appointment as a fellow, he had written a book very different from the one on Plato. This one, almost conversational in tone, attempted an analysis of political philosophy – not as it had been explored in the great writers of the past, but as it was *now*.

The book was not merely popular with his students. It was one of those surprising examples of a serious intellectual work catching the public mood and becoming a bestseller. There were profiles of Oliver Gold in the newspapers. He was written about as the Ruskin or the Mill *de notre époque*. He was hailed by the right-wing newspapers as a hero, and even fell into the trap, briefly, of writing for them. Other aspects of his thought were considered very left-wing, and one of his old pupils, writing about him in a liberal newspaper, saw him as a sort of anarchist in the tradition of Tolstoy.

This step into populism came to be regarded by Oliver himself as a personal disaster. Not only did it make most of the dons dislike him as much as he was idolized by the young; but it also made him feel that he came before the public covered with labels, none of which gave a realistic picture of where he stood. The truth was, that his mind was on the move, and he sat down to write a much denser book about the relation between private ethics and public morality. His intention in writing this book, written in uncompromisingly academic language, and with many allusions to philosophers of whom the general reader had probably not even heard, would kill his rather damaging reputation as a populist, and enable him to progress through a tangle of thoughts which he was finding intensely difficult. But the book never got finished, and he had no sooner finished a chapter than he found that he had changed his mind about it. Many unfinished drafts accumulated.

The expectations had been too great, his own expectations and those of others. The more Oliver struggled to be the genius whom his young admirers believed him to be, the more he felt his capacities shrink.

Then, during one summer vacation, he reread much of Hegel, his hero. He had often lectured on Hegel, and he had frequently taught him to his pupils, so there was a sense in which he had been reading the German philosopher ever since, at the age of twenty, he first opened *The Consummate Religion* – a strange place to begin such an intellectual adventure, but that was that.

On this occasion, aged thirty-five, while staying in a borrowed Suffolk farmhouse, he gave himself up to the fertility, the power, the sheer greatness of this other human mind, rather as if he were alone in the farmhouse with Georg Wilhelm Hegel himself, and hearing him talking. He did not make notes, or not many. He read, quite rapidly, almost as if he were reading fiction and not attempting to grasp every twist and turn of the argument, but inhabiting, rather, the imaginative world view of those extraordinary works – *The Philosophy of Right* (which he read in German, often reading it aloud) and then some of the *Lectures on Aesthetics*; all the *Lectures on the Philosophy of History* (these he read in English) and finally, *The Phenomenology of Mind*. (This he read in German.)

When he began this great reread, the trees were still in their summer freshness. When he finished, the leaves in the garden were on the turn.

Two things happened during that almost solitary summer. (The friends who owned the farmhouse occasionally came to stay, and to see that Oliver was 'all right', but although he was polite and friendly, they missed his fluency of conversation; he was so completely absorbed in the mind of Hegel, and in his own spiritual crisis.) The first thing which happened, quite early during his reread, was the discovery that he, Oliver Gold, had nothing to say to the human race. Nothing. The fluency with which he had written his early books, and with which he lectured, or spoke at dinner tables, flown with wine, now appeared to him an appalling futility. The sheer fertility of Hegel's mind, so much greater than his own, its size, expansiveness, subtlety; the exuberance (if such a word can be used of such an intelligence) merely made Oliver shrink into silence, a silence which was so deep that the owners of the farmhouse, on one of their visits, wondered whether Oliver was indeed 'all right', or whether he was having a nervous breakdown.

It was absurd to have thought of himself as a potentially great philosopher, in the same league as Hegel himself; but such was the parochialism of the university, and the power of personal vanity, that Oliver discovered that he had entertained this conceited belief for a number of years. He had considered himself to be a great thinker who, if he had only been allowed the time, would be able to produce a master work which would not merely excite the admiration of his fellow philosophers, but would change the way that the human race thought about itself, and arrest the catastrophic effects of popular culture in the West. He had believed that he possessed some quality of insight, akin to mystic knowledge, which would capture the *Geist* of the present time and resolve the conflicts which threatened the unity and stability of society, the conflicts of race and class and the sexes.

In the present state of society, it was impossible to say anything serious which would have a wide or deep effect. It was clear to Oliver Gold where society was getting things wrong, which was why he had initially been so popular with the right-wing newspaper editors. But the conflict between Left and Right, particularly since the collapse of Marxism, now seemed one of ridiculous pettiness. The quality of the men and women entering politics, the puerile level of political debate in the newspapers, the fatuity of religious leaders and the absolute void left by the diminishing popularity of religion meant that it was almost impossible to imagine that the human race would ever hear again those tones of grave and interesting ethical discussion which had characterized the last century. He had set out with the belief that he could break through all this, all the time-wasting mind rot which made it so difficult for his contemporaries (television fed) to hear. The Young Hegelians, Marx, Ruskin, Tolstoy – they had all spoken with loud, popular voices – and they had found a response to the profound seriousness, the urgency, of what they had to say. He had been under the considered impression, after the success of his early books, that there might be a generation of disciples who would similarly awaken the world to a sense of its follies, its wickedness, but also to its capacity for goodness, and its beauty.

The puniness, the sheer ridiculousness of this hope was borne in upon him by the time he had finished reading *The Philosophy of Right*. There would be no young Goldians, as there had once been young Hegelians. By spending the summer with Hegel, Oliver had discovered that he was little more than a pygmy. This sense was sometimes accompanied by something close to a physical hallucination, as though he had shrunk to the size of a walnut.

The kind family who had lent him the farmhouse had the habit of switching on their radio at breakfast and talking to one another simultaneously. Either their hearing system was much more sophisticated than Oliver's, or they were in fact listening, neither to one another, nor to the broadcast. This became a paradigm for him of the human condition in the late twentieth century. No serious person could be heard above the din. When the family had gone, and he was left alone to his silences, he tried to imagine Hegel talking (difficult and indeed incomprehensible as the great philosopher's words would be); or Tolstoy talking,

or Ruskin, about a return to simplicities, a recovery of the
'heart' torn out of humanity by industrialism, nationalism,
and the sheer ugliness of modern life. He thought of these
great men talking, not, as they had done in life, to their
friends, or their silent lecture audiences, but on a radio
show; forced to squeeze their reflections into three-minute
sound-bites, interrupted by jingles and traffic news; and,
when actually transmitted into people's homes, talked
through by families having their breakfast. That was the
twentieth century in its late decadence; not an age like the
nineteen thirties when dogmas of almost boundless vulgar-
ity were fed into the minds of the masses by loudhailers in
Moscow or Nuremberg; but a trivial mindless jabber, in
which the noise of traffic and pop music, and the apelike
chatter of human families drove out reason itself; sound,
but not even fury, signifying nothing.

There was a second, and quite different thing happening
inside Oliver's head, as he continued to read Hegel hun-
grily, by now addicted to the quality of the German's voice,
but no longer really attending to its meaning. It was a very
simple problem, which he had hoped to resolve by intense
concentration upon his favourite philosopher. It was a question which Hegel himself had addressed with great urgency
and which, thereafter, had obsessed all the intellectuals of
the nineteenth century. It was the basic ethical question of
how we distinguish between right and wrong; and the
somewhat different question of how society decides what
is right and wrong.

This was the subject of Oliver's unfinished book, but he had been thinking about it, as any intelligent person must, since his adolescence. Like many people, he had been arrested by the assertion in *The Brothers Karamazov*, that if God did not exist, anything is permitted.

As an undergraduate studying law, he had been a convinced utilitarian, happy to turn Dostoyevsky's paradox on its head and say: What is permitted, we deify, and make into 'the will of God'. The question of ethics was not helped, in any case, by dragging God into it. (Did any but a handful of atheist polemicists believe that 'God' was wicked? So God's will = what is good? So we are still left with the question, what is good, and how do you define it?)

He found himself, during that Suffolk summer, unable to frame a form of words which would embrace a paradox. The paradox was this: we persist in the idea of moral absolutes because they are useful. The concept of the Good, or Good and Evil, are mystical concepts, which can only be declared, shown, not proved. We believe that pity is better than cruelty, generosity better than meanness of spirit, and so forth. But we hold on to these ideas not because of a disinterested or mystical love of the Good, but because like all systems – language systems or theologies or philosophical systems – they provide a useful template against which to measure ideas and notions. Embrace a totally utilitarian ethic and you end up by losing the sense of a moral imperative; deify the Good too rigidly, and you end up with rigid theocracies – a supposedly Catholic

Ireland where thousands want to divorce, an Islamic republic where many would see nothing wrong with drinking a glass of wine.

It was old ground, of course. He had worked it out, the following term, by giving a lecture on *Hamlet*, a Christian play whose *raison d'être* was belief in the virtue of a Christian vice, namely vengefulness. In Racine's reworkings of Greek tragedy, Oliver told his audience, the conflict is between two virtues – a private loyalty clashes with a public loyalty. In Shakespeare, something much more disturbing is at work. If we respond to the play properly, we should *all* become Hamlets, with our consciences turn'd awry. The Prince feels guilt for avoiding something which by Christian standards is a sin: revenge.

Hamlet is the first existentialist masterpiece, he told his students. It is the first picture of an individual in metaphysical isolation, a man who is paralysed, and even driven mad, by moral solitude; who cannot act because his own sense of moral problems is totally at variance with the systems in which he finds himself. Dante wandering through Hell itself still remains firmly within the system. But modern individuals are no longer like that. The systems are all breaking up. They don't work unless people 'believe' in them.

In describing Hamlet, Oliver knew that he was describing himself. This explained why he was both so popular, and so disconcerting, during the period when he allowed himself to become what is known as a media don, and to write articles for the newspapers and to give broadcasts about ethical questions. In some respects, he appeared to be defending 'the system', to be saying that unless we all, as a society, agreed on a firm set of rules, we should break up. At the same time, he betrayed a consciousness of why this simple picture could not hold, not because there were so many more wicked people in the world than there used to be, but because we had all become isolated individuals, isolated not merely from one another, but metaphysically alone, confronting the universal blank of nature. 'We like having Oliver Gold on the show,' one radio producer had said. 'He seems to be a tremendous reactionary in some ways, but you never know which way he will jump.'

His last wireless broadcast had been on the modish subject of child abuse. It was a debate between four people – Oliver himself, a female rabbi, a social worker with special experience in this distressing field, and a teacher. Oliver's contribution had created a storm of angry reaction from the listeners; but there had also been a dozen or so sad letters from those who wanted to thank him for speaking up, as they saw it, 'for them'.

The position advanced on that broadcast by Oliver Gold was this: the sexual taboo is the area of ethics where general consensus is most clearly required if the taboo is going to 'work'. In the nineteen fifties in Britain, it was supposed that the only acceptable form of sexual behaviour was monogamous heterosexuality. This notion had only been sustainable with a great deal of hypocrisy. Tolstoy in the last century had reckoned that the eighty thousand prostitutes in London had been the people who made it possible to sustain the system of respectable bourgeois Victorian marriage. Without these women, the men who returned to their suburban houses and upheld the standards of family life would have taken mistresses and there would have been widespread divorce. In the nineteen fifties, there were, perhaps, fewer prostitutes, but there was more need to turn a blind eye to what was going on in adulterous and unhappy marriages. Divorce remained difficult. Homosexuals were imprisoned. Abortion was unobtainable except in the 'back street'. All this was cruel, but it had the advantage of being clear.

It rather seemed, at this point of the radio discussion, as if Oliver Gold was going to defend the *status quo* in a rather more rigid manner than any of the three panellists with whom he was holding the discussion. But just at the moment when the social worker was asking him, 'You surely aren't suggesting that we still send homosexuals to prison? For heavens' sake, Oliver . . .' he had allowed himself to expand on what he was saying.

Up to the end of the nineteen fifties, he said, the situation was quite clear. The law had been framed to protect marriage and the family. There were perfectly sound economic reasons for this, and you could say that societies which insisted upon such standards were more stable than ones which allowed a free-for-all.

Once society had changed its concept of the law, Oliver

argued, a free-for-all was the logical step, and it should not be partial. The law now allowed homosexuality, and the moral climate was one in which this was not a grudging allowance but a celebratory one. 'Homophobia' was a modern sin. Loveless marriages could be ended with the ease of dissolving any other form of contract, and it could be done with total disregard for the feelings of the children or the friends of the couple who were separating. Okay. That is what we want, or is what we said we wanted – freedom to do as we liked.

How, then, can we justify the maintenance of the last taboo, concerning the sexual feeling of children? He was not speaking of those who forced children to have sexual experiences against their will. No one would wish to justify rape or enforcement, either of adults or of children. But why should what we call 'paedophilia' be regarded as the ultimate wickedness? Suppose a child and an adult wanted it? In many societies, it had been deemed perfectly 'normal'. You did not have to return to ancient Rome, where 'paedophilia' was, you might say, the most normal of all sexual acts. What about nineteenth-century England? Even the Archbishop of Canterbury, Benson, had chosen his wife when she was twelve years old. Lewis Carroll took nude photographs of his little friends with their full and delighted consent . . .

It amazed Oliver Gold afterwards that he had allowed himself to become so carried away. The producer took him aside after the programme and had asked him not to discuss the subject again, and he inwardly resolved not to appear on any more radio programmes. In purely logical terms, he felt that he had won the argument. There was nothing which the rabbi, the teacher or the social worker could say in answer to his question: *why should you claim that a child has no free will?*

They had shrieked at him, of course, and averred that children were too young to make up their own minds. He countered this by asking what age had to do with it? Weren't the divorce courts full of adults saying that they had got married at twenty, thirty, forty, and claiming that they had made mistakes, or that they did not know what they were doing? Were they saying that a sixteen-year-old knew her own mind, but someone aged fifteen and a half did not? Well, if they weren't, what of a twelve-year-old? What of an eight-year-old? Had they no recollection of their own childhoods? Did they think that sexual feeling only dawned when they had reached the legal age of consent? Did they really think that children were incapable of falling in love, or of having sexual feelings? In which case, they were going against every piece of evidence from psychiatrists since Freud. By what logical criterion could they make 'paedophilia' illegal which did not also apply to indecisive adults? And if they felt so strongly about upholding 'childhood innocence' and 'family values', were they not really advocating a return to the old restrictive pre-nineteen sixties morality? Fine, if that was what they wanted – let's ban divorce, ban abortion, ban homosexuality, lock up teenagers for having sex, as they had started to do in some of the American States . . .

Oliver did not mind questioning commonly held moral assumptions; nor did he mind upsetting people. That was in part his job. It had been the job of all moral philosophers since Socrates. But he did mind having revealed so much of himself.

When he listened to the tape of the programme, he could scarcely believe that he had been saying into the microphone, and hence to millions of listeners, things which he had kept in the most secret recesses of his brain for years. There was no one, not a doctor, nor an analyst, nor a personal confidant with whom Oliver Gold had ever shared his secret. This was not because he was ashamed of it. On the contrary, he had long since come to the conclusion that what we call guilt in relation to sexual behaviour was almost entirely chemically related. He had noticed this even as a child. When in a state of arousal, no moral argument could dissuade him from the delight contemplated. When it was over, he would feel depleted, and a sensation usually called guilt would overcome him. He soon recognized that these guilty feelings vanished as soon as he felt aroused once more, and that these feelings were not in fact moral at all. They were quite different in kind from the feelings he would have if he betrayed a friend or committed an act of cruelty. (As it happened, there were hardly any immoral acts which he could remember having committed in his entire life, and – one of the reasons he found Christianity such a puzzling belief system – he did not find the practice of virtue remotely difficult.)

It made perfectly good sense that society should wish (particularly in straitened economic times) to insist that the only acceptable sexual life was heterosexual monogamy. But everyone knew that beneath the surface conventions, we concealed other selves which paid no heed to the publicly accepted morality. From an early age, therefore, Oliver Gold had developed a common sense view of sexual behaviour, determining that whatever highs or lows of sensation he might have, he would not mistake them for moral experiences. (Periods of extended lust made him almost deranged, particularly in young manhood, but he had learned, or almost learned, to cope with them.)

Obviously, most of Oliver's experiences of sex (but this was true of most of his experiences, aesthetic, musical, gastronomic, intellectual) had been solitary. There had only been four exceptions to this pattern.

His initiation happened when he was nine years old, when the fondlings of a stepmother had gone beyond conventional bounds. Whenever he heard or read descriptions of 'child abuse' by ignorant people, Oliver tried to match his own memories to their hysterical clichés. Sometimes, he privately conceded that there was some point in their moral outrage. For the episode with his stepmother had been something he had to keep secret. It was not simply that he was cuckolding his father. There was something of necessity furtive about the affair, more than adult love affairs are of their nature hidden. The actual discovery of the hidden places of his stepmother's body seemed in retrospect to be a paradigm of the emotional experience of which it formed a part. There are areas of ourselves which it is unnatural to reveal or to discuss, other than in exceptional circumstances. It had only dawned on him quite slowly, as the intimacies became more and more intimate, that he was doing something which might have been displeasing to his father. The discovery led to the end of his father's marriage. Perhaps Oliver and his father would never have been friends. After this, they never were, and as a boy he had suffered violence, both from his father and his second stepmother. There were certain after-effects of the affair, which were to colour his sexual outlook. The only time he had come close to revealing this had been in the Senior Common Room at the age of about thirty. The dons were talking about Ruskin, and the horror felt by that Victorian sage on his wedding night when he discovered that women had pubic hair. Their condescension towards Ruskin (a man whom Oliver passionately loved, almost as if he had been a friend) horrified him and he had left them in a silent fury as they knowingly simpered about 'poor Effie' finding happiness with her second husband, John Everett Millais, and 'poor Ruskin' having formed his ideas about female anatomy from studying Titian's nudes.

Their vile conversation awakened buried images – the fun he had had with his stepmother, when it had been simply a matter of kissing and fondling, and of her running her wonderful smooth hands over his wonderful smooth little body; the softness of her breasts, and her nipples.

Lick Beaver, Ollie, lick till Sonya comes. Those hands on his neck, thrusting his little head beneath her skirt . . . It had been a sleepless night, pacing the streets of the university town and watching the cruel moon cast its heartless light on spires and cobbles, after his colleagues had laughed at John Ruskin.

Five years had passed, after Sonya left his life, before another person had such relations with Oliver Gold. This time, it was when he had just turned fourteen and the lover was an older boy, in fact the head of his house at boarding school. The delightful overture, someone else's hand in his pyjamas, the sensation itself (why was being touched so much nicer than touching oneself?) and the sweet knowledge that, by allowing this to happen, it was he, the younger boy, who was somehow in charge of the situation, had recalled instantaneously the first delight of the earlier experience, the delight of being touched by Sonya before he was required to go further. He knew that the older boy was in love with him. They took such risks, rising early in the morning for their trysts, when the other boys were still in their dormitories, and sometimes repeating them during the afternoons in hidden places, cricket pavilions in winter, deserted classrooms, even, on one occasion, the school chapel. This liaison was never discovered and it lasted for about a year. It was a true love affair, but when James left the school they did not keep in touch. (After Sandhurst, James became a Major in the Coldstream Guards. He married and produced children, but he was bowler-hatted early. Oliver sometimes wondered why. James was something in the City now.)

Shortly after going up to the university, Oliver Gold decided that it was time to prove to himself that he was 'normal'. He had made up his mind that this procedure should be got out of the way as soon as possible and he chose a female undergraduate quite arbitrarily after an evening of drinking. It was a silly thing to do – they had only lately met at a lecture, and they both belonged to the Italian Club, so that after the fiasco they had to choose between the hideous embarrassment of facing one another, or forgoing the genuine pleasure of pasta evenings, and talks by visiting speakers on such interesting subjects as Dante, the painters of the Trecento, and Garibaldi.

The catastrophe, from the purely mechanical viewpoint, had been absolute, as humiliating as possible on both sides. It had been the first time for the unfortunate young woman, and in later years, when Oliver saw her making appearances on the television news – she became a very right-wing MP – he decided that it had also been her last time too.

He had assumed, until the terrible hour in his college room, that it was always possible to make the body perform its tricks, regardless of what fantasies might, in solitude, pass through one's head. The absolute disparity between the partner of his dreams and the naked young woman in his arms put paid to this misconception. He had made the further mistake of trying to invent excuses and, when they had hastily got dressed again and were drinking instant coffee, he had rehearsed an embarrassing catalogue of possibilities – that they were perhaps too drunk; or perhaps he found her *too* attractive. When, years later, he saw her on someone else's television screen vigorously defending the nuclear deterrent or harsher prison sentences for delinquents, he could only remember a slightly greasy-haired girl gazing wretchedly into a mug of instant coffee and saying, 'I'd rather not talk about it, if you don't mind.'

The truth was that he had already, by the time of this disaster, entered the world of his own sexual personality. Twice (with Sonya and with James) he had been the 'passive' partner. Something developed in the meantime which made it clear that, the next time, he must be the active initiator of proceedings. He knew perfectly clearly by now the nature of his sexual ideal. Long before his disillusioning conversation with the dons about Ruskin, he had understood that Victorian man's intense love for a little girl, Rose La Touche; understood that Ruskin, the over-protected only child of elderly parents, was imprisoned in childhood and would never escape.

At this stage of dawning awareness, Oliver knew a good deal more about his own sexuality than he knew about Ruskin's. *Peter Pan*, a book to which he was obsessively devoted, was for him a sexual tract. Whereas the 'normal' majority forget their childhood sexuality, telling themselves that the 'kiddies' are sexless beings, waiting to mature into erotic adults, for Oliver such ideas were all the wrong way round. Sex for him was inescapably connected with the pleasures and secrets and emotional intensity of boyhood. While he passed through his twenties and thirties, he knew that his only chance of finding emotional satisfaction was with a child. Equally, he was realistic enough to know about the world into which he had been born. Keep we must, if keep we can, these foreign laws of God and man. He was terrified of a scandal, and of wrecking his career, since he had no private money and was entirely dependent on what he could earn. (His father and his second step-mother had nothing to do with him. They had two children of their own, and when his father died, Oliver was not mentioned in the will. Nor did he attend the funeral.)

Perhaps the two crises of Oliver's life, the two dark secrets, were related to one another: his inexpressible philosophical ideas, his intellectual 'blockage', and his secret pining for a love which truly could not speak its name and which had, in any event, never found an outlet? He accepted that he was one of those many people in the world whose tastes or circumstances did not allow them to be anything but celibate. While his career was being a success – first as a barrister, then as a philosopher – the celibacy had been a positive advantage. He kept unsocial hours, often reading and writing deep into the night, and it was hard to imagine this manner of living reconciling itself with married domesticity.

Nor did the celibacy do anything to diminish his popularity. He had become something of a cult figure largely because of it. His pupils, in the early, self-confident days of his fellowship, had basked in his affection. His secret, being impossible to express, released him, both emotionally and intellectually, to be sympathetic in a way that no married tutor could be. There were many who were devoted to him, and not just Catharine Cuffe, though it was she who appeared to have made devotion to him the pivot of her life.

Oliver Gold had been aware, within the first hour of meeting that pale, thin, long-haired redhead, with her snub nose and her intense, imploring Irish eyes, that Cuffe was in love with him; but the discovery that pupils, or indeed total strangers, had developed such a fixation was not, at this juncture of his history, anything unusual. That such awareness should go to his head was inevitable; but something which immeasurably added to his allure at this date was that the head was the only place to which it did go. Ten years had passed since the 'fiasco', and he was a proud man. He would never risk the repetition of such a scene. The fiasco had happened to an unheard-of undergraduate. Now he was Oliver Gold, the most popular lecturer in the university, and, within the tiny compass of that place, famous.

There was a sexual danger in this; fame, even of this

parochial variety, is attractive to others; and vanity could have made him risk a repetition of the fiasco, had it not been for one very simple fact. Celibacy had concentrated his sexual imagination, and he knew now, with perfect clarity, that he could be happy only with the 'dream children' inside his head; children whom he did not possess, and whom he would never be allowed to possess.

Sometimes, with truly Wildean folly, he thought it would be worth going to prison for his love. He had heard of how such men are treated in English prisons; how the warders turn a blind eye while the other prisoners show what they think of those who abuse children. Oliver sometimes thought that there would be a Christ-like dignity in enduring it all – the violence, the urine in his tea, the brimming chamber-pots rammed on to his head, the insults and the shame – for the sake of one hour of what his heart craved. One hour of reciprocated love with a child. One hour of sharing with the dream child the certainty that, as far as they were both concerned, in that beautiful moment, *there was nothing wrong with it*.

But a celibate he remained, with no wish to repeat the fiasco and no opportunity to meet one of his little dream lovers. This state of things lent a burning intensity to his friendships when they were allowed to develop. His pupils and disciples enjoyed a quality of friendship which a Victorian man would perhaps have regarded as normal but which was most unusual in late twentieth-century England.

His relationship with Cuffe was a case in point. When he

recognized that she was an intellectually serious person, the tutorials came to last two, three, even four hours. He took to buying picnics of cheese and fruit so that their discussions need not be interrupted by hunger.

'This is a true symposium,' she said one day at the end of the Dialogue; and a dialogue it always was. Cuffe was no one's fool; she did not sit meekly mopping up the guru's words of wisdom; she answered back; she questioned; she was even abrasive and rude, which he liked, since she was not rude with the self-conceit of the young, but because intellectual intensity and passion made manners for the time superfluous. This woman really *minded*, she really wanted to get right those questions which had exercised the greatest minds. The first time he became aware of this was during a discussion of her essay on Hume, and the conundrum of how human beings can lay claim to any knowledge whatsoever. Though epistemological questions had never been the ones which interested him most, as a philosopher, he could not fail to be excited by the intelligence of this young person, so much more vividly concerned with philosophical questions, so much more acute, so much deeper and better read, than most pupils he taught.

So experienced a teacher as Oliver Gold knew by then that what we think is in large degree a manifestation of personal character. The ratiocinative faculties show what we are like as much as our tastes in music or our personal habits. The intensity of Cuffe's scepticism – she was trying to outHume Hume during that hour, and was advancing a position of extreme empiricism which was truly absurd – appealed to him. It was common for the young to strike attitudes; it was decidedly unusual for anyone of nineteen to have entered so profoundly into the empirical-sceptical mindset, to question knowledge itself and the uses we make of it, to know how to do philosophy. During that intense symposium of cheese and olives, they had moved from being teacher and pupil with a crush on one another into a profound friendship. He knew that he was safe with her, as he had never been with any other woman. If she was in love with him, she was as much in love with David Hume. The love was of a kind which would demand no fiascos.

There are many types and intensities of emotional involvement which only the celibate can know and explore. The great bear-hugs which were to become their mode of greeting never threatened to become sexual embraces, but there was always a strongly physical element in their attachment. He certainly, from his perspective, loved her beauty, the strength-in-frailty of Waterhouse's Lady of Shallot.

Only in her family (father the manager of a carpet factory in Kidderminster, her mother one of that last generation of middle-class women who did not go out to a job, the comfortable neo-Tudor house in the suburbs where Oliver and Cuffe now spent Bank Holidays and Christmases) did he feel that they were giving a false impression, and doing so knowingly. There were various phrases used by bachelor friends who needed to provide the world with the belief that they had a regular partner of the opposite sex. At the university, there was no shortage of young women who were prepared to be the 'walkers' of such men, to attend dinners with them, or to accompany them to balls without the bore of enduring a pass being attempted in the shrubbery during the small hours. 'A beard' was the most vivid of these phrases. Since, at this stage of his history, Oliver's own beard began its appearance, it became, by an irrational association, his habit to think of himself as 'Cuffe's beard' even before it became quite plain that she would never be going in quest of male lovers.

He loved her, of that there could be no doubt; but he always loved her with a lesser intensity than that with which she so evidently loved him. And it was this which enabled him to enter into the deliberate deception of her father and mother. They obviously thought of Oliver and Catharine as lovers. Although Mrs Cuffe was an observer of old-fashioned conventions, there was clearly some hope in her facial expression, the first time Oliver went to stay, that her daughter had moved on, in the way that young women of their class and type had done, with regard to bedroom arrangements.

'This is the bathroom –' they were a family with one bathroom, and upstairs was, like most English houses, something of a squeeze, with bedrooms cheek by jowl. 'And you can be – where would you like to be, Oliver?'

She had hovered by the door of Catharine Cuffe's bedroom. It was a room where such fervent tidying had taken place, during the long spells of the daughter's absence, that most traces of Cuffe's teenage self had been expunged. Even so, he had felt he was glimpsing his friend's past, in a more intimate way than any verbal recollections could have summoned it up for him: that so recent past when she had wanted to put posters of Bryan Ferry on her walls; and a more remote time, when, still in the pre-pubescent chrysalis, Cuffe had been an addict of those Enid Blyton stories which his eye at once spotted on the shelf, and when a smooth hairless little body, winceyette-clad, had pressed itself against the pink donkey with wobbly ears, which still lay there on the young woman's pillow. For the first time, erotic fascination had dawned, not for Cuffe as she now was, but for the dream child which she had been; and perhaps something of this feeling had communicated itself to Mrs Cuffe who made the surprising remark that they would probably want to make their own arrangements about where Oliver slept.

Afterwards, Cuffe had said how astonished she was that her mother had been prepared to let them share a bedroom. They did not discuss, but must have noticed, the look of disappointment on Mrs Cuffe's face when he had hastily opted to sleep in David's bedroom (Cuffe's brother, at that date doing a 'year out' in Zaire with VSO). Whatever the conventions which Mrs Cuffe had observed since the nineteen fifties, whatever her church-going habits and her wish to do what was right in the eyes of the world, the instinctive longing that her kind should be reproduced, that her daughter should marry and give birth, had been stronger in that moment than the desire for respectability.

On all subsequent visits to Holmwood, Oliver and Cuffe slept separately. When David returned, Cuffe took the sofa-bed in the sitting-room, and Oliver had the secret pleasure of a few nights in Cuffe's bedroom.

'I do believe he was hugging the pink donkey,' Cuffe told her mother once over breakfast. And they had laughed, and Mrs Cuffe had said, 'Missing you, I expect.'

Because of his unhappy relationship with his own family, Oliver had forgotten the importance of home. He enjoyed helping Mr Cuffe in the garden, wheeling the barrow, passing the secateurs, mowing the grass, forking bonfires. He happily accompanied him to the local pub, leaving the ladies to prepare the lavish roasts and multitude of vegetables which were prepared at festal times in Holmwood. Mr Cuffe was a shy man. His intelligence was (presumably) wasted, managing carpets in Kidderminster, but he belonged to the polite generation which saw no point in questioning destiny. It was not for him, old enough to have fought in the war, to set out on a path of his own. He had married, bought a house slightly more comfortable than that of his parents, and taken the sort of job needed to pay for it. Intelligence, application, a knowledge of chemical engineering which would have put some of the dons to shame, were all directed by the quality of obedience, not obedience to his bosses or the conventions of his class so much as to the nature of things. He had never been visited by the troubling fantasy, which possessed so many of Oliver's pupils, that he could do anything with his life – edit a newspaper, found a pop group, work for a few years in advertising and then write a novel, go into politics . . . People in Mr Cuffe's world came home from the war and the rest of life was determined by the need to earn enough money to pay for Holmwood, the annual holidays in Tenby, the leisure to belong to the tennis club.

Holmwood had excited in both Cuffe and himself the dream that they might one day, in some form, live together and share a life of domestic innocence. The intellectual crisis in Oliver's life, his tremulous awareness of a direful void whenever he tried to press forward in his intellectual journey, was one of which she knew little, since by then she had moved to London, and much of their talk and their correspondence was of her work, or of books which they were both reading. Their letters did not discuss the tumults passing inside Oliver Gold, and had more to do with the conflicts of English nineteenth-century thought, the journey from Utilitarianism to Idealism, and on, or back, to common sense and G.E. Moore. She had not been made privy to the journey he was making against this gentle stream when, having discovered in his own mental chambers the locked barricades of common sense, he was trying with many a rattling of doorknobs and exasperated false turns down unlit corridors, to retrace a path to an ethical philosophy which would be distinctively his. Sometimes he allowed her a glimpse of what was happening to him when they tried to thrash out together what was going on in the new fads of continental thought. But Cuffe was so impatient of Foucault and Derrida, and so firmly of the view that even the most difficult concepts must be intelligibly expressed, that much of his journey had to be made alone. She accused him more than once of egotism; of a failure to accept the common sense view of things; of some tormented need to be 'famous', to cut a dash, to explore positions merely in the hope that future histories of philosophy would contain chapters with titles like 'Gold and the New Beginning'. The remarkable thing about twentieth-century philosophy, in her view, was that there were no new positions to be advanced. She had reached the position of believing that their job was simply a matter of resisting nonsense and, in her phrase, 'tidying up'.

In his crisis of intellectual loneliness at this juncture, while Cuffe made her name at London University, and he was left behind in college, only old Arnold Maar could help him. Maar had discovered his own limitations at about the time that Hitler had deprived him of the professorial chair which he had occupied so young. Like so much in Maar's life and person, the switch had been seamless. The college fellowship had been made available to him at the time of the *Anschluss*, and he had therefore been an Englishman for forty years when Oliver's *crise* came upon him. Maar's slight, well-clad figure, the dapper little blue bow-ties, the perfectly cut double-breasted suits, had become as familiar a sight to generations of students as the medieval architecture itself. There were few college offices which Maar had not willingly and gracefully held. (He liked to joke that he had done almost everything, except be the chaplain, and that he would have filled this post with the greatest happiness had it been offered to him.) He was a legendarily kind host. His accent all but unmodified from the moment of his arrival at Croydon airport; his taste in flowery white wines unmodified by the increasing sophistication of other late twentieth-century palates, he was the last of the gentle men.

It was Arnold Maar who had seen the approaching crisis in the mind of Oliver Gold, for it was Arnold, even more brilliant in the arts of kindness than in his intellectual pursuits, who was prepared to subscribe to the heresy that the intellectual life was not everything.

'My dear, you need a complete break –' What strange things his old palate could do to that word 'break', how guttural and rolling was the 'r' in it, how melodiously unEnglish his version of the diphthong. 'This, as I have told you, happened to me. At one moment, the mind is advancing, advancing, advancing –' The pronunciation was *atvantzink*; it sounded like a purely German word. 'And at another, one is confronted with an impenetrable wall. For some eighteen months after I came to this college, I brooded on this. I raged against those who had disturbed me. That truly was how I saw things at the time, when the

95

whole of Europe was being plunged into flames. Of course, none quite guessed what was happening to my dear father and mother whom I'd left behind –' he had held up his soft, manicured hands to express the inexpressible horror – 'but I was so desolated, so selfishly preoccupied with my work, and with the madness of interrupting it. Yes, there was persecution, of course I knew it. But I was the great Arnold Maar, and that was so much more important than the political situation. How could these people have deprived me of my peace of mind? That was how I saw it at first. Of life, I knew nothing. And then, once I had begun to teach here, there opened at my feet a yawning gulf. It was as if all I had ever known of mathematics was at an end. There was *nothing*. Simply nothing. It was the decision of an afternoon. The college librarian rescued me, dear Timmy Cross, a saintly Tractarian clergyman coming to the rescue of this alien being from Austria. "In the library," said he, "we have a precious copy of the *Arithmetica Universalis* – so why not do a learned edition?" As simple as that. He asks one question, and he solves the very dilemma of my life. In one stroke. I had, of course, only ever read *about* Newton, I had never read Newton. But that very day I went into the college library and I began to read the *Arithmetica Universalis*, and by the end of the week I had decided to do the edition, and by the time I had finished editing it in nineteen forty-seven, I had stopped worrying about the great Arnold Maar. Once in two hundred years such creatures are born, a Newton, a Russell. I was not one of them. So what? The whole of Europe and all my family had been destroyed. And the knowledge released me – before that, I had no idea of the world outside my brain; and at last I was filled with a determination to make a better world, and to help with refugees – and this is when I did my work in UNRRA, and went to the camps and so on and so forth. And I knew I could be happy here, writing the history of mathematics, and teaching, and being the Junior Dean, and the Dean, and the Sub Warden and everything except the chaplain! Well, you are brilliant like me, and you are as vain as the young Arnold Maar. Perhaps, who knows, you are the Saviour, as all your young friends think. No, my dear, I am not mocking you. God knows, the world needs some Saviours. But you will drive yourself mad. Reading Hegel is bad for you. You want my advice? Stop trying to wrestle with ideas. Do something different. Go and live somewhere else for a year or two. Go to London.'

Oliver repeated these wise words when he next met Cuffe for one of their evenings of pasta in Bloomsbury. She had told him that she now lived in Muswell Hill with friends, but the nature of the establishment had never been spelt out to him. She now made the suggestion that he should become Janet Rose's lodger.

'But I first met the Roses years ago. Janet's an intellectuals' moll. She collects people as if they were cigarette cards.' He stroked the beard, it was a long one now, and said, '"I'm so glad you like that wallpaper – Stravinsky chose it when he came to supper with the Emperor of Japan."'

Cuffe laughed.

'I've mentioned Michal?' she checked. 'I told you that I'm living with Michal. Janet is Michal's mother.'

'Actually, the cigarette cards were never in that league; it was more, "Freddie Ayer once ate my peanuts."'

'Actually,' she said, 'it helps, your knowing Janet. You know Hensleigh's dead.'

'It's years since I went to one of their parties.'

You would not have guessed this was the case when she took him back to 12 Wagner Rise.

'But Oliver and I go back *years*!'

Janet had been so over-excited, gabbling about some broadcast of his and expressing enjoyment of an article she claimed he had written in the *Independent* (it was in fact some years since he had done any journalism and he had never written for that particular paper), that he had wondered whether he could endure life in her house. Or was he being unfair? Was her sprightly 'Oliver and I go back *years*!' simply Janet's way of being friendly? Janet's way of being friendly was so very unlike the Cuffes' way at Holmwood. He had never once supposed that Mr and Mrs Cuffe regarded him as a cigarette card to stick in the album: he was simply their daughter's friend; the fact that he had written books or spoken on the wireless provoked good-humoured comment, but not crowing. The cast of mind which, after a lifetime with dear Hensleigh, had become habitual to Janet, would have been regarded by Mr and Mrs Cuffe as impure; the notion that one wanted anyone in one's life for any reason other than that they had landed there by chance was vulgar, and the Cuffes' circle was limited to friends made at the tennis club, neighbours and relations.

Janet's 'Oliver and I go back *years*!' posited an intimacy which had never existed. She had named two or three persons of whom he had either never heard or whose names he had forgotten. 'You used to come here with Claudio, and Clarence, and Margot.' Then she had named two prized cigarette cards, a poet and a painter, with whom it was alleged that he and Janet and Hensleigh had enjoyed dining at their local trat in the old days. (In all the seven years he had now lived in Janet's house, he was never to see either the poet or the painter cross the threshold.)

But the proposal was what he needed, and he had moved in. He was forty-three when he moved into Janet's attic; Cuffe was twenty-eight, and so was Michal; Janet was fifty-five and Bobs was barely three.

It is a curious fact that though the three-year-old was running about Janet's room when the final details of the arrangements were being discussed, interrupting the grown-ups and trying to introduce Oliver to her teddy bear, he did not imagine that she would ever come to replace the dream children in his head. He had been so worn out, intellectually, so frayed, that he wanted the healing balm of release from university and college routines. And after a year or two of it, his mind had begun to heal.

What began to unfold was the most delicious danger, the

most heart-rending miracle. Now, looking back, he did not choose to put dates on the affair or ask himself when it had all begun. It was the central fact of his life, the knowledge that he and Bobs were made for each other.

Bobs had certainly been the person of whom he saw the most during his first year of residence at 12 Wagner Rise, and so it was perhaps inevitable that he should have seen a lot of Bobs's mother, and that Michal should have fallen in love with him. When he discovered this fact, he had been irritated, thinking that he would have to move out of the house just when he was beginning to become acclimatized. But he had been able to handle the situation with tact, and to assure Michal that theirs would always be a very special friendship while insisting that it was simply not fair to Cuffe if he and Michal enjoyed clandestine gropings.

Cuffe he continued to love, both as a being and as a body. There were many occasions when, had it not been for the fact that he remembered the fiasco with such searing clarity, he would have liked to try the experiment of sharing her bed. (There were times when they had done just that – shared a bed, fully pyjama'd, and hugged one another – during a tour of Norman cathedrals, when there had only been one room left in the hotel.) He felt no such desire for physical intimacy with Michal, and this would have been the case even if he did not find her smell displeasing. It was not that she 'smelt' in the vulgar use of the term. Presumably, the smell of her body, which was not that of sweat, simply of her, was alluring to Cuffe.

He wondered, during those early years, whether little Bobs timed her sudden entrances into rooms to prevent her mother making passes at Oliver. Did she, even at five years old, his angel-temptress, his putto, his little cupid, his carefully sculpted mixture of knowingness and innocence, did she know that she was his maiden-mistress who possessed his heart and had complete control over him?

Did she even know it now, aged ten?

He had abandoned any attempt to make sense of his love affair with Bobs, any more than he bothered to trace how it had progressed. Anyone else who got to hear of this totally secret affair would presumably want to assert that it began when the first physical intimacies got out of control. But Oliver would wish to say that this was a false description. He had always delighted in her, and she had always loved their romps. When he had held her upside down until she giggled herself silly, and her skirt had fallen down over her head to reveal her little knickers; when he had read her stories in her bath and dried her with a towel before helping her into her pyjamas; when they had lain on the carpet tickling one another and laughing – were those not moments of physical intimacy? And had she not known, just as well as he, where they would lead?

Bobs was now ten, and he was fifty, and they were lovers. In his eyes and, he knew, in hers, this was the most beautiful, the most joyful, the most wonderful thing in life. It was as innocent as if they were both thirty. He in no way regarded it as a vice since it had been a mutual pleasure. He had no doubt that Bobs loved him as much as he loved her.

And yet he knew that this love affair was potentially catastrophic. Not only did he know that if it were discovered, he would be expelled from the house at once. Janet would in all likelihood summon the police. There was even a part of him which believed the propaganda of the age. Naturally, they did not understand, how could they, what an enrichment was given to men like himself when he found a willing, giggling, pliant child lover. At the same time, he knew that those who frowned on such activities could make out their case. Did not the experience of sex during childhood cause unhappiness or emotional arrest in later life? Did not his own oddness stem, in part, from childhood experiences? He was unable to extricate himself from the cycle of memory and moralizing when he asked this question. Some of the time, he felt – well, we are all as we are, some of us like tall blonde women, and some of us like dark men, and I happen to be one of those who likes little girls; and I have had the incredible good luck to have found a little girl who likes me.

But at other times, he could hear inside his head all the cliché-mongers, the newspaper leader writers, and those sadists who bang on the side of the Black Maria when such men as Oliver are brought to court, and who scream out abuse when, with blankets draped over their heads, such men are hurried into police stations. 'You are sick. You have infected an innocent child with your sickness. You must bring this thing to an end. You must escape her. You must leave the house, for you cannot trust yourself to go on living with Bobs in the same house. And there is only one way of leaving the house which will provoke no questions. You must find someone who will marry you.'

So, that was the point of Camilla Baynes, the dear little mousy one who now sat beside him listening to *Rigoletto*. She was so small and bony that it did not feel, when he hugged her cardiganed torso, that she had developed as a woman at all. Thanks to her simple biblical faith, there were some mysteries which he would have to wait until after the wedding to fathom. Was it not possible, after they were married, that with a little alcohol, and with the lights out, he might be able to imagine that this sweetly flat-chested tinikins was a little friend who could take the place of Bobs? The illusion was plausible that evening, for when the gruesome operatic tale was over, and the father had inadvertently killed his child to the apparent delight of the audience, Camilla's fine mousy hair did not move from his shoulder; her little lids, which he bent to kiss and tickle with his beard, were closed in unheeding sleep.

Chapter Six

'I can't think why Cuffe says that jersey is hideous.'

'Two immediate reasons come to mind,' said its wearer.

'It's only because Camilla bought it.'

'That's the first reason.'

'It is mean of you to search for a second reason,' said Bobs. 'Beauty's in the eye of the beholder, we are told. Cuffe says it is a Young Farmers' Association jersey. What's that?'

'Luckily, I don't notice what I'm wearing.'

'You make a tremendous fuss about your simple outfits.' Bobs laughed delightedly at this fact. 'And you'd notice if you were wearing no clothes at all.'

'You cast me in the role of Andersen's Emperor. All too cruelly, all too plausibly, all too probably. My new clothes are symptomatic of my being found out at last.'

'Found out?'

'As a fraud?'

This was dangerous territory. Feeling the humour fizzle,

sensing that indeed something too like truth was being approached, Bobs reverted to the controversial garment.

'Cuffe says she likes you in dark, plain colours. She must have bought you half a dozen of those navy-blue guernseys.'

'It is your grandmother who generally gets in first with the dark-blue trousers. Cuffe buys the guernseys to match.'

'They like the way your beard grows over your guernsey.'

'Don't you?'

'Josh and I will bite it off, won't we, Josh?' She bared her teeth and came towards him with the white rat, holding its face towards the beard as if it were a razor. Josh showed no great interest in Oliver's beard, and appeared happier when she turned his red little eyes to face her own. She ran him over and over again through her hands as if they were a treadmill, and then stuffed him up her own jumper, so that he made interesting mobile woolly lumps up and down her front.

'It only touches the guernsey,' continued the beard's owner, who, perhaps for want of a rat to play with, was stroking this growth. 'To say that it grows *over* the guernsey implies a parasitic adherence, such as mustard and cress on blotting paper.'

'Amanda Wilkinson!' Bobs momentarily became Miss Scott, a teacher who had taken them for Nature Study at her previous school. 'You're not scattering enough seed on your blotting paper. Look at the lovely tufts on Leslie's paper – but then Leslie always keeps it damp.'

When mirth had subsided, Bobs pursued, in her own voice, 'Where did she buy it? The jersey? Camilla?'

'I really could not possibly imagine.'

'Harrods, Michal says.'

'Why, then, did you need to ask?'

'I think those orange zig-zags really suit you.'

'It is comfortable.'

'Cuffe says that if it goes on at this rate, Camilla will dress you from head to toe in hideous clothes, and Michal even says she'll shave your beard off.'

'What would she do with it?'

'She could make a purse. Michal says that weddings always bring out the worst in everyone. Much worse than divorces or quarrels about deaths, Michal says.'

'But we don't generalize, do we?' he reminded her.

'I forgot that. Oh, stop it, Josh. He bit me really hard.' Bobs contorted her face into parodies of pain, but seemed to be laughing none the less.

'By "bring out the worst", it is hard to know what your mother means. It could mean "worst possible" or "worst yet".'

'Worst yet, according to Granny, is the idea of having Camilla's mother to stay here – for a whole month.'

'There are many reasons why Rosalie should come here. Camilla's flat is too small to accommodate the pair of them.'

'It'll be too small for you, then, when you marry.'

'And she can't be expected to stay in a hotel for a month. It would be too expensive.'

'Even with all their money?'

'I think it was your idea that the Bayneses were millionaires.'

'Granny believes it anyway.' This made Bobs giggle all the more. When she spoke again, it was to say, 'Get on and move, by the way.'

'I'm sorry, I thought it was your move.'

With a long bony finger, he moved a black draught forward. She immediately moved a white.

'Cuffe says that everyone should stop worrying 'cause the wedding isn't going to happen anyway.'

'Why did she say that, when Camilla and I had told her the opposite?'

'I suppose she meant, she hoped it wouldn't happen.'

His long fingers drummed on the table, then moved another draught.

'Oh, do concentrate,' she said, as she took three of his pieces and 'huffed' them. 'Maybe Michal's right, and the wedding is bringing out the worst in them. They're all in foul moods. Granny's upset 'cause she says you accused her of rummaging through your things.'

'I never accused her.'

'You asked her if she'd seen some notebook or other that had gone missing.'

'That isn't to accuse someone, to ask if they have seen something.'

'She said she never rummaged, and that you were all cold and angry and agitated when you asked her. It was as good as accusing her.'

'She exaggerates – or you do.'

'Was it your diary?'

'I don't keep a diary.'

'She guessed it was your secret diary. She thought that was why you were so agitated. No one knows where my diary is.'

'I didn't know you kept one.'

'It wouldn't be secret if people knew about it.'

She blushed. He found it hard to know whether the confession had been blurted by accident, or whether it had been something she had been trying to tell him for some time.

'I hope it isn't indiscreet.'

'What's indiscreet?'

'When you say too much, or in this case, write too much; when you let out more than is wise; when you write things which it would be better that no one knew.'

'I'd heard the word,' she said. Her momentary silence, and her thoughtful expression, suggested that she was considering its aptness as a description of her journals. 'Aren't diaries meant to be indiscreet? Isn't that their point? You put things in them which you wouldn't want to say aloud to anyone else.'

'So, you've never shown it to anyone?'

'No prisoners,' she said, as she romped across the board, taking two more of his pieces. 'So did Granny pinch yours? Your diary?'

'As I say, I don't keep one.'

'Then, why accuse her of pinching it?'

'A couple of notebooks went missing – things I was working on. That's all. And a poetry book from my desk. That's all.'

'We could all search for them. They're probably just mislaid. Oh, here's Lotte. I know, Lotte – you want me to come downstairs and eat my tea.'

The Austrian au pair entered. Janet always attributed Lotte's poor complexion to nerves, insisting that no one who ate her wholesome food could suffer such dire facial effects. Bobs never told her grandmother of Lotte's addiction to chips, a craving fed by regular visits to Burger King or McDonald's on the pretext of 'slipping out to do some shopping'.

There was a dog-like vulnerability about Lotte's face, its large brown eyes, its oval shiny red cheeks, its frame of hair which always looked in need of a wash. She was thirty-five years old, a walking embodiment of the untruth that such skin and hair difficulties vanish after adolescence.

Janet, who usually spoke of Lotte as if she were a genus of domestic animal rather than a human being, was given to saying that 'they' were happier if a companion could be found for them. No one quite liked to give the obvious reply that Lotte was mysteriously lacking in sexuality. Another person with identical looks (even if afflicted with comparably severe acne) would have turned heads as she walked down the street. She was tall, shapely and fair haired, all supposedly attractive qualities. She had what are called good legs, and a well-developed chest. But there was something missing. Everyone felt it. She must have been aware of it herself, and it presumably contributed to her habitual low spirits and that absence of self-esteem which made her neglect her appearance.

'Amanda telephoned,' she said in a thick accent. 'She wanted you to telephone her to go through your chemistry homework.'

Amanda was not a friend. Bobs did not really have friends, of the sort who came to stay for the night in order to watch videos or eat pizzas. But it was obligatory to choose a partner for chemistry, and Amanda had been chosen for her by the teacher.

'I said you were busy,' said Lotte.

'I'd better ring her. But we're finishing this game first.'

'You must put Josh away in his cage before you go down for tea,' said Lotte.

'What makes you think that Josh is here?' asked Bobs. 'Lotte, what an extraordinary idea!' She did not say this with any intention to deceive. The little bulge was visible, running up and down inside her jumper. The fact that Lotte never understood this form of humour, this deliberate stating the opposite of what was visibly true, always made Bobs snigger.

It was not difficult to finish off Oliver on the draughts board. His defence was feeble.

'Great! Great! Total annihilation!' exclaimed the victor.

When she had gone ('Might do,' her impertinent reply to Lotte's repeated instruction to put Josh in his cage), Oliver began to address Lotte in her own language. His German was good from a grammatical point of view, but his accent, as Arnold Maar had often said, was laughable. It was of Arnold they spoke, as so often when speaking his language: a remarkable fact, since it was Lotte's language too, and they never spoke of her.

'Today I very carefully cleaned the bowls which your old friend, the distinguished professor, gave to you.'

'He departed them.'

'Truly?'

'That is to say, he bequeathed them. Not departed. Lotte, it is not good to clean them so vigorously. It will damage them.'

'I break the bowls? This is not true.'

'No, Lotte. It is not a question of breaking. You know that on the outside of the bowls, there is something?'

'There is dust, so I wash them.'

'No, there is another thing. Oh, my God! Thunder and lightning! I do not know the word.'

'If one of the bowls is broken, it is another who broke them. Perhaps the rat jumped up into the bowl. Rats can jump high. In Vienna after the war, my parents had rats in their apartment.'

'No one has broken a bowl. But you know that on the surface of each bowl there is something smooth, yes?'

'That is the glaze.'

Oliver struck his forehead with his palm and repeated the word. *Glasur, Glasur, Glasur.*

Then he said, 'It is so old that it is fragmentary.'

'Fragmentary, how so?'

'It does not stay near the bowl.'

'I do not understand.'

'If you wash them, if you wash the bowls in very hot water – yes? – with the soap, the glaze becomes weak and it goes away.'

'The colour, yes, is weak. It is faded, this colour. I think once they were a bright blue those bowls. I saw some Chinese bowls once in a museum, and they were bright blue.'

'There are different colours. This colour is called *ching pai*. It is like a duck egg. It is one of the distinguished colours of the Sung period. No? It is delicate and pure. It is like the sky in winter, grey but with only a little blue.'

'As I said, this colour is weak. The bowls in the museum were a very rich blue.'

'This colour goes away if you rub, rub with the soap.'

'But I tell you, they were this colour when they arrived. They have faded with age – it is not my washing them which makes them pale.'

'Since the Middle Ages, since Frederick Barbarossa was alive, these bowls have existed. It is very sad if we, being very kind, and wishing well, should rub, rub, so that we destroy them.'

'I did not wish to destroy anything.'

'I am sorry, Lotte. I did not want to make you sad.'

The ensuing silence, however, was sad, whether or not he wanted it.

To fill it, he went on, 'Tell me, Lotte, are they all as cross as the little girl says?'

'Mrs Rose, I guess, is the most cross. But all of them are sad because they love Oliver very much.' She smiled coyly. 'Even the little miss. She is perhaps saddest of all.'

'She does not show it.'

'Sometimes we feel things but we do not show our feelings.'

'I think it is a good thing for Bobs that I should go away.'

Lotte shrugged, as though there was no benefit to be gained by asking her.

'I fear that the time comes when, with me as her best friend, she cannot grow, like a flower. You know that a young person needs to change, to develop, to grow.'

'When I came here she was a tiny baby, and now she is grown so much in the last year, she is almost the little woman. She will miss you.'

'I shall miss her.'

'But not in quite the same way, I think. You fall in love, you go away with Camilla to live in America.'

'Who told you that?'

'She's American, isn't she? Mrs Baynes who is coming here next week, she comes in from America, from Detroit, I think?'

'Yes, she is fleeing from Detroit.'

'How so?'

'She flees from Detroit, but she lives nearby, some ten miles.'

'What is the danger, that she flees?'

Oliver knew what each word of this sentence meant but, since it made no sense to him, he assumed it was an idiom.

'But Lotte, you live here and your parents live in Austria. So why should not Mr and Mrs Baynes live in America, and she live in London with me?'

'She will have a baby, and then she will be homesick. This is what makes the house so sad. Mrs Rose is sad, and Michal is sad, and Miss Professor Cuffe, we are all sad. Very sad.'

'You are wrong. Camilla and I will not flee to the United States as soon as we are married.'

'That is what you believe. Camilla will want to take you and make you into an American. This she wants, and what she wants, she gets. For seven years you live in this house, like the family. Then you go. This is very sad for us all.'

'It is sad, of course it is, Lotte.'

'Yes.'

'I hear that Mrs Rose is angry with me because I asked her a question and she thought that I accused her of being a thief.'

'Oh, this is the very *indiscreet* diary.' She said the word in English.

'Do you always listen at doors?'

'Often.'

In the ensuing silence their positions changed. There was something of triumph in her smile. It would have been too strong a word to say that he felt as if blackmailed, but he certainly felt cornered.

'At your door I listen. At that of the Miss Professor, when she is with Michal.' There was no shame in these confessions, none; merely an infantile knowingness. 'And I hear Mrs Rose on the telephone to her friend Miss Reisz? These books which are stolen, she says they are your master work, very important. But Bobs believes they are *indiscreet*.'

'If you are going to listen, you should listen properly. It is true that some exercise books have gone missing. Lotte, they are very important to me. You must help me. You must help all of us.'

'If the others see these books, they will be angry, no?'

'You do the cleaning. You go into every room. If these books are hidden somewhere, you can help me find them.'

'You want me to be a spy?'

'Lotte, I will offer you anything if you can bring those exercise books back to me.'

She moved very close to him. The downy white mohair jumper which enclosed her firm round breasts was almost touching the orange zig-zags of the Young Farmers' jersey. Her lips were parted.

'You make a promise,' she whispered. 'If I find those books, you will not go to America? You will not marry Camilla?'

Chapter Seven

'It's absolutely nothing, really. I'll go change right away.'

'But it's not just on your mackintosh – it's got on to your trousers. Even your handbag's sticky.'

Janet Rose fussed about the visitor with a damp cloth.

'Oliver could not have been more apologetic,' said Mrs Baynes. 'Isn't he an adorable man? He said he'd left the car with the roof open on the lot overnight. So? Some kids got in and had a little fun. They'd have smeared worse on a car seat in Detroit, I can tell you.'

This was a plucky face to put on things. Janet disliked the intimacy it seemed to have created between the guest and her future son-in-law; she disliked the bustle and the palaver, too. She had envisaged that their guest would arrive from the airport by mid-morning at the latest. She would receive her alone. She had planned to give them both space to consider the momentous union of Oliver and Camilla. She would never have chosen such an entrance, their guest sticky from the car, the kitchen full of the whole complement – Bobs in her school uniform, Cuffe, Lotte. Even Michal had returned in the middle of the drama.

'We became worried,' said Cuffe, speaking louder than normal, as to a foreigner unsure of the language. Her eager friendliness was disconcerting to Janet, who had heard Cuffe's entirely disobliging views of Camilla. 'At first we thought the plane had been delayed . . .'

'We came in right on time, and there was Oliver, waiting for me. I thought maybe he'd be holding up my name, you know like the chauffeurs do at the barrier? But I recognized him at once from his photographs, and I dare say it was pretty obvious who I was. He can't get crazy American women waving enthusiastically at him every day of the week.'

'I wouldn't be too sure,' said Cuffe.

A little larger than her daughter, and considerably more handsome, Rosalie Baynes looked the reverse of crazy. She had thick, silvery-blonde hair, well coiffured and cut quite short, animated blue eyes, spectacles. She wore a little discreet lipstick and a gentle, pleasing scent emanated from her person, mingling with that of the honey which clung to her white mackintosh, her oatmeal trouser suit.

'Perhaps it would have been better,' said Michal, 'if Oliver had fetched you in a taxi. I do not know how you managed to fit that suitcase into his little car.'

'I balanced it. It was a squash, but the other bags fitted into the trunk, more or less.'

'And then, on top of all that, the car broke down,' said Michal, repeating what everyone knew already.

'We got two flats. Presumably, the kids thought it wasn't good enough just to pour sticky honey on the front seat of the car; they'd have a little fun fiddling with the tyre valves.'

'Could you have been killed?' asked Bobs.

'Well, of course it was dangerous, but so's driving a car.'

There was something spirited in Mrs Baynes's enunciation, which implied that conversation should aspire to the condition of epigram.

She continued, 'Oliver says it always vexes him when it is assumed that intellectual men have no practical knowledge. Wittgenstein was an engineer before he was a philosopher, and Oliver said that if he was clever enough to teach classes on Hegel, he was clever enough to change a flat tyre.'

Janet, who had never allowed Oliver to change so much as a light-bulb in her house, perhaps subscribed to the commonplace view that the life of the mind was incompatible with practicalities. She looked distinctly displeased by Rosalie Baynes's narrative, by the fact that this set of minor calamities had made the visitor so very much the centre of attention.

Mrs Baynes continued, 'Of course, he could change one tyre, but with two flats and one spare, that wasn't much help to us. But the police came along, and they were charming, and it was in its way a very charming lay-by. You know, we could even glimpse Stoke Poges church? We stood there, waiting for the breakdown truck to fetch us away to the garage, and there were cars and trucks whistling past us on the freeway, and airplanes coming into land practically over our heads, and in the midst of all this concrete horror and motorized mayhem, there's Thomas Gray's country churchyard. No ploughman homeward plodding his weary way today – just us. But here we are. We plodded.'

Over here! The phrase had almost been uttered, the conquistadorial watchwords of the GIs half a century earlier. Once more, with amiable self-confidence, the Yankee came to claim another European conquest. Janet, worn and older-looking since the previous evening, had been doing her best to save her treasure for the old world, to prevent the export without a struggle; but she found in Rosalie Baynes a bundle of unlooked-for qualities (for example, intelligence) which would make the struggle a difficult one. And, as on the previous occasion when they had come to lay claim to Europe, it was the more difficult to resist those who came, supposedly, as allies.

'Now,' she said, mistress at least in her own house, 'it's a strange time of day to be offering you anything, but we didn't touch the casserole for lunch, and it's still warm in the lower oven.'

'No, truly.'

'Auden always said that tea was the only thing he wanted when he was jet-lagged.'

'Really? Where did he say that?'

'In this kitchen actually.' Janet felt she had better give the visitor some impression of the kind of household she was coming into.

Whether Rosalie Baynes detected the lie, or whether she felt the allusion was merely a little ambitious, she chose not to rise.

'Well, maybe some coffee, if anyone else is having some. Would you have de-caff?'

It appeared that Cuffe kept decaffeinated in her quarters and she went to fetch it while Janet switched on the electric kettle. While the stainless steel vessel murmured into life, Janet involuntarily recalled the previous evening's effort to win Oliver back. She had been feeling deeply silly all day, trying not to think about it.

The idea had come to her in the bath, as she lay drinking brandy in the steamy waters. These solitary evening booze-ups, when the others had all retired to bed, had become something of a routine. She did not usually get drunk, just lightly sozzled in front of the late television news pro-gramme. Then, with the remains of her brandy, she would slip into a bath. On this occasion, though, she had replen-ished her glass, and as she lay in the scented waters, the fantasy was so strong that she could almost believe that she was Oliver's lover. It was good, sometimes, to forget that she had not had sex for thirty years. The third glass of brandy, and the steam, were conducive to a reverie which had felt like reasonable mental processes. The poor man was lonely. That was the explanation for his choosing this unsuitable bride. If he had only realized that Janet was available, he would have found nothing to tempt him in the American girl.

The bathtime fantasy was completely specific. She would go into Oliver's bedroom and find him sitting up, propped against the pillows in his pyjamas, reading a book. She would sit on the bed and gather him into her arms.

She wanted to do this for her own gratification – that went without saying – but she had also persuaded herself that it was, quite simply, the best thing for them all. He had been living under her roof for nearly eight years. He could have been her husband all this time, or at the very least, her lover. They had all assumed that he was a celibate, or a man who preferred his own sex. Young Camilla Baynes had exploded this theory, and revealed to them an unattached and beautiful male who was lying in his bedroom night after night, theirs for the asking. Of course, Michal and Catharine Cuffe had one another – they did not want him as a lover. It was Janet who must offer herself. She was not much older than he was. The decade or so which separated their ages became, in the course of the bath fantasy, little more than years.

If she, Janet, could give him what he wanted, there need be no more talk of his going to America. Everything had worked so well until Camilla had entered the scene. Now, he had changed. Instead of the philosopher in cycle clips, wearing the chaste blue guernsey and the corduroy trousers, the cycle helmet and the luminous sash, the true London cyclist, he had become a laughable figure in a whole range of unsuitable, incongruous outfits, who drove a stupid little car. It was not a philosopher's mode of transport. It was that of a bimbo.

With the change of car and clothes had come the change of sympathies. The Old Oliver would never have accused Janet of rummaging about among his belongings, or stealing his notebooks. The very idea was preposterous, that Janet, of all people who understood about writers and thinkers, should have done anything so clumsy. Hensleigh had never been able to write a review if someone else was in the room. Janet knew about the necessary secrecies with which a writer surrounds the process of composition. But Oliver, in his wild agitation, appeared to have forgotten this. He had all but accused her of stealing. Then, during another frenzied, whispered questioning, he had said, 'I suppose you know their contents by now?'

He had seemed slightly insane when he asked this – so unlike Old Oliver, *their* Oliver, who would surely have welcomed one of the women taking such an interest in his work that they should have sought a sneak preview.

It was all this painfulness, this barrier of distrust which had grown up between them, which Janet, in her boozy bathroom reverie, had resolved to assuage. They would make love! All would be well! This was what he had been wanting, needing, all those years. She had a very specific sense of his body, at this point of her fantasy. She remembered him in swimming drawers at the local baths, and on seaside holidays. She remembered him, hand in hand with Bobs, running into the waves at Polzeath – his bare bony shoulders, his white back, his long, spindly, hairy legs, his surprisingly broad and masculine chest, with its tufts of shaggy fur. Oh, she wanted it, she wanted it; and in her erotic mindplay, she had satisfied, not only a longing in herself, but the problem which beset them all, this impending marriage. In one delicious act of sexual passion, she would resolve the whole crisis. She would bring back their Oliver, reclaim their lost hero, and at the same time have an experience which she had been missing, last enjoyed, if that was the right word, when Hensleigh had been very drunk after a party.

Towelled and talced and pomaded, she had slipped her naked body into a dressing-gown. (Neither she nor Hensleigh had nightclothes, having heard from one of their bohemian friends that such things were bourgeois. Their nakedness in the same bed had been one of the more poignant features of their nearly sexless marriage.) She knew what she had to do. Quite steady enough to walk, and to climb the stairs barefoot, she must *confront* him. This terrible thing, this engagement, had come about because of American brazenness. (The fact that Camilla was so obviously unbrazen, so retiring, timid, mouselike, did nothing to diminish Janet's belief in the young woman's conquistadorial skills; she had marked out territory at once by buying things, and no doubt, in private, she had made comparably overt sexual claims. And this, clearly, was what

123

the shy Englishman wanted, needed.) She had been resolved then, the naked, dressing-gowned figure of Janet on the stairs, to come at him quite openly, to offer herself.

When she tried to recall the scene next morning, she could not be sure whether or not she had heard voices from Oliver's bedroom, or whether she had merely heard Oliver's voice. If he had indeed spoken, was it because he was speaking to himself? Or because there was someone in his bedroom? Or just because he had heard her coming up the stairs? The truth was, that though she had been able to walk, she had been quite far gone in drink. She knew that this must have been the case, since – there he was! He had heard her coming up the stairs, while she was under the impression that the pink feet, whose little toes were distorted by corns, had made a silent ascent.

'Janet – is everything all right?'

Oliver had not been in bed, as she hoped. He was standing outside his room, with an expression of anxiety on his face. He had been wearing striped pyjamas. A few sprigs of chest hair were visible above the crimson and white collar of the pyjama jacket. She had thought she had sensed the shape of his manhood beneath the trousers, as though he had emerged from his bed in a condition of semi-arousal. Honesty compelled her to recall that if this had been the case, then she had caught it in mid-descent, rather than the opposite.

'I'm not going to eat you, you know,' she had said.

'It did not cross my mind that you would.'

This exchange, spoken aloud by herself, whispered by Oliver, took place on the landing.

'Don't you think you should ask me into your room?' she had said.

'Can't this wait until morning?'

'Let me in, Oliver. Be a sport.'

In response to this piece of ribaldry, he had directed her quite firmly, not towards his bedroom, but to the little sitting-room, which did not have so much as a sofa. She had still felt confident that they could do it there as well as anywhere.

'You've been quite distant with us since Camilla came into your life, Ollie. Of course, we love Camilla – we all do. Lovely girl.'

'You've all been – marvellous.'

'But we love you more, Ol. We love you. Ol, pet. Think what you're doing. Think of little Bobs.'

A curious expression – panic? rage? she had not been able to read it – had passed over his face.

'You've forgotten about Bobs, haven't you? She'll miss you, it won't just be your three groupies who'll be sad. You've helped her, brought her on in so many ways.'

'I know it will be hard for us all, saying goodbye,' he said.

'We love you, Oliver.'

'I know.'

'Come on, Ol.'

If his pained expression had been worthy of study when she mentioned Bobs, words could not be found to describe the terror and surprise that he evinced at her next casual gesture, as she unloosed her girdle and revealed her naked state.

And he had reached out – put his hands on her shoulders, so that it really seemed as if her bathtime fantasy was about to be enacted.

'Touch me, Oliver. Feel me. You know it's what you really want. Feel me, Ollie, feel me, wanting you? Can you? Oh, I want you so much.'

Words like this really had fallen from her lips as he had gripped her shoulders.

'Have you been drinking?' he asked.

'I had a little drop.'

'We shall have forgotten this in the morning.'

This had sobered her up. She could remember with painful clarity all that followed; the fact that the night air on her nakedness felt, not erotic but simply chilly, as she regirdled herself; the fact that the varicose veins on her left leg were so disfiguring; the fact that her pubic hair was grey and her breasts were shrivelled. How could such a scene be forgotten, in the morning, ever?

'Shall I help you downstairs?'

'No, no. I shall be all right.'

'Good night, Janet.'

His words had been so matter of fact, as if she had merely come upstairs to bring him a cup of cocoa.

In the morning, they had met in the kitchen. She had made him an early cup of tea before he drove in the Mazda to fetch Camilla's mother from the airport. There had been no possibility of discussing what had taken place. He certainly did not want to do so, nor did she. In the light of day, Janet wondered how she could have made such a blunder, one calculated to drive Oliver away, even if he did not have the arms of Camilla as his refuge.

And now, only hours after that cold exchange over the early-morning tea mugs, Janet found herself confronted by the mother, who had somehow managed to make the calamities of a tedious journey serve to her advantage in the emotional competition which had now been made so embarrassingly overt.

'And while I'm up in this part of town, I thought I'd have a look at the Freud Museum,' Rosalie Baynes was saying. 'A friend of mine went last summer and told me it is absolutely fascinating. You see the great man's collection of totems and fetishes all over the room. And the famous couch. There's even a little movie they show you, of a birthday party? Something like that, and you see his dogs and all running up to him. I love that kind of stuff.'

'It's down in West Hampstead,' said Janet. 'We are, strictly speaking, Muswell Hill.' None of the women had in fact visited the museum, but at least they knew the geography of London better than their visitor.

'It's near Frognal,' said Rosalie Baynes, not with the air of someone who needed to put another down, but with the easy, and in the circumstances tactless, desire to place the

Freud Museum on the map. 'Maresfield Gardens. I reckon I'll go to Finchley Road and walk. When I was still working as a librarian, we used to have some very good friends who lived up in Canfield Gardens? It's the other side of Finchley Road, I guess.'

No one had discovered, before her arrival, that Rosalie was a former librarian. Having consigned her safely to the world of vulgarian plutocracy, it was annoying to have to bring her closer to the intellectual fold.

'Hensleigh came on the scene *just* too late to know Sigmund, but we all knew Anna, of course, and Lucien and Clé have crossed our paths at different stages.'

'There's a man called Freud on *Just a Minute*,' said Bobs. 'It's a really funny radio programme,' she explained to the visitor. 'You have to speak for a minute without deviating, without hesitating – and what's the other one?'

'Repeating yourself,' said Janet. 'That's our friend Clé, on the show.'

'I didn't know you knew Clement Freud.'

The child, normally bored by the namedropping, seemed genuinely impressed.

'I could take you to the Freud Museum,' said Cuffe.

Janet shot her a glance. She had a bleak sense of a marvellous world, their lives with Oliver, dissolving. Before, they would have stuck together. Now, it was every woman for herself.

'I'm rather ashamed I've never seen it,' continued Cuffe. 'One doesn't have to be a Freudian to be interested in it.'

'What's a Freudian?' asked Bobs.

'I don't know,' said Mrs Baynes. 'In spite of myself, I *am*. Okay, a lot of it is nonsense, but he's the one who really got us thinking about this strange thing called self we are all carrying round inside us, the bits we've forgotten, or buried; the bits we think we remember, but don't want to remember in the way they really happened . . .'

'Well, these are deep waters to have sailed into,' said Janet airily, scarcely able to understand their visitor's absence of interest. Mrs Baynes had been told, albeit untruthfully, that W.H. Auden drank tea in that kitchen, and that Hensleigh and Janet were on nodding terms with the Freuds. She had not raised an eyebrow.

'You've not had time to change your things,' said Janet, but just too late to interrupt Cuffe's, 'I can't buy penis envy.'

'Well,' said Rosalie Baynes, 'there are things I've envied more, certainly.'

'Is that what Freud thinks?' asked Bobs, extremely amused. 'That women want to have *those*?'

'It's one of the things he thought,' said Cuffe.

'The main thing he believed,' said Rosalie, addressing her remarks this time expressly to the child, 'is that when grown-up people are unhappy, it's very often because of a bad thing that happened to them when they were children. And if this unhappy person goes to see Dr Freud, and talks and talks about his childhood –'

'Without deviation, hesitation or repetition,' giggled Bobs.

'Well, then they can find out what was bugging them. Often it may be something so awful that they'd buried it away down inside them and forgotten it.'

'I remember now,' said Bobs. 'Oliver had an idea about that chap, didn't he?'

'It would be very surprising,' said Cuffe, 'if Ol did not have an idea about Freud. He has an idea about most things.'

'What if you weren't messed up?' asked Bobs. 'What if you could remember your childhood, and there were some bad things and some good things but you didn't see any point in letting them get you down?'

'Well then,' said Rosalie, 'you'd be a very lucky, well-balanced person and I guess you'd be wasting your money going to see Dr Freud.'

'There are plenty of other things to see in North London,' said Janet. 'There's Hampstead Heath, of course. There is Kenwood House, where there are some wonderful pictures. Oh, many things.'

'I often explored Hampstead when we stayed with Tom and Lizzie, the friends in Canfield Gardens,' said Mrs Baynes. 'It's just I never got round to the Freud Museum.'

'What sort of memories would they be?' asked Bobs, unable, it would seem, to leave the subject. 'The ones which were too horrid to remember? Would it be things like the war? Or people being really, really horrid to you?'

'Well, the whole point is that they are so horrid you've forgotten about them,' said Mrs Baynes gaily. 'So you bury 'em away like a dead body in a cellar, but the smell keeps on coming up the stairs.'

'Poo!'

'So all your fears come out in other ways – in dreams, in funny kinds of behaviour patterns.'

'I expect it's a bit like hypnosis,' said Bobs. She began to tell Mrs Baynes about a recent television programme in which a man was hypnotized and made to perform all manner of undignified actions, for example, believing that the chair on which he sat was scaldingly hot, or that an old mop on a wooden handle was a beautiful woman. She had difficulty in recalling the programme without splutters of mirth.

'I love that sort of show. It just sounds hilarious,' said Mrs Baynes.

Oliver returned to the kitchen with a plastic bucket full of water on whose soapy surface a sponge floated.

'I think I've got it all off,' he said, 'but it's hard to know until the seats are completely dried whether some stickiness remains.'

'Well –' Mrs Baynes shrugged – 'that's inner-city kids for you.' She repeated that the children of Detroit would have been able to devise something steamier, gamier.

'Mrs Baynes has been telling us about Clement Freud,' said Bobs. 'You see, everything's locked up inside you, and you forget it all because it's too painful to remember, and then he puts you into a kind of trance.'

'It was entirely my fault for leaving the car roof open overnight,' said Oliver.

'I think that if something really awful had happened to me at the age of three,' said Bobs O'Hara, 'I should prefer not to remember it.'

'There's much to be said for that point of view,' said Mrs Baynes.

But Janet said to her, 'Now, Rosalie, we've kept you long enough. You really must go upstairs and change, and Oliver will take those clothes to the dry-cleaners for you this afternoon.'

Chapter Eight

Michal Rose and Catharine Cuffe lay in bed together, in the dark, eight hours later.

'You don't think,' asked the child's mother, 'that Bobs was responsible for smearing the car seat, do you?'

Cuffe was silent. Complaints about the sprog's behaviour were allowed when they fell from Michal's lips, but it was a different thing if Cuffe ventured even the slightest criticism. Then Michal could become a tigress defending her cub. Cuffe recognized that a delicate balance needed to be held between expressing a kindly (and insincere) interest in the development of Bobs, and the equally powerful necessity to keep a tactful distance. Any reply made to Michal in her present, tense mood must be supportive of all the mother's emotional responses, while not appearing to collude in any condemnation. While she considered her words carefully, Michal spoke again, and it was clear that she had interpreted the silence as accusatory.

'So! You think she poured honey all over the inside of

Oliver's new car, and you said nothing? You think she fiddled with the tyre valves – it could have killed him, for Christ's sake! That's really extraordinary of you, Catharine.'

When Michal loved her, she called her friend 'Cuffe'; it was only in wrath that she used her first name.

'We've all shown, in different ways, how upset we are about Oliver,' said Cuffe. 'I mean, my God! When I heard her at supper going on and on and *on* about the house she's having built for them in Connecticut, I just felt so angry, Michal. This is such a waste. The most brilliant man of his generation, for Christ's sake, and she's putting him in a wooden hut with that *chipmunk*. I mean, imagine all the interesting work of which he'll be capable, with *that* going on as background noise all the time.' She adopted an atrociously unconvincing rendition of Rosalie Baynes's voice: '"Would you believe, you can buy an entire wooden house, ready made, prefabricated? They just build the whole thing in Detroit and stick it on the back of a truck and drive it to wherever you want to live. And that's what these folks'll do. They'll just drive off and find a nice little plot and –"'

'But you haven't answered me. You think Bobs vandalized the car. You think Bobs tried to kill Oliver.'

'We're all very unhappy. I didn't even know they were thinking of living in America until she came out with it at supper. I mean, I thought at least they'd live in London. So of course, we are all unhappy. You and I, Mike, at least we've shown it, at least we can admit it to one another. But Bobs is different. She's feeling as much pain as the rest of us, but she can't let it show. You're always saying she's no friends at school, no friends of her own age.'

'What's that supposed to mean?'

'It isn't meant to mean anything. I am just saying what you often say.'

'Well, don't. Maybe Bobs is just more polite than we are, more grown up, more anxious that Oliver should be happy.'

'Michal! That kid has lived in Oliver's shadow for the last seven years. Completely. He has been her constant companion. The minute she gets back from school, she runs up to see him – assuming he hasn't been to meet her at the school gate. They've eaten their meals together. They've played Snap, tennis, Monopoly, Lexicon together. They read the same books. When we all went to the Cornish cottage, they even slept in the same bed.'

'Someone had to share with her, and she said she didn't want to share with Granny.'

'They're so close, she and Oliver. And now he's getting married, he talks quite calmly of going away, he doesn't even tell us that he's going to live in *America* –' her voice rose to a shriek – 'and what's her reaction? Bobs is happy as a lark. It doesn't make sense. Something is going to snap – that's all I'm saying.'

'Maybe she's not really upset. Children are weird. I work with them all day, remember. They never react as you'd expect. It could be that she simply doesn't mind Oliver going – not in the way you mind. You think she's got to be upset because you are upset.'

'We are all upset.'

'We are all upset, granted. But maybe you are the most upset. After all, you are in love with the man.'

In the dark bedroom, Cuffe's response was a sigh.

'You always were in love with him. You have never been in love with me. Just leave my child out of it, will you?'

Cuffe reached across her lover's shoulder to comfort, to reassure. But Michal would not be held. She shrugged off the advance, and pulled herself upright against the pillow.

'Look, you know how I feel about Oliver,' said Cuffe. 'I've never made any secret of that. He was my mentor, my god, my hero. But, of course, I've grown up since I was an undergraduate. In some ways, I grew out of Oliver years ago. In other ways – well, you don't grow out of a thing like that.'

'I don't want to listen. You've told me so many times. We've had to listen to your feelings about Oliver morning, noon and night for the last ten years.'

'Darling, we haven't known one another for ten years.'

'Don't condescend to me.'

'I'm not. Oh, Mike. Be as angry as you like, but don't be angry with me.'

There was a long silence.

Then Cuffe repeated, 'Don't, Mike. Don't be angry with me. I need you now more than ever.'

'You started it by accusing my daughter of pouring liquid honey over that foul little car.'

'I *didn't*.' Cuffe had ceased to be the sweetly reasonable philosopher and had sat upright. She repeated stridently, 'I didn't. It was you who started talking about the car.'

'*You* said that Bobs –'

'I didn't say anything, Michal, until you started to talk about it.' Once again Cuffe tried to hold Michal, and once again she was repulsed. And now the Irish dander was up and the redhead flew from the bed. Standing beside it, she shouted, 'You are so *childish*. Did you know that? So childish – much more childish than Bobs. Perhaps it was you who messed up the fucking car.'

'Oh, I like that. I'm to blame for everything. It was you who brought him to live here. It's just been a cover, all along.'

'What's been a cover?'

'You *are* lovers!'

'What are you talking about?'

'You and Oliver are lovers. You and Oliver make love. Then he found Camilla, and you were so jealous that you behaved like a maniac, you started destroying his things!'

'Mike, that is just the craziest . . .'

'My God, how could I have been so stupid? It's been going on, in this house, under our noses, and I'm –'.

Cuffe grabbed the duvet and wrenched it off Michal.

'What the hell are you doing?' Michal yelled.

'I'm going to sleep in the chair,' said Cuffe, marching

137

across the room with the bedding and throwing herself into an armchair by the fireplace.

'Oh, Cuffe, don't sit there. You're on my shirt, fuck you! I ironed that shirt, and I was going to wear it in the magistrates' court tomorrow.'

Rosalie Baynes lay in her shadowy, unfamiliar room, wide awake. She decided, if the noise continued much longer, that she should switch on her light and open the volume of Elizabeth Bishop's poetry with which she liked to travel. How did anyone sleep in this house with a din like that going on? Why, those women were shouting at the tops of their voices!

Still, she lay in the dark, hoping that her body, in spite of the racket, would assert its need for rest and take her off to sleep.

Camilla had explained about the household at 12 Wagner Rise in her long letters, written in that small, regular hand, covering leaf after tissuey thin leaf. She had nevertheless implied, without overtly stating, that Oliver led his own life; if not in his own apartment, then anyway separately, in the house of these women. Rosalie had been unprepared for the cheek-by-jowl, hugger-mugger nature of existence here. She was even having to share a bathroom with those two.

'*Look, why not admit it? You've been in love with Oliver for fifteen years. Moving in here with me was just an excuse, to let you live under the same roof as him . . .*'

Rosalie's feelings about her daughter (so different from her closeness to her son Frank, cheerfully, and for a second time, married, with kids and an excellent job, the only drawback being that the job was in Sacramento, too far for frequent visits) were raw-toned, inhabiting that swampy emotional territory between anger, guilt and simple incomprehension. Rosalie had always wanted to be Camilla's friend, but there was this little wall of sadness about the girl. When the prestigious sale-room who employed her in New York had suggested, or offered, the move to their London branch, the feelings of Camilla's mother would have been difficult to define.

Initially, there had been a sensation like relief, but it had been a relief shot through with the sad recognition that she had failed to get through to Camilla in the previous quarter of a century. If she moved to England, there was a chance that this 'getting through' would never happen. She had not felt relief because she was not fond of Camilla. Rather it was that Camilla had always constituted in her mother's bosom a weight of bother, the sense that she was a problem; and the knowledge that her daughter was to be shipped, like one of the precious cargoes for which the firm was celebrated, from Manhattan to London conveyed briefly the hope that the weight of the problem would be taken too. Perhaps Camilla would learn the art of happiness in England? Lighten up a little? Meet a nice man?

Such miracles had happened before, when young people crossed the Atlantic. On her visits home, Camilla had seemed jollier, almost from the first. If, as her father had intolerantly remarked after the first Thanksgiving visit, it appeared that all her acquaintances in London were goddarned fairies, this was, Rosalie had tried to explain, a professional hazard. Both parents came to recognize that in the two years she had spent in London, Camilla had discovered that she was seriously good at her job. That must have accounted for part of it, the burgeoning self-esteem. But still, no beau had entered the story which she episodically relayed in her airmail letters. It did not take much imagination to guess that there had been attempts, escapades, evenings which came to nothing. Camilla was attending a church. Howard did not greatly like the sound of it, but at least there were men there, and it might have been hoped that some of them – a banker called Derek who had taken her to a Bible class, a doctor called Graham who had invited her with a party of like-minded Christians to stay in Suffolk – would have come up with the goods. In two years, however, there had been no hint of any serious takers.

The suddenness with which Oliver Gold's name was introduced into the epistolary narrative came as a shock to Camilla's two readers in their attractive suburb ten miles from the centre of Detroit. Here was a figure who burst on to the scene, full blown and unexplained, a picaresque trick which jarred on the aesthetic nerves of one reader who was used to Edith Wharton, and another whose daily diet of prose came from the *Wall Street Journal*. Hitherto, the neat-handed narrations took as their theme the politics of the sale-room, and the lives of a chosen few, loosely connected with the commercial side of the art world, whose supper parties were more amusing than the staider non-alcoholic meals of the Grahams and the Dereks. Ross, Scott, Jim, Brad, Chuck (a fellow-countryman) and their various squabbles and alliances gradually became known to the readers, though one of the readers wondered why all the young men were so darned monosyllabic. Howard did not like what he read between the lines of the young men's habits, but except for the occasional episode when work and pleasure dramatically collided (Ross and Scott's purchase of a magnificent seventeenth-century bed, said to have belonged to a Duke of Abercorn, was an example) it was usually possible to leave the more disturbing sides of these friends' lives as a matter of inference. Rosalie felt pleased, at least, that solemn little Camilla had met some friends with a little colour, openly preferring those letters which dealt with these aesthetes to those which related the sermons preached at Camilla's place of worship.

And then – Oliver had taken her to Gluck's *Orfeo*. There was no, 'I've met a man called Oliver and'. Simply, 'Oliver took me to *Orfeo* last night.' The next week it was a stupendous production of *Parsifal*, staged by a visiting German company. Then a theatrically absurd but musically rich *Götterdämmerung* at Covent Garden. Soon, the letters became mere chronicles of Oliver's opinions. Rosalie found herself missing Scott's tiffs with Ross, and Chuck's lucky finds in the Portobello Market. There was Oliver on opera (Gluck was the greatest composer of operas, it appeared – 'That puts Verdi in his place,' Howard had said); Oliver on the decline of modern culture (all the fault of the Americans, it would seem); Oliver on ceramics (nothing worth writing about between the Ming dynasty and Bernard Leach, the stupendous masterpieces of Meissen or Sèvres being branches of confectionery, not art); fiction – almost nothing which was any good in English; poetry – stick to the Greeks and the Germans. There had been so much of Oliver (and all this since her last visit home) that their decision to be married hardly came as a surprise.

Howard's view that Rosalie should go to Europe at once and check this guy out had nevertheless seemed like horse sense. Why, for instance, had their two holidays together been kept a secret till they were home again? There had been twelve days in Switzerland, and a visit to his old university town, lasting several days. In all her carefully documented accounts of mountain walks, or medieval architecture, or the arcane rituals of an academic dinner, there had been no hint of his marital status. Rosalie Baynes decided that the likeliest explanation was that her daughter had gotten herself entangled with a married man. It was painfully obvious that Camilla was serious about him, but it would not be possible to sound out Oliver's level of seriousness without crossing the ocean.

There was an inheritance from a grandmother; not 'pots',

but enough to establish a degree of independence for the affianced couple, if independence was what they wanted. It had, in fact, been Camilla, and not her mother, who raised the possibility of a prefabricated log cabin, to be set down in rural Connecticut; she had heard about them from a colleague. Oliver, it seemed, was anxious to get away from England. He needed this for his sanity. He had tried the experiment of leaving his university job and establishing himself as a recluse in Muswell Hill *and it had not worked*. This much had been established by Camilla's letters home.

There was an ambiguity about all this, though, which confirmed Mrs Baynes's view that she should see the situation for herself. For this reason, she had accepted Janet's invitation to stay at 12 Wagner Rise, rather than putting up at her usual and favourite London haunt. What exactly were their plans? Would they live in the log cabin or simply go there for summer vacations? Would they buy an apartment in London? In New York? Camilla had neglected to give specific answers to these questions when they had been put to her on paper or on the telephone, answering as though they did not affect herself, only Oliver. Wherever she was, she hoped to do something in the ceramics line. Sure. The essential thing, Camilla had tried to convey, was that Oliver should write a book, one which was worthy of his genius. She had explained to her mother that it was Oliver's last chance. If it failed, well, they would think again in two or three years' time; he would find himself a job in some university, on one side of the Atlantic or the other. As for herself, Camilla would be just fine, fitting in with Oliver's arrangements.

This acceptance of Oliver's agenda fascinated Mrs Baynes. She hoped she had brought up Camilla to be a good feminist; insofar as this affected personal life, however, it had never cropped up. Camilla, in all her college years, and her period in New York and London, had shown no particular interest in either sex, and had remained without a regular companion. What fascinated the mother, then, about Camilla's readiness to fall in with Oliver's arrangements, indeed to plan her whole life around him, was not a departure so much from principle as practice. It was a change from a lifetime's habit of melancholy self-absorption, and consideration of no person but Camilla herself.

'It's you *who are in love with him. Not* me.'

'Me *in love with Oliver? You must be* joking!'

This exchange was yelled out in the next-door bedroom. Back home it was round about ten in the evening; here it was the small hours. Howard would be walking Rocket round the yard, smoking a last pipe; checking the burglar alarms; pouring himself a modest malt, and maybe watching some stupid thing on TV. Already, Mrs Baynes had seen and heard enough to make the few remaining hairs on Howard's somewhat monastic-looking skull stand up on end.

To begin with, Oliver's age, which had never been mentioned to them in letters, had come as a surprise. She had been told to expect a man at Heathrow who was bearded. But she had not expected a man whose beard was long and flecked with grey. Why, this fellow was Rosalie's own age! And it was much worse than his being married, with a wife and kids to support – far worse than that. He had never been married at all! He was a bachelor, for godssakes.

He had been extremely friendly, though it was an act of extraordinary thoughtlessness to meet someone at an airport in such a tiny sports car. Had it never occurred to his philosophical brain that she would be dragging a suitcase which was larger than the trunk of the car itself? And how truly astonishing that this snazzy little vehicle had been the gift of Camilla herself. It must have cleared out the little ninny's life-savings. She might even have been forced to borrow to pay for it. Once arrived at 12 Wagner Rise, Rosalie had been quick to pick up the belief in this household that Camilla was some kind of an heiress. True, they were comfortable, but no more than Janet Rose appeared to be. The little girl prattled as if she thought the Baynes family were in the Getty league of wealth. Then again, all that stuff about huntin', shootin' and fishin'. The child had quizzed her as if she had represented herself as a duchess with rolling acres, seldom out of the saddle. Howard did have some cousins down in Virginia, and they'd once or twice taken him out hunting. Rosalie herself had, once or twice, shot duck and snipe. She had never claimed to be a landed aristocrat, and it was difficult to imagine that Camilla would have wished to paint this misleading picture. Rosalie had thought this worth explaining at the supper table, and Camilla herself had twitted the little girl for overstressing the Bayneses' interest in rural pursuits. Nevertheless, Rosalie had read in the hostile glances of the adult females both a disapproval of blood sports (understandable enough these days) and the accusation of fraudulence, as if the family Baynes had been selling itself as something it wasn't.

That journey from the airport had been the least comfortable of her life. It was a great contrast to her normal, nifty London routine; the trundling of the large suitcase on its wheels to the underground station; the speedy Piccadilly line direct to Knightsbridge. How could that bearded loon have been so absorbed in his own thoughts as not to notice that he had a slow puncture in two tyres, and that the passenger seat of the Mazda was coated with honey?

Rosalie Baynes, throbbing with tiredness throughout the unpalatable supper, had been scarcely aware of what she was saying. She could not make sense of this set-up. She had never seen Camilla in love before, so glowingly, so blindly, so painfully cheerful. She formed the sense that the household was an emotional harem; not one where sexual licence was practised, but one where females, the silly grandmother, the truculent Michal, the disconcerting friend Miss Cuffe, whose tone of irony spoke continually of a joke she was keeping to herself, the weird little grandchild and the Austrian nurse, all worshipped her future son-in-law.

Oliver had done his best to put Rosalie at her ease in the initial stages of the evening, but he had quickly forgotten his manners and become abstracted, even irritable. Rosalie did not see much sign that he loved Camilla. There was something theatrical about the doting way he addressed her, and then lost himself once more in thought. When the supper had broken up, and Camilla had made steps to depart, he had merely waved her goodbye. No smooching in the hall, no seeing her into a taxi. Rosalie had felt perfectly idiotic, prattling about their ludicrous log-cabin scheme as if she considered it the sweetest idea in the world. She had merely wanted to convey that she gave a mother's blessing to the union. Inside, however, she had misgivings. Something was wrong. Even before she had retired to bed – and what an uncomfortable bed, with no support in the mattress, into whose softness she sank with the ominous dread of future back pains – she did not feel happy about the arrangement. It was horrible to say that she smelt a rat – though, as Bobs had told her, this was quite literally what she could smell, together with a chicken, a budgerigar and a rabbit. The house did not feel right; and she knew this even before she had spent those insomniac hours listening to the women in the room next to her own, shouting at one another about Oliver.

The abusive sounds had by now become more affectionate. Having decided to jump up and down on the loose floorboards (or that was what it sounded like) the lovers had gone back to bed to effect a reconciliation. There could now be heard ecstatic groans and the movement of bed-springs. The stiff, feathery pillow was the best thing Rosalie could find to wrap round the back of her head to muffle her ears. Wide awake with exhaustion, she whispered, 'Oh, my gosh.'

Chapter Nine

Oliver also lay awake, but with the sleeping form of Bobs in his arms. He loved the smell of the child. There is a point in the physical development of any human being when the odours given off by its body become repugnant. This point perhaps would soon come to Bobs. There was a certain event of which he lived in dread; he feared that when it happened, he would be unable any longer to hold her in his bed as he did now, savouring the smell of her hair, and the hot, lithe body as it lay, clad in her pyjamas, in his arms. Dogs and cats and horses retained the sweetness of their own smells, as children did; even their farts were sweet by comparison with the rank odours produced by adults. As for grown-up sweat, and grown-up breath . . . How could any pair of adults wish to share a bed? (This was a matter which had never cropped up with his fiancée, and he hoped to deliver it, as he was able to deliver so many other injunctions to that obedient young woman, as a *fait accompli*. But all in good time.)

He kissed the sleeping head of Bobs, and the sweatiness of her brow and head, that fever which all young children have in sleep and which was not symptomatic of unhealthiness, made him tingle with physical love. It was extraordinary that a dream child, *the* dream child, who had been inside his head for upwards of twenty years, should have become incarnate for him. He knew no greater joy than he knew now, and no greater sorrow, for he had made up his mind, if his notebooks had indeed been read by another member of the household, that he would commit suicide.

Aware of the devastation which this would cause to his beloved, he was plunged into a tormented conundrum, unable yet to decide whether he should die in absolute solitude and selfishness, or whether the kindest thing would be to take Bobs with him, to kill her first, and then himself.

The logic of the position was inescapable. While the women were under the impression that he was engaged on a great philosophical tract, he had, for a number of years, been keeping a detailed journal of his love for Bobs. The notebooks must have run to at least half a million words, though not every page related directly to Bobs. He had typed up a hundred and fifty thousand words or so, and these versions he kept in a locked black metal deed box under his bed. It would have required a crowbar to open this box. Yet, while he kept this more polished version so tightly secured, he had, with a recklessness which he now regarded as insane, been accustomed to keep the written notebooks on his shelves, arranged by number, upright, together with his philosophical notebooks, offprints, scrapbooks and other academic jottings. It had seemed safer to hide them by not hiding them, than to draw attention to a considerable body of secret work by purchasing several lockable trunks, or by secreting them in his chest of drawers with his clothes. In spite of his protestations that he wished to be personally responsible for keeping his own shirts, socks and jerseys tidy, Lotte and Janet both had the habit of coming into his room with freshly laundered items and replacing them in this object of furniture. They also, in spite of the fact that he had asked them not to do so, were in the habit of dusting and tidying his desk. But the shelves were sacrosanct, and he had never had any reason to suppose that anyone had ever plundered them before.

When he had first come to live in the house, he had filled the notebooks with reflections about Dante. Guided by Arnold Maar, he had decided to discipline himself by not writing any philosophy. He would channel his writing energies into a new project, which was the setting down of his thoughts on *The Divine Comedy*.

Oliver had been a reader of Dante since his schooldays. He had bought a tiny dark-blue pocket version of the *Inferno*, the Temple Classics edition published by Dent, with an English translation on the recto pages, and the Italian, a language he did not then know, on the verso opposite. He had found, with a schoolboy knowledge of Latin and French, that it was easy to acquire a reading knowledge of Italian, and this was brushed into shape by attending a course at the British Institute in Florence after he left school.

Since then, he had read the *Commedia* every year, and usually kept a copy of one of the Temple Classics volumes in his pocket. When mugging up the drier points of the law in chambers, or when, at a later stage, he had wrestled with logic and the task had seemed so arid that he felt his brain drying up like sawdust, the Italian master brought deep refreshment. At first, he read the poem for the sense of uplift it brought him, and for the idea that Love, first encountered in humankind, was an inexplicable psychological-cum-spiritual mystery which, for the medieval author, led to a penetration of the meaning of life itself, and the purposes of God.

Gradually, Oliver, who did not believe in God, developed an interest in Dante's own life, his biography, his friends, his family, the history of thirteenth-century Florence. He had periods of revulsion against the *Commedia*; the relentless and self-confident malice which consigned Dante's enemies to hell, for example, became more and not less distasteful to him with the years. And there were times when, to Oliver as a philosopher, the medieval mind-set – the belief that everything fitted together, everything was of a piece, everything made a shape or a pattern – seemed nothing but a wearisome game. At other periods, however, when the very different, modern ways of doing philosophy became repellent for contrary reasons (that it was too bitty, too negative, above all, too dry) he enjoyed inhabiting the greatest imagination of medieval Europe in the way that one might find refreshment by stepping off some hot street into the cool shade of a vast Gothic cathedral. Here, love, astronomy, lust, the theology of St Thomas Aquinas, personal disappointments and resentments, history, gossip and religion all fitted neatly into a beautiful Gothic toy theatre in which the modern man could profitably play. There had been no doubt, then, when Arnold Maar had suggested to Oliver that he forget the idea of a book outlining his own philosophical ideas, what he should write instead.

He did not intend to do research for his book. He would leave that to the Dante scholars. He intended, rather, to attempt a reading of Dante, and of his life and times, based on good general knowledge and a quarter of a century's general reading and reflection. Perhaps he started to write too soon, for quite early on in the work he discovered that, rather than taking a holiday from philosophy, he had written twenty thousand words on Aquinas's theory of knowledge – not a brand of philosophy that had ever interested him before. But he had become obsessed, for about a year, by the idea that there were analogues here between Thomas's distinction between understanding (*intellegere*) and knowing (*ratiocinari*) and Wittgenstein's breakthrough, when he contrasted *showing* and *saying*. Wittgenstein had demonstrated the impossibility of a private language, but had he, and all philosophers since, been able to discover a common language in which metaphysical propositions could make sense? Could philosophers work outside a system? Oliver's Hegelian hungering for a new system, one as cohesive as medieval Catholicism, had taken possession of him again and given him something like brain fever, until he had consciously stopped the work, and forced upon himself an encyclopaedic programme of medieval reading, this time limiting himself to poetry and history, and consciously avoiding any philosophical theme. He read *The Romance of the Rose*, the *Chanson de Roland*, Waltharius, Saxo's *Gesta Danorum*, the *Ancrene Wisse*, and Chaucer's *Treatise of the Astrolabe*. He kept copious notes, for it was only by working all the time on this task that he could stop the brain racing after its Hegelian schemes.

During this period, Bobs had been growing up, and the Dante book became a project which he laid aside. And then, in a new notebook, he sat down one morning and wrote the sentence: *When Dante first met Beatrice, she was a child of eight years old.*

He had never told anyone about his dream children, still less about his love for Bobs, but he quoted the sentence to Arnold Maar, when he next met the old man, who was buying him dinner at the Athenaeum.

'This is a poem about a child!' he had said excitedly. 'If we look for parallels, it would be in Ruskin's passion for Rose La Touche.'

'Is that quite true?' Arnold had responded lightly, with no obvious suspicion that they were discussing a matter very close to Oliver's heart. 'Would it not be necessary to add: true, she was a child of eight years old when Dante first met her; but then he was himself a child of nine. If the *Vita Nuova* has a modern parallel, it is not in the Victorian men who became obsessed with little girls, still less in *Lolita*, but in dear John Betjeman's "Indoor Games near Newbury".'

But a modern parallel was not what Oliver sought. Rather, he discovered (Bobs herself was eight when he wrote the sentence; it had been her eighth birthday) a profundity of truth which was missed by the attempt to reduce Dante's Beatrice to a mere symbol. What Dante said, on his first glimpse of that actual child, was that he had been crushed by a power of greater magnitude than himself. It was the beginning of the Vision of God – *Ecce deus fortior me*, behold the God who is stronger than I, *qui veniens dominabitur michi*, and who in his coming will rule over me.

As soon as he had written the first sentence of his new notebook, Oliver's great work changed. There were days when he continued to write specifically about Dante, but most of the time he made only cursory references to the Italian text. He felt, in fact, that just as Virgil, the greatest epic poet of the Roman age, had led Dante through the infernal and purgatorial realms, only to part from him as he entered Paradise, so Dante himself had led Oliver through all the intellectual and emotional journeys of his life only to convey him to this brink, where he glimpsed his Beatrice.

The book henceforward became a journal of his love for Bobs, and once he had begun, tens of thousands of words flowed from his pen.

If only he had limited himself to writing about Dante! If only the eyes of the thief who had purloined two of his notebooks were now reading about Guelphs and Ghibellines, or the feuds between the Adimari and the Donati! Instead . . . It did not bear thinking about, but he could think of nothing else.

What would they *do* when they found the incriminating evidence which could be deduced from those pages? He tried to picture the reactions of the women: the rage, perhaps violent rage, of Michal? The cold disillusionment of Cuffe? The brainless fury of Janet? Worst of all, perhaps, would be the 'understanding' of Margot Reisz, who, among other proofs of her worthiness, was a prison visitor. Worse even than the pain caused to the women, he considered the shame of it all being made public. Terrible images played in his brain: of the pages being pored over by lawyers and policemen, of their being read aloud to boot-faced juries, and quoted, with loud vulgar headlines in the newspapers. He saw his own face in the tabloids, emblazoned with words like 'sick', 'devil' and 'pervert'.

His obsessive chronicling had not been a matter of the will. He had written because he had to write. There had been other books in the past, such as Hazlitt's *Liber Amoris* or parts of Rousseau's *Confessions*, which attempted the degree of self-analysis, confession and disclosure which had been Oliver's sole literary preoccupation for the last couple of years. But he had come to believe that his own book was in an altogether superior league of importance.

It might be, in fact, one of the great books of the world. He felt, when viewing the task in this mood, that many of the things which he had been struggling to say in his unwritten, unwritable, philosophical reflections were being said obliquely in this great story. For it was, he was convinced, not merely the most important thing in his own life but, quite simply, a great love story.

It was a story which very few people would ever be intelligent, or pure, enough to understand. Plato would have understood it; indeed, there was much about the book which overlapped with the *Symposium*; but it had the advantage over Plato of being an enormous day-by-day chronicle of a near-perfect union between two souls. Oliver was in love with Bobs, but not in the essentially ephemeral way that his friends had been in love: the hectic taking up of a boy or a girl, the ups and downs of their passion descending into mere repetitiveness, quotidian affection punctuated by domestic irritability, or ending in resentment and separation. His love for Bobs, by contrast, had been a daily unfolding of joy and strength, giving him peace of mind at last, after those years of intellectual struggle when but to think had been to be full of sorrow, when the thinking-machine had been clogged and unequal to its task. If learning to think had no value unless it taught us to live, then Bobs had taught him something which had been denied by twenty years of philosophy. For she made each day pass, as it must for the animals and plants, *natürlich*. Time itself had been suspended since his love, his friendship, began. The concept of wasting time had gradually died, and with it the old metaphysical encumbrances such as the superstition that days, months, life itself, should have a point, or an explanation, or a justification.

Their physical delight in one another, and this was what Plato would so well have understood and appreciated, was no more than a part of their total spiritual union. Only for about six months of their nearly eight-year relationship had sex played a large part in a love which still remained tactile, and physically demonstrated. True, there were still days when, grotesque as it seemed, they 'did things' for which he could be arrested by the police; but these days were not distinguished in his mind (nor in hers, he was sure) from those days when their hugs, their kisses, their hand-holding, were of an order which magistrates and police would deem in the modern cant word 'acceptable'.

The fact that, physical lovers though they still were, holding and kissing and stroking were more important than individual sexual acts, did not make him sad. No doubt, if they had been grown-up lovers of the same age, it would have caused distress, but there was no such awkwardness here. Desire in Oliver was failing. He was still visited, on a few days each month, by an undirected and overpowering lust. If Bobs could satisfy this, so much the better; if not, he remained in its narcotic thrall for hours. Such involuntary

visitations to, or from, his psyche were very much less frequent than in early manhood. That was one reason why
marrying Camilla was a possibility. And Bobs herself was
changing. Soon she would grow away from him; and this
was another reason for wishing to escape, to make a sweet
wrench, rather than a gradual frigorification. From the day
he first met her, as a very young child, there had been
something bittersweet in their love, and he was convinced
that her perpetual giggling frivolity was her way of handling
this. It was the very fact that, unlike him, she was too young
to weep about it in solitude that made her the stronger of
the partnership, the one who could laugh at some of the
'games' of which grown-ups would have been so disap-
proving.

The plan had been laid in his heart for the inevitable
break to be disguised as a wedding. And Bobs's merry
acceptance of this had been so much less panicky than that
of Janet, Michal or Cuffe precisely because, in her imma-
turity, she was wiser than any of them. The transition was
to have been pure; the intense pain caused to both of them
on parting could not prevent its inevitability.

Later, perhaps: ah, they could both dream of a later. He
had sometimes fantasized about Bobs coming to live with
him and Camilla, as their adopted child. And she had been
saying for years, on and off, with giggles, that she wanted to
marry him.

But now a different transition was threatened and he
did not know which would be worse, the shock felt by his

fiancée or the anger of the other three women. The hurt caused to Bobs would be worse than either, of course. And as he lay in bed with her, he kissed her hot head, and squeezed her thin shoulders, and felt tears stream down his fevered cheeks and into his beard as an image cruelly fixed itself in his mind: Bobs sobbing, on a video film, as she was interrogated by police psychiatrists; Bobs being forced to choose between denouncing her lover or keeping quiet for his sake. Almost more poisonously painful than the idea of her pain was the thought of these evil, lumpen people, who understood nothing, persuading her by their psychiatric tricks that she had been 'damaged' by the previous seven years, luring her to hate, not merely Oliver, but her own self. They would try to persuade her that she was a victim, and that the love of her life had been nothing better than an abuse. All their merry conversations, their hours of play and gossip and their perfect communion and companionship would be represented as something dirty, something for which she had to apologize, or from which she had to be cleansed. It was this which he found unendurable: better that Bobs should be dead than that she should suffer such a disillusionment, which would be on a level with Iago's corrupting the mind of Othello, or with persuading a contemplative nun, who for years had adored the Blessed Sacrament, that there was no God.

When Oliver contemplated the inevitable destructive solution to their difficulties, he felt nothing but rage against the army of phantom policemen and journalists and social workers who had destroyed his peace of mind. His life had been a dedicated pursuit of virtue – not merely intellectual truth, but virtue. After a crisis in which his mind had been threatened with the clogging of cynicism – that cynicism which ruined the more worldly or the more stupid of his academic colleagues who tired of the struggle and opted to waste their lives on college business or footling research or social climbing – he had chosen a braver, a purer path. He and Bobs had found this path together and it had been good.

Its goodness was the secret which he had written down, in hundreds of pages, intending, fully, that human eyes should one day read them; he wanted posterity to know of the perfect love between himself and Bobs. Future generations would find it as hard to believe that men like Oliver Gold were persecuted in the twentieth century as that homosexuals had been persecuted in a previous generation. It was the burning goodness, the perfection, of his love which the pages recorded. Many times in the pages of the notebook, he had spoken of the martyrdom which the good endure in each generation. The good which they perceive is regarded by the world as evil. Jesus and Socrates are killed for corrupting youth. He had not recognized what reserves of courage would be needed, since his own martyrdom required the sacrifice of Bobs. The divine voice required the sacrifice of Isaac. He had decided to lock his notebooks away, to bequeath them to his old college library with the instruction that they should not be opened until

fifty years after the death of Bobs. Now the day of that
death was near; and the stupidity and prejudice of the
policemen and the journalists, and the jealous closed minds
of the women with whom he shared a house, were forcing
that life of dedicated virtue to end with a murder and a suicide.

Chapter Ten

Catharine Cuffe's journey from the North Library to the Parthenon Marbles was a fight through armies of tourists. The crowds were solid, and as she squeezed through, she had time to wonder whether the British Museum had been the best place for a private meeting. It had the advantage of supreme convenience, since this was, for her, a research day, so that she could see him without wasting journey time. Nor could anyone have been surprised had they been glimpsed together.

A married woman with whom Cuffe had once had an affair had advised her: 'Public meetings should always be in places where your friends would find nothing odd about seeing you both together. They won't think twice if they see the pair of you having lunch at the restaurant in Notting Hill which you use habitually. But if you both happened to be spotted in a motorway café outside Basingstoke, then the world would *know*.'

Not that an act of betrayal was planned in the British

Museum that day; Cuffe had in mind, instead, a dramatic readjustment.

He was there early. When she saw that fastidious Oliver was wearing a pair of trainers on his long narrow feet, she could hardly believe her eyes. At least he still wore the dark-blue linen suit which she had helped him buy at Liberty's two years before; though the effect was rather spoilt by the sporty, white aertex shirt, with the soft collar and the three little buttons at the throat.

'The crowds are simply unbearable,' she said.

He shoved up and found room for her on the bench. Sitting close, she saw an expression in his face which was not far short of desolation. His cheekbones stuck out. They were almost skeletal. In the fortnight since Mrs Baynes's arrival in London, Oliver had surely lost over a stone in weight; and he now looked more wasted and depressed than he had done eight years before, when Cuffe had rescued him and brought him to Wagner Rise. The weight loss was so dramatic that she wondered about AIDS, and inwardly asked herself whether, with the particular suggestion she had in mind for that day, she had come too late.

She had dressed herself with care for this interview and had spent a good half-hour, after leaving the North Library, in front of a glass in the Ladies. The hint of mascara on her upper lashes was only a hint. The pinkish lipstick was so delicate that to a man's eye it could have been lip-salve; and no man would have realized that there was any other make-up at all on the pale, clear, slightly freckled Irish face and the cheeks which appeared by nature to have burst into the very faintest of blushes. Nor was there any waxiness about her upturned and surprised nose. The thick red curls fell from that intelligent brow on to green velvet shoulders. It was like a riding jacket, exaggeratedly waisted and small, worn over a brilliantly white shirt. The tight black trousers had been worth paying for: they were a perfect fit. So were the knee-length boots.

'You haven't got to teach this afternoon?' he asked her.

'I don't have to teach, and there are no meetings. It is almost the only day of the week in term of which this can be said.'

'I think I know why you have summoned me.'

His voice was quavery. It was in fact quite difficult to hear what he was saying. It was little more than a hoarse whisper, and he shook as he spoke.

'Well, if that's true, it will save a lot of time,' she said.

He said: 'I guessed it had to be you. Only you would have taken such a degree of interest in my written work.'

Two parties of Japanese, each being instructed by their tour guide, passed in opposite directions, so that although Cuffe could be said on some literal level to have 'heard' each word he spoke, it was only the last five words which made any impact.

'Oliver, listen to me. Perhaps it is chiefly of your work that I have been thinking. I want to remind you of something.'

'Oh, God!'

He had covered his face with his hands. She believed
that he was about to weep, or that he was already weeping;
and her heart revived, for this was surely a sign that he was
ready to listen to her.

'You've been a hermit in Janet's house for the last seven
years, and I want to remind you . . .'

More Japanese, never in groups less than fifteen, now
jostled for the space in front of them with a party of loud
Italian teenagers. And a group of English schoolchildren,
too small to have much hope of glimpsing the marbles that
day, had joined the *mêlée*.

'Keep close by me, children. Oliver!'

The teacher was yelling at a recalcitrant child who
threatened to get lost in the crush. But Oliver Gold had
glanced up instinctively at hearing his own first name. He
looked as if the whole company of tourists and young
people had come swarming into that great exhibition hall
to denounce him.

'And of how important and inspiring,' Cuffe was saying,
'you continue to be to your pupils. Other lecturers and
tutors taught us things. Well, that's all right, I suppose, we
all like to know *things*. Formal logic, for instance, is a useful
thing to learn, nor does it do anyone any harm to master
how Kant arrived at the idea of transcendental deduction.
You've got to do this stuff, you've got to master it, before
you know what philosophy is. And that's what I'm doing all
day long with my kids –' her head jerked, supposedly in the
direction of Gower Street – 'and I try to make it fun, and I

try not to waste their time. But you are and were one of those different people . . .'

Oliver continued to keep his face covered with his hands.

She just caught the words 'failed you all', which he appeared to have mumbled.

'Oliver, that's *not true.*'

'Failed . . .'

'Look. You changed lives, Oliver. You made us know, from the very first moment that we stepped into your room, that we were engaged upon a series of terribly important exercises. We were learning how to think, that was the first thing. Sometimes a machine could not work, you told us, until the mechanic took it to bits and cleaned each of its constituent parts. Your function, in that first term as our teacher, was to take to bits, and to expose, all our foggy prejudices, all our logical incapacity, and to make that machine work, to make our minds come alive. Any of us who survived the blast of that first assault –' Cuffe extended one of her white hands and adopted a voice, nothing like Oliver's but evidently meant for his – '"Why do you say that? Notice, I did not ask, why do you think that, because no one, strictly, could think what you have just said . . . I don't know what you mean by mean, and I suspect that you don't, either."

'Any of us who did not have a nervous breakdown after such demolition jobs had been performed inside our heads, emerged from the experience better people – not just sharper witted. We had glimpsed how vitally important it was to tell the truth, and to learn how to do that is painstaking work. We had understood why philosophy is a high, noble calling; we saw that it isn't just important for philosophers, but for everyone.

'"The world needs to know what only we are trained to know; we have to do their knowing for them." Do you remember saying that? Do you remember that train journey, the first time you came home to meet Mum and Dad? And we talked all the way about the need to talk philosophy in non-technical language, wherever possible, so that intelligent general readers could engage with us, the way they are starting to engage with popular science –'

'Catharine, there's no need to draw out the torture.'

'You never call me Catharine.'

'What do you want of me? You have clearly asked me to meet you here because there was something you could not say in Wagner Rise. We both know what that is. Did Michal agree that you should meet me here, on neutral ground? Or Janet perhaps?'

'They don't know I'm here. Look, Oliver. It really is too crowded to talk in here. Shall we try to have that walk?'

The central entrance hall swarmed with an even greater throng than had the Egyptian exhibition rooms through which they had struggled. Both hardened users of the Museum, even in the high tourist seasons, they knew that it was easier to make an escape from the back entrance than from the front steps. They walked through the King's

Library and, having negotiated yet another opportunity for buying postcards, they came to a large galleried room in which many English manuscripts, from medieval to modern, were displayed.

Though neither of them had ever read *Beowulf*, they were momentarily arrested at the cabinet displaying the slightly charred MS Cotton Vitellius A. xv, unaware of its lucky escape from a fire in 1731, but conscious of the more generalized and exciting truth that some remarkable product of the human brain could survive and touch us after nine centuries. This little brown book was about the same age as Oliver's celadon Sung bowls.

'I used to come here when I was a boy,' he volunteered.

It was the first childhood memory he had ever shared with Cuffe. It was strange that although he had so often been to stay with her parents, none of them knew so much as where he had grown up.

'With your parents?'

'My father used to come to London on business. He used to stay at the Hotel Russell.' He smiled.

'I remember looking at these manuscripts in their glass cases; and apart from liking handwriting for its own sake, what fascinated me was this hope, which I had discovered in myself. At really quite an early age, I wanted to write a book famous enough to be placed in a glass case.'

'You still could.'

He turned away with disgust. Without looking at her, he spoke.

'I had already planned to go away. You must believe that. It was a necessity. I've only got one thing to ask of you, and that is, that you let me go quietly. Don't let us talk about it – not any of us, not Janet, not Michal. I promise to go. Talking will make it worse.'

'Dear Oliver.'

Just momentarily, she touched his hand. He flinched.

'I think we are agreed, that at this particular moment, I am in your power. I ask you to be merciful, that is all. That way, the fewest people get hurt.'

'That seems a melodramatic way of seeing things.'

'Hardly.'

'Talking of manuscripts . . .'

'Don't. Please, don't.'

'Why, Oliver! There's no need to look so frightened.'

She drew back the cloth which protected *Beowulf* from the light, and they marched towards the back entrance of the museum. But about halfway down the long gallery, he stopped and looked deep into her eyes.

'There's no need to prolong the agony. Let's get this over.'

'I was going to ask you to look over a manuscript. Something I came across the other day.'

'This is cruel.'

'I had not forgotten writing it; but I had forgotten its existence. I remembered writing it, and rewriting it; and then I assumed it had been thrown away. In fact, it was tucked inside a paperback – Geoffrey Warnock's *Kant*.'

'What was tucked inside? How could you fold it into a book?'

Cuffe looked at Oliver, and began to wonder if he had been drinking. Very little she said appeared to be getting through to him.

'You asked me,' he was saying, 'to meet you in secret because you wanted to discuss something you had written? Not something I had written?'

'Oh, God, Oliver. Why are you crying? I wanted you to read it. I wanted your eyes to play over the actual page I wrote. It must be fifteen years old – I think I was twenty when I wrote it. Never dared post it, of course. Will you?'

'What?'

'Read?'

Having put it into his hands, she allowed herself a squeal of girlish embarrassment. She pirouetted on the heel of one boot, and walked away from him while he stood, trans-fixed, by the sight of her twenty-year-old handwriting. How well he remembered the writing, and the fact that her essays were scented, like love letters.

Dear Oliver,

I am writing to ask you to marry me. This is a perfectly serious proposal and I beg you not to throw this letter aside before you have finished reading it.

There are those, and perhaps you are among them, who would say that you do not need a wife. I guess (tho' this is very impertinent of me!!) that you are a celibate, and that you do not desire a mate, or anyway a female one. This doesn't bother me. I am a homosexual . . .

'I'm afraid one can be very pompous at twenty,' she called across.

Let me explain to you why I think we should marry. Philosophers need to think on their own, but they also require a very attentive audience. This need is much greater for them than for poets or novelists. This is not just egotism. They need someone who is sufficiently advanced in their subject to follow their train of thought. They need to be challenged and questioned as they make their solitary journey to the truth; but challenged in a sympathetic and totally engaged way; they do not need the destructive criticism of jealous rivals, nor the sycophancy of a groupie. Russell needed Wittgenstein when he was trying to work out what was wrong with the Principia Mathematica, *just as Wittgenstein needed Frank Ramsey when he was trying to work out what was wrong with the* Tractatus. *Plato's greatest tribute to Socrates is to have got him wrong, to have undermined his arguments.*

I have managed to enter your mind in a way which you must find helpful. There is no possibility that another human being could ever know your mind as well as I do. To have me on hand, day and night, will be of immense value to your work in the future. I am prepared to devote my whole life to your work; to make my work, your work.

This is, as you must know, because I am in love with you. I would give you friendship, solace, sympathy and companionship. In times when you were lonely and tired and too frayed to work, I would be there to support you, and to make you laugh. When you wanted to be alone, I'd obediently bugger off. This offer never closes. Even if you read this letter in ten or twenty years, I shall still mean it. I do not want to marry anyone else.

With my love,
Catharine.

He turned and looked at her. At twenty, she had claimed she knew his mind. It was no longer true. She could not imagine what he was thinking as her thirty-five-year-old eyes met his. And when he turned to leave the museum, she could not be sure that he wanted her company, or whether he was running away.

They walked silently together, and at a considerable pace, down Malet Street, through Gordon Square and Tavistock Square. She remained at his side, which meant teetering, almost at a run. At length, he sat on a bench at the edge of a little communal garden. Some pink flowering currant sprayed its pungent, cat-pissy smell beside them.

'Am I to keep this?' he asked, holding up the letter.

'If you like.'

'Was it really your reason for wanting to see me today?'

She nodded; he had not seen this kittenish aspect to her nature.

'You wrote it fifteen years ago, and it's still what you think?'

'Yes.'

'Not the rubbish about Plato deliberately undermining Socrates?'

'That was not the most important part of the letter.'

'No?'

'Oh, don't play games, Oliver. This is your life, my life, we are talking about.'

'Back there, in the museum, you praised me as a teacher. You praised my ability to teach young people the rudiments of how to think for themselves. Don't you think it is possible that this is all I'm good at?'

'How do you mean?'

'Why do you think I came to live at Wagner Rise?'

'Because you wanted to get away from teaching and write a really serious book.'

'I did it because I'm lazy. And because I am vain. I did it because there were enough people who shared your crazy delusion that I am a great thinker that I had even come to believe it myself. The last seven years have been an unmitigated disaster.'

'How can you say that?'

'Good people are people who do good things. Nurses are good people. Priests, sometimes. Conscientious financial advisers, wise policemen, teachers. Perhaps when I first began to teach I too had the chance to be a good person, but being a good teacher went to my head; I wanted to make myself into a guru. It is very easy to hoodwink the young, and to hoodwink oneself. I have wasted the last seven years and I have done great damage.'

'I don't know about that.'

'Don't you?'

When he turned and looked at her, there was something of madness in his intense gaze.

'Are you really saying that you don't know?' he asked.

Frightened, sensing a revelation for which she was not emotionally prepared, Cuffe spoke with a quivering lip. 'What are you saying?'

He let out a long sigh. First he looked at her. Then he looked away. The silence seemed endless.

'Well?' she asked.

'I don't think you have worked out the implications of your proposal,' he said. 'Imagine the disruptive effect in Wagner Rise if you and I were to marry.'

'I have imagined it. This is the solution that will cause least pain. Believe me.'

'And Janet will be pleased?'

'Everything will go on as before – so of course she would be pleased.'

'And Michal would be happy if you were to marry?'

'Oliver, I am not suggesting that you and I should become lovers. I know that such a thing would be completely impossible.'

'Then why should we get married?' he asked. 'Unless to spite Camilla?'

'That's not fair. I'm trying to salvage something from all this. There are three others in this thing, you know, three who will be desolated – desolated, Oliver – if you go. I'm trying to suggest something which will ensure that you stay, so that Janet will still know she has you in her attic, her pet hermit; so that Michal will still have you around – have you any idea how fond she is of you? And so that Bobs . . . Oliver, have you thought of the implications of all this for the sprog?'

'They've crossed my mind.'

'But has it occurred to you what you are doing to the child?'

'Explain.'

'You have been the closest thing she ever had to a father. In case you haven't noticed, she absolutely worships you. But you don't ask yourself how it will affect her! You just calmly talk about going to live in America.'

'We might get a place in Connecticut for the summer vacations. Might. That isn't "going to live in America".'

'Oh, come on. You can see what that woman wants. She'll get you over there, and Bobs will never see you again. I ask you again – is it fair to her?'

'Which woman are you talking about? Which woman wants to "get me over there"?'

'They both do, mother and daughter. They've got their claws into you.'

'That is a ridiculous way of talking. Don't you think you should try to come to terms with the reality of the situation? That is, I am in love with Camilla. I love her. I am going to marry her.'

'Even if it drives a little child mad with grief – oh, come on, Oliver, think what this will do to me, if Michal is having to mop up the kid.'

'Bobs seems remarkably cheerful and well balanced to me.'

'How can someone be as clever as you are and so stupid at the same time? Don't you remember what it was like to be a child?'

'Not very well.'

'Children act. When they can't cope with a situation, they put on an act.'

'I thought that was grown-ups, but at the moment I am muddling the two; so are you, perhaps.'

'Who do you think tried to wreck the car by pouring honey all over the seat? Who has been playing all these pranks on Mrs Baynes? Is it a wonder she's gone to live in a hotel?'

'You truly suppose that Bobs put the honey in the car, and the stink bomb in Rosalie's bedroom?'

'You think it was Janet, I suppose, or that Margot Reisz came round and did it? Look, the sprog's unhappy, Oliver. She is threatened by the Bayneses. She wants Mrs Baynes to go away, Camilla to go away.'

'No, my dear. You are threatened by Camilla – not Bobs, but you.'

'And you are saying I let your tyres down so you might

have been killed on the motorway? *I* put a chicken in Rosalie's bedroom? A live chicken?'

'We never did establish how Cuthbert got in there.'

'You're going to say next, you never could establish who shat on her bed. It was chicken shit, if that helps you make up your mind. Look, Oliver. I'm not saying my proposal is the only solution, but it is one solution. You are just trying to shut your eyes to what is going on at Wagner Rise. Okay, you have three hysterical women to cope with; but you also have one very disturbed little girl, and you are simply refusing to open your eyes to this fact.'

When he said nothing, she said, 'At least tell me you'll think about my idea. That we should get married.'

He had stood up before he replied, and he was on the move, walking away from her in the direction of Euston. She almost had to run to keep up with him.

'Oliver? Please!'

He said, 'I don't see how I could avoid thinking about it,' and that was his farewell.

Chapter Eleven

'I cannot tell you the relief, the sheer blessed relief, to be back at the dear old Basil Street! Uh-huh. Yes. The hall porter greeted me like I was an old friend . . . Well, it's a little small, maybe, but it's clean. There aren't any chickens running around the place looking for a place to use the bathroom. It's got a lock on the door. And proper plumbing! You know the shower works here? And the toilet actually flushes – three days we had in that house with only one toilet that flushed. You know what the plumber said when he finally fixed it? Someone had put Tampax down there – can you imagine anything so dumb? I was just going crazy in that place . . . Yes, one more practical joke and I'd have . . . yes. Well, of course it was the girl, but confront a child's mother when she's out all day and in bed with a woman all night? I don't exaggerate . . . Well, I mentioned some of the big things to Janet, of course I did, but the little things, I just decided to let them pass . . . Well, they call them apple-pie beds, don't they? A good joke the first time

179

it happened, you get into bed, jet-lagged, a little lonely in that strange house, and you want to stretch out your legs . . . The third and fourth time it happens . . . Yes, positively hilarious. No, dear, what'd be the point? There'd have been denials and hurt feelings, and there was quite enough of all that stuff in the atmosphere without . . . Howard, I know. Yes, I know . . . I wish so too, honey, it would have made it a whole lot easier if you were here . . . Well that's true too. Oliver? Well, maybe I should've talked to him. He's been like a father to this child since she was just so high and as far as I can see, he's more or less been responsible for bringing her up while her mother helps hoodlums and has affairs.'

Rosalie's voice wailed in amusement at the response to this observation.

'You'd never say that, if you were over here,' she laughed. 'They think we've all gone crazy on political correctness, but you should hear . . . Well, I know. So, poor little girl. She's jealous. Wouldn't you be? She seems to get on well with Camilla, that's the funny thing. Well, Camilla always was good with children . . . Howard Baynes, that's unkind and untrue . . . Okay, then, unkind and true . . . So, she doesn't do anything to Camilla, she takes it all out on me . . . Oh, no, she's perfectly *polite* to me. It's what she does when we aren't face to face . . . Yes, maybe she figures that if this old witch from the United States'll just get scared, she'll pack her bags and take Camilla home and everything'll be as it always was . . . You know the way kids' minds work . . . Well, maybe you're right, maybe none of us do. I sure don't know the way *our* little girl's mind works . . .

'. . . She's okay, Howard. Well, that's still true. Yes. There's the church crowd, and then there are the artistic bachelors.' Rosalie Baynes laughed again. 'They're not that kind of church, honey. No, it's some place not far from here, very enthusiastic. Yes, course I went. I told 'em afterwards, we're Presbyterians, we're used to something a little more formal . . . Yes, they testified. Waved their arms. Half of them in some trance or something . . . Don't ask me how she got into all that stuff, she says it's quite normal here – bankers and doctors and lawyers all go to this place . . . I don't know. You old cynic. It's certainly true she's cooled off it a lot since she got engaged to Oliver.'

She laughed again.

'No. Ross and Scott don't go to church. Or not that church, anyhow. She met them at work . . . China, pictures, it's all the same, isn't it? . . . As far as I know, yes . . . They have been good friends to her, only that particular crowd of young men . . . Just a little.' (More laughter.) 'And you know, like, they have the same haircuts, the same shirts – yes, you know those little sports shirts, with short sleeves and three buttons at the collar? . . . That's right. I've met about six or seven of 'em so far, all wearing 'em. And all with these great heavy shoes, as if they've been digging roads . . . No, they haven't. Ross is in a gallery. Scott does something architectural. Chuck's in the same auction house as Camilla, and Jim . . . You get the picture. They're not all misogynists, but Jim explained to me what a manuscript was last evening, leant over and explained. Helpful, wasn't it? Oh, I don't know, some medieval thing he'd been working on, thought I might not know about the Middle Ages, coming from the poor benighted States. Sure. That's what I mean . . . Well, I'm not such a submissive person as Camilla, in case you hadn't noticed. No, I think that's one of the reasons she likes that crowd . . . Yes, she likes to be a little brown bird among the peacocks. Maybe, who knows, deep down inside that funny, earnest little daughter of ours there's something we never winkled out, never even knew was there . . . I miss you too, baby. Oh, I do . . .

'I just wish you could meet him, that's all. It would help me figure him out . . . Pervert? Did I say that? Maybe I shouldn't've. But, Howard, there's something about him. There he is surrounded by all these women, and they've all gotten the hots for him. No question . . . Well, maybe Charles Manson's going too far, but certainly a touch of Rasputin. Sure. But you see, hun, I don't think he does. As a matter of fact I don't think he does with *anyone*, and that's kinda worrying. He wants to be worshipped all right, and he's gone to the right house for that. He's gotten Janet slavering over him. And you should see the way the maid looks at him with her great sad eyes – Lotte, yes. Then there's the little girl, getting all ready to join the fan club, and Michal. And there's the red-headed . . . Yes, only she's no broad, she's thin as a greyhound.

'Howard, why did our little girl want to go and get herself mixed up with this lot of weirdos? I mean, they're not going to let him go without a fight and that's for sure . . . Well, is he worth fighting for? Hey, I can hear her at the door. Yes, I told you, she's taking me to this dire party of Janet's. I'll tell you about it tomorrow. Love you too. Bye now.'

Mrs Baynes went to the door of her bedroom in stockinged feet to admit her daughter.

'You've just missed your Daddy on the telephone. He sends his love.'

'Mom, we're going to miss the party if we don't set out soon. And look at you – not even dressed.'

'Well, I'm ready, except for my shoes. This pant suit'll surely do?'

Camilla had, in her mother's eyes, overdressed, ridiculously so, considering that Janet had insisted that the party would be 'very informal, just a few very old, dear friends'.

'Claudio Lewis will be there,' said Camilla.

'Darling, until I went to stay with Janet I had not even heard of Claudio Lewis – or the little magazine he edits.'

'It's the English *New Yorker*. Well, kind of . . .'

'Darling, I could pass an exam in Claudio Lewis, His Life and Times. There's no need for you to fill me in. But since when did you have to dress up to meet a writer?'

There was such a thing as trying too hard, making oneself ridiculous. Camilla, in a scarlet dress bought that afternoon at a distinguished Knightsbridge store, looked about eight years old. The dress did not fit. Rosalie Baynes wondered how any sales assistant worth the name could have allowed Camilla to walk out of the store four hundred dollars the poorer, and with a thing which stuck out at the neck, stuck out at the chest (which Camilla didn't, poor little thing) and which created a highly confusing bag of air at her waist. The uncompromising vermilion of the ensemble drained what colour there might have been in Camilla's cheeks, and the asymmetrical dabs of blusher on each cheekbone only emphasized the true pallor beneath. A girl of eight who'd been playing with her Mom's vanity bag, that's what Camilla looked like.

'Come here,' said Rosalie.

'Mother, we are going to be late.'

Camilla froze, allowed herself to be hugged, rather than responding to the parental embrace.

'Honey, are you quite happy?'

'That's a tall order.'

'You know what I mean.'

'Is this some kind of an attempt to run my life for me?'

'It's not an attempt. We just wondered, your father and I, if you are really sure. We're pleased for you, honey, honestly we are. Only, you've not known Oliver very long. That's all. He's a nice man, and you are still at the exciting stage. You've been dating, what, six months? You've barely had time to find out if you are compatible.'

The mother's sharp look brought forth a true blush in the daughter's cheek. Camilla did not meet the inquisitive gaze.

'You are compatible, aren't you?'

'Mother, I don't think this is your business. I know that sounds very rude, but . . .'

'Just a little rude,' her mother conceded. 'And just a little untrue. You are expecting your father to build you a house in Connecticut, where you can live with your philosopher. That makes it our business.'

'Are you saying you'd rather I married a man for his money? I mean, how grubby can you get?'

'We aren't suggesting anything of the kind. I just think you owe it to yourself to know your own mind – hopefully, to know Oliver's mind, too. We only want you to be happy, darling.'

'Oh, Mother.'

Like a little quivering bird, that was how Camilla felt, as she stood in her mother's arms. Was she weeping?

'If only I could get to grips with why you want to marry him, that's all. It's more usual nowadays to live together for a while, and then marry if it works out. I mean, if you are in love . . .'

'Can you doubt it?'

There was fire in the girl's belly after all. She pushed herself free and looked angrily into her mother's face.

'Can you really stand there and doubt it?'

'You tell me, honey.'

'Of course I am in love with Oliver. We are in love. He wants to marry me because he is in love with me. Could anything be more simple? Why should you be looking for sinister motives when this whole thing is clear as day?'

'I don't know, Camilla. Maybe because I'm just a very foolish old woman, maybe because I love you.'

There was silence between them, a long silence. They could hear one another breathing.

'Do you want children real bad?' asked Rosalie at last.

There was a sort of gasp as, with streaming eyes, Camilla looked up and said, 'Oh, Mom! I'm thirty-six years old, Mom!'

Perhaps there was nothing better the two of them could do than to stand and hug one another; perhaps it was for this cause alone that Mrs Baynes had flown the Atlantic. The sobbing seemed to go on and on. It came from the depth of Camilla's gut. It was as though her oblique and delicate personality had for a while been wrenched, plundered, by the primeval need of the race to reproduce itself. From the pit of her groin to the top of her skull, she shuddered and wept with a pain which communicated itself terribly to the older woman; terribly, since the mother had the one thing the daughter so tragically lacked, her own child in her arms.

The strength of Camilla's response to so basic a question took Rosalie by surprise. Rosalie took it for granted that most women wanted children (perhaps all women in some part of themselves?). But tiny, delicate, porcelain Camilla, she who seemed so well suited to her own professional world of glazed, brittle objects and human beings of a comparable quality, had always seemed to her mother to be a figurine set apart. Her boyfriends had been few, and her

mother had guessed that she was a virgin. Her brother
Frank, in every way a more normal character, had poured
scorn on these college friends, openly opining that if Cam
could bring such creatures home, she did not have her
mind on the business, a coarse judgement with which their
father had agreed.

Rosalie had not, then, been surprised when Camilla
accepted the posting in London. She knew that home had
ceased to be home for Camilla, perhaps never had been.
The chance to value china in London could now be seen as
a cultural adventure, a perennial repetition of the need to
sample a few years in Europe, and perhaps to find a mate,
which had been the theme of so many American lives.
Neither of her parents had been optimistic of her chances,
since Camilla was such a very quiet woman, who showed
no signs of being able to mix outside the confines of work
or church. Now having met samples from both these
worlds, a mother had reason to be grateful that Camilla had
fished in other ponds. Among the ceramicists and auction-
eers it would have been unrealistic to seek many young
men in pursuit of a wife; among the evangelicals, it would
have been hard to find many congenial golfing partners for
Howard.

That Oliver Gold was possibly not one of nature's golfers
was the least of a mother's objections to him. Rosalie, however, had been unprepared for the depth and strength of
Camilla's need for a child. But here she was, weeping and
shaking. Rosalie had been all set to have it out with the girl.

She had promised Howard, and indeed promised herself, that she would ask some blunt questions. Had it occurred to Camilla to ask whether Oliver were homosexual? If not, what other reasons would she adduce for a man being fifty years old and unmarried? Where did he come from? Had anyone met his folks? If not, why not? And just what kind of a set-up *was* 12 Wagner Rise?

But all such questions were silenced by Camilla's sobs and shakings. It was almost as if some deity had picked up the poor young woman and cruelly rattled her, shaken her up like a puppet. In its fevered, panicky and tearful condition, Camilla's slight, bony body seemed pathetically ill-suited for the end she craved.

It felt as if something like an hour had passed, although it was probably only a few minutes, before Rosalie dared to come out with: 'Have you talked with Oliver about having a baby?'

'Oh, Mother, I fell in love with him. He came in one day with these boxes of china, and he was so nice, so sympathetic, so interested in what I had to say – in what made me *me*, in me as a person. And when he took me out on one of our early dates, do you know what he did? He brought the kid along. He brought Bobs to tea at Fortnum and Mason, and we all sat there at the bar, like three kids, having ice-cream sodas. And oh, Mom, if that man didn't want a kid of his own, I don't know who does!'

'So, you talked about it?'

'We don't need to talk about it.'

'Well, it's your life, honey. But in my experience you always need to talk about things. It doesn't do to take things for granted. I'd never know what was going on inside that old head of your father's unless I made him own up to what he was thinking! You're not pregnant, are you, darling?'

'Mom!'

The shocked tone in which Camilla spoke confirmed the hunch that she was a virgin. Rosalie asked herself how she, a woman of normal, healthy impulses, had managed to raise such a Victorian prude. She had never been the sort of mother who taught Camilla that sex was wicked, or that the possession of a human body was anything to be ashamed of. So how did it come about, this terrible frigid stiffness which advertised itself in almost every gesture? Rosalie realized that the most damaging evidence against Oliver was his desire to marry Camilla, for no man – no normal man, at least – could fail to notice this *cordon sanitaire* with which the poor young woman was surrounded; and since it was so apparent, so obvious, what could be a man's motives for wishing to settle down with her?

'Mother, I'm going to marry Oliver, d'you hear? You've probably made yourself a list of things you dislike about him. That's tough. Maybe I have, too; but don't let's talk about those things. I wasn't born yesterday.'

'What does that mean? What is it you suspect?'

'Okay, I'm not kidding myself, nor anyone else. If I wasn't desperate to get pregnant, I should not be in a hurry to get married to anyone; and maybe I wouldn't get married to the first kind, lovable, eccentric man who happened to come in and have his china valued. Maybe, I'd shop around a little. But I am thirty-six years old, and believe me, Mother, there are just not a lot of men out there. It looks like there are, but there aren't. I don't want to marry a married man.'

'Why not? I did.'

'I don't want to marry a homosexual.'

'And you're sure that's not what you're doing?'

'Oliver is not homosexual. Whatever put that in your head? No. If an unmarried, kind, heterosexual man with a beard falls in love with you, you don't hang around, okay?'

Rosalie looked intently at her daughter, peered into the frightened squirrelly eyes and felt for the first time closer to penetrating their secret, closer to feelings of affection for her than she ever had before.

'I didn't know you liked beards,' she said. Such sororal tones had never been known between them. Rosalie had envied those friends with daughters who swapped confidences on such matters as sexual preference.

'I don't like beards,' said Camilla. 'That thing's coming off the first morning of our married life.'

Chapter Twelve

Oliver, who had been turning the leaves of a volume of Lewis Carroll's photographs, had found the one which usually did the trick, and was concentrating upon it with intensity. By looking at the photograph with the simple attention of an Orthodox mystic contemplating an icon, he could lose any sense of his present surroundings and be subsumed entirely in his fantasy. The actual surroundings, his familiar room, the bookshelves, the chair, the trees outside the window, the totally unerotic sight of his blue corduroys at his ankles and of his bare legs concealed beneath the Victorian desk, all these prosaic externals were lost in the daydream which the photograph could summon up.

With a sufficient dislocation of dream self and common-sense self, he could even forget that it was his own fingers at work, and imagine those of the child.

The picture was very familiar. The head tilted on one side of naked shoulders. That quizzical expression which showed total ignorance of the feelings it evoked, yet at the same time was all commanding, all powerful. The child-mistress; the innocent, yet knowing one; innocent because, like an animal, she knew about this, this, *this*; loved it; had no shame about it; it was the secret game which she wanted to play with him, only with him. Eyes wandered to her flat pinprick nipples, her smooth, androgynous little belly, and to that perfect, pencil-sketched division between the marble legs, that mark of a thumb-nail in smooth clay.

In addition to the images themselves, and the dreams they inspired, it always added to the pleasure to indulge in this activity in the unlocked study; the pleasure was enhanced by the knowledge that someone, anyone, could come in and discover him. This final lunacy – the notion that there might be something exciting, rather than embarrassing, about Janet or Lotte bursting in – was revealed immediately for the deception it was by the time he was reaching in the desk drawer for the paper handkerchiefs. The crazy comfort of his dreams and his dream children was replaced by his constant companion, fear, and by the sick sense that everything was closing in upon him.

It worried him that, since the disappearance of the notebooks, he had retreated more and more into these solitary sessions of fantasy. He had almost returned to the state of addictive erotomania and delusion which had been troubling him at the time of his great mental *crise*.

As a man who had never much liked his own sex, and whose best friend had been a septuagenarian and fastidious bachelor, Oliver had no method of testing whether these passages of overpowering erotomania were normal, or whether he was in a position where it would be wiser to commit suicide, or to hand himself over to a psychiatrist. Every so often, in the conversation of others, one heard of a man who had amazed everyone by going 'off the rails'. Some supposedly happily married man would behave in a way which was laughably or tragically (usually both) out of character. A supposedly heterosexual man of good standing would be found in a public lavatory giving fellatio to a vagrant; or some pillar of rectitude would be found with a prostitute. Janet, when she spoke of such episodes, needed to retain her bohemian credibility by suggesting no element of shock; but such stories would have no place in our imaginative lives unless they were seen as aberrations from the norm.

Biographies and even autobiographies which dwelt on this interesting theme actually enhanced this view. Even truly outrageous books such as Simenon's *Mémoires intimes* or *Montherlant sans masque*, both of which Oliver had read with furtive frequency, were actually rehashes of the idea that the man of genius is somehow different from the generality of the human race, his hyperactivity in the sexual area being as unusual as his literary fecundity.

But what if this was all piffle? What if all men, or all men at some periods of life, were like this? When in this particular frame of mind, it was difficult to concentrate upon anything which was not an erotic daydream. It was, in fact, as if one were suffering from the effects of a drug which numbed awareness of all other things. In this state of mind, Oliver could sit for hours on end contemplating photographs of children, or merely looking out of the window and seeing the whole world as a teeming and unending sexual dance. In this frame of mind, he did not need to focus on the particular physical type of young body which attracted him: he had only to look out of his window and the dull suburban street became a bacchanal. Faces glimpsed in houses opposite were imagined attached to bodies, writhing like the thickly encrusted erotic forms on Indian temples. Even old ladies drawing back their curtains after breakfast could be imagined being penetrated from behind by great black men, or dogs. Walks, when such was his vision of things, were dominated not so much by thoughts, as by a sort of tunnel of sex. Sometimes, when he returned from such a walk, and he had, through the usual process, momentarily cleared his mind, he had sighed with relief that he had not been arrested by the police for *doing* something – doing what, he did not know or remember, but something unseemly. The parks were particularly to be avoided on such occasions, as was Queen's Wood. Here he would pass young lovers, in this warm weather uninhibited, kissing on benches, lying on grass, fondling one another's groins. The toilets – not that he wished to explore them – were, he knew, full of men exposing themselves. Any open space in London became a great playing-field of sex. And although Oliver tried, in such moods, to retreat from the scene lest he make a fool of himself, he was always led inexorably to that high-pitched strain, that sound as melancholy as seagulls and as hopeful as the dawn, caused by children at play. Netball, the little legs jumping in the air so that one saw up their skirts, was best; but all games had their charms. A drizzly games afternoon was most suitable to his purpose, since it enabled him to wear a mackintosh and to complete the necessary business while he watched, rather than recollect in tranquillity.

Even at the height of such erotomania, he could glimpse a life in which he was free of it. Like an alcoholic who knew what life would be like without the bottle, he could imagine clear, unfettered days in which he was liberated from this demeaning slavery. The paradox was that Bobs had given him this freedom. During their slow development as lovers over the last seven years, he had shaken himself free from generalized sex mania. While he concentrated on his love for her, he had felt almost no need for Lewis Carroll's photographs, and there had been very few drizzly walks by children's playgrounds. Only since his engagement to Camilla, and his attempts to cut loose from Bobs, had he found himself becoming once more a slave to sexual fantasy. And the anxiety which had oppressed him since the disappearance of his notebooks had plunged him back into the hell of addiction. This type of rampant, unfocused, insatiable sexual desire was, he was certain, something which could come upon almost any man or boy at some period of their lives. Luckily for most, such phases did not last long. For Oliver, there had been a period in his twenties when he said that he found it difficult to work, to concentrate first on law, then on philosophy. He often alluded in conversation to this difficulty, without adding that its reason was simple: he was thinking concentratedly and continuously about sex.

He did not believe that even queers (and his belief was that most men became queer not because they preferred men but because they were so highly sexed, and gay sex was more available) were at it all the time. Those cases you heard of, before AIDS changed the gay lifestyle, of men going out to bath-houses and having five, six, ten lovers a night, could not have been anything but episodes even in the lives of the most highly sexed; and this was one of the things which made such mortal contracts so poignantly sad. There is a dark side of the moon. The Temptations of St Anthony, so often depicted in art, describe a reality. The sickness which destroys in the noonday was a recognized peril of the monastic life. Those who suffered, in the Inferno, because of simple lust, undoubtedly suffered; Dante was not writing whimsical tales.

Every now and then, in the cycle of the moon, there was a partial eclipse, but it never lasted long. What seemed to have happened this time, and what was so truly alarming, was that Oliver felt himself slithering down into an abyss of darkness from which there might quite possibly be no recovery. The sky was darkened. It was like the worst period of his depressions fifteen or so years before, but much worse, since, while feeling totally isolated, and unable to concentrate on the simplest things which were said to him, he also knew himself to be in acute danger.

Just as minor danger (the fear that Lotte might come into his room with her mops and dusters while he tossed off) could stimulate excitement, so the fear of total ruin produced a clouding of the brain which was close to madness, and which was accompanied by rampant sexual desire. There had never been a time in his life when it had been more imperative to *think clearly*. Yet as often as he said this to himself, he felt that he had become a victim of chance and circumstance, that events were out of his control.

Sometimes he tossed off with the clinical intention of clearing his head, just for twenty minutes, to allow himself to think, to plan a strategy for that moment when he was finally confronted and accused. Each time he forgot (how could one forget a lesson learnt thousands of times since the age of eleven?) that sexual appetite, unlike the appetite for food, was increased by what it fed on, that wanking, though it might momentarily diminish desire, did not release the brain from sexual thoughts, but produced sensations of excitement, lassitude, panic, which were hardly conducive to rational processes. (How right Victorian headmasters and Catholic priests were, to regard masturbation as a sin.)

It was in such a state of mind that he now sat at his desk. The murmur of Janet's confounded 'gathering' came up through three floors. He knew that, eventually, he would have to go downstairs and join in, but before he did so, he must try to clear his head.

For the last week, he had been in a state of spiritual pain which had never in his life been equalled. The meeting with Catharine Cuffe, which she had herself suggested, had been something he dreaded. (Once – it was one of those playful conversations with Bobs which came close to philosophical investigation – they'd wondered if it was possible to create units of measurement which applied to stress, just as other units measured weight or length. The unit of dread was called a 'dentist', and was measured on a scale of one to ten. The knowledge that you were handing in shoddy homework and could be upbraided by a teacher was half a dentist. Having to admit that you had broken Granny's video machine was two dentists. And so on. The meeting with Cuffe in the British Museum had been a ten-dentist meeting.)

For so long, he had rehearsed things in his head, planned one particular conversational theme. When Cuffe had had her say, though, he had almost nothing to reply. He had been quite sure she was going to confront him with the notebooks. He could even imagine the excuses she would have made for spying – that she had needed to set her mind straight on some philosophical point, and had searched among his *cahiers* for guidance . . .

It would not have mattered how Cuffe had read the incriminating evidence. What would have mattered was that she had done so. And, since she had not raised an immediate hue and cry, it could be said that things might have been worse. He assumed that she had kept the secret to herself, and not told the grandmother or the mother that the little girl had been having an affair with their philosopher He had gone to the British Museum certain that Cuffe was nursing this information for her own purposes. Obviously, she would not have proposed a meeting unless she intended an ultimatum: what would be her terms?

When no allusion was made to the notebooks, none at all, and when it became clear that Cuffe had merely summoned him to the Museum in order to dissuade him from marrying Camilla, he had been, for a time, heady, excited, joyful. But this sense of euphoria could not last. Cuffe was, as his few remaining vestiges of common sense told his agitated mind, his best hope. If Cuffe had been his notebook spy, she might have strong motives to keep the information secret. She might insist that he had therapy, or that he went away, but the knowledge that he had been to bed with the sprog would, in Cuffe's terms, simply be a weapon she would use in order to get him for herself. Her proposal of marriage had not surprised him. There was, indeed, a strong case for it. And there had been several occasions, during the week since their meeting, when he had read the proposal as a coded allusion to her knowledge. For obvious reasons, Cuffe wanted Camilla to go. Camilla represented more of a threat than Bobs, simply because she was of marriageable age. Had Cuffe been making him a simple blackmailer's offer as they sat there on the bench: 'Marry me and I shall say nothing about the notebooks'?

Reluctantly, he was forced to conclude that this was not what she had said. There was actually no reason to suppose that Cuffe had stolen the notebooks, read the notebooks or even that she knew they existed. There was no reason to suppose that Cuffe knew about him and Bobs. And this forced upon him the tormented knowledge that there were now only a limited number of explanations left.

It remained possible that he had been mistaken; that he, one of the neatest and most punctilious arrangers of his own books, had mysteriously and most uncharacteristically mislaid the notebooks. Might he not simply have slipped them into the wrong shelf? Such a theory had been tested by hours and hours of searching. Duster in hand, he had taken out, and replaced, every one of his eight hundred or so books, his two hundred notebooks. Each volume had been opened, dusted, and its pages riffled. He had turned out his neat clothes drawers twenty times. He had searched in his duvet cover, and under his mattress (for he sometimes read his own works in bed, when Bobs had left him of a morning, and crept back to her own room). He had lifted the rugs on his floor. He had even (for the despair of his loss made him believe that the notebooks could be *anywhere*) turned over the rubber footmats in the car.

Another possibility, that the notebooks did not in fact exist, had made its siren appeal to his exhausted brain. Was it not possible that he had been so *distrait* that he had forgotten to write his journal for the last few months, that he had merely believed that he had done so? But, no, he could so distinctly remember writing in the new exercise books – *Volume XXXV* and *Volume XXXVI*. He had a distinct visual recollection of the blue ink as it had formed the Roman numerals and dried on the surface of the page.

There was no comfort to be found in lying to himself. He had neither lost the books, nor dreamed them up. He had written them, fully and frankly as ever, a confession of his secret nature and his secret love. He had put down on paper things about himself which no one had ever heard him say aloud. There was a sense in which even Bobs did not know the things of which he wrote, since she could not possibly, at her age, be in a position to understand his generalized obsession with the dream children. And these books, these barings of his soul, these incriminating confessions which could be read by the police and which could send him to prison, had passed out of his hands. Either, an inconceivable supposition, they had been stolen by a stranger; or they had been taken by someone in the house. Cuffe, his best bet, was now ruled out of the running. Surely his little American nymphet would have been neither so naughty nor so wise, on one of her two visits to his quarters, as to have appropriated the notebooks? Her mother had been bolder, during her fortnight in the house, coming into his room for chatty interludes; but had Rosalie read even a page of the notebooks she would not have remained silent. Bobs herself? What would have been the little girl's motive for such a theft? Lotte? Surely not. Janet? Michal?

This was the part of the calculation which, in his present emotional condition, was unthinkable. He could not tolerate the idea that any of these people had plumbed his secret, so his mind refused to concentrate on the certainty that one of them had done so. Had any of them read the books, he could not imagine a motive for keeping silence. Surely, whoever she was, the thief should have denounced him by now? Or claimed some advantage from her knowledge? The silence was what chilled his heart, causing him to fear not discovery, merely, but death itself.

He had not known that he was so afraid of death. He had always been able to speak of it so airily. He had studied all the great deaths in literature, from Socrates's onwards. He had even, once upon a time, given a lecture course on death. As he confronted the inevitability of his own death, and that of Bobs, he found himself reduced to shaking liquid. Not jelly. He would have liked some of what went into the lavatory to have had the consistency of jelly, but, like the psalmist, his bowels gushed out like water. He minded so. He minded that his death, which would define his life, would make those left behind see his whole existence in terms of what they would deem sexual perversion.

The Knowledge of the Good, which he had made not merely his own study, but that of generations of grateful students, and which he had even tried to inspire in his radio audiences, had been his primary business and aim. Cuffe, in one of her early, gushing letters, had quoted a remark made about Wittgenstein: 'He conjured up a vision of a better you.' This really was how Oliver had tried to live; it was why he had tried to live. For the mere loss of a couple of blue exercise books, covered with squiggles of ink, he would be fixed in the minds of those who knew his name, not with the pursuit of good, but evil.

This angered him as he approached his death; but much worse than this was the fear of death itself. Twenty-five dentists. The slave of his body, he did not believe himself to be a soul inhabiting a shell of flesh, but to *be* that body. Now squatted humiliatingly on the lavatory, now in the possession of sex, now dry in the throat, now nauseous, he had a perpetual physical consciousness of what death was. It was all these functions stopping. The long legs and the long fingers would be stiff and lifeless. He was more than ever aware of himself as a collection of physical sensations, nerves, muscles, fats, bones which, among their other prosaic functions, produced the mysterious phenomenon labelled consciousness; he was aware of their imminent dissolution, and sick dread hung over him. He remembered Arnold Maar in hospital in that final week, so resigned to it all. How could he be? How could anyone be?

And yet Oliver could think of no escape other than his plan of a murder and a suicide. He knew he was not in a state conducive to sensible thinking. He longed to devise a way of killing his beloved without breaking his own heart, for the dead body of Bobs was more than he could bear to imagine, even if he only lived ten seconds to see it. Nor could he allow her to know him to be her killer, and her last minute alive to know a mystifying betrayal by the one she loved best.

He had thought of their both drinking poison, but he knew nothing of pharmaceuticals; and nothing worse could be imagined than the botched attempt, and coming round to face a police inquiry. He had thought of disguising himself in a balaclava helmet and attacking her on her way home from school, perhaps dragging her into some bushes and cudgelling her from behind. But this idea was impossible. How could he cudgel the head he had caressed so often? How could he endure her screams? The closest he could come to a possible solution was a seaside walk on some high cliffs; a sudden push in the small of her back as she stood on the edge. And then he would jump to join her on the foaming rocks below. The very thought sent him retching to the bathroom. For when it came to the point, would he possess the courage?

Chapter Thirteen

'German books – yes, these I read,' announced Margot Reisz confidently. 'It is years since I speak German very often, and very quickly I am, that is, absolutely, I become tousled.'

'Lotte can speak English,' said Bobs (in this language). 'Would you like some dip?'

'Ah, wonderful, wonderful,' persisted Miss Reisz in her eccentric German. 'The dictionary, you understand? It becomes very. I forget my dictionary.'

'What word do you want to look up?' asked Lotte. 'Maybe I can help.'

'Excuse me, please?'

'Well, to save you the trouble of looking up the word in a dictionary, why don't you just ask me? Say the English word, and I'll tell you what it is in German.'

'Words,' said Margot Reisz, 'I forget words.'

'But this is the same, or very nearly the same in German,' said Lotte. '*Worte*.'

'Words I know, but I have only a little dictionary.'

'Do you mean a small vocabulary?'

'*Vokabular? C'est ça!*' affirmed Miss Reisz loudly.

Bobs wondered whether the change of language heralded the danger of Margot getting on to the subject of her house in the Dordogne.

'Ah, yummy!' added Margot. With a savage gesture, she used a potato crisp to scoop some of the green gunge which Bobs held in a dish. 'How's your French coming on?'

Bobs simpered.

'We've got up to Book Two of *Parlons français*. Only, it's mainly about shopping, which is really boring.'

'That's right! Nothing like having a go! I always remember your grandfather saying, it doesn't matter how badly you speak a language. Foreigners are always amazed that English people should try to speak their language at all; jolly grateful when we make the effort. I can't stand these Little Englanders who don't even try to speak French. You know, last year in Bergerac – well, you remember the lovely market there, Bobs, because Granny brought you with me to buy the vegetables, didn't she? Do you remember? There was this pair of Brits, really Surbiton.'

'That's Camilla,' said Bobs. 'You haven't met her, have you?'

'Isn't she charming? Can we catch her? What's she going out of the room for?'

'She's going upstairs to fetch Oliver. He's probably too shy to come down.'

'That's our Ollie!' said Margot Reisz approvingly. 'Never did like a crowd.'

It was debatable whether 'crowd' was the right word to describe the dozen or fifteen grown-ups who stood awkwardly in Janet's kitchen-diner. Unlike Janet, Margot Reisz wore her grey hair up. She wore a black top embroidered with threads of an unsparing turquoise, an object bought on a cruise some years before. The espadrilles which she wore on her feet ('The most comfortable shoes there are!') also suggested an air of holiday. The truth was that, since retirement from the Civil Service, Margot had been on permanent vacation, which was why her suppers with Oliver, in her flat near Alexandra Palace, had come to mean so much to her.

Bobs wondered whether all parties were of their nature boring, or whether her granny had bad luck with her friends. The expressions of exultation – 'I *say*!' '*Thank* you!' 'Mm, olives, wonderful!' – whenever Bobs stood beside one of them with a dish suggested that it did not take much to make them happy; but perhaps there was something a little sad, to be quite so uplifted by the sight of avocado dip?

Perhaps none of these people had known love? Granny talked of missing 'darling Hensleigh'; but when she did so, it was to reminisce about the boring things they had done together, such as having dinner with famous poets. She never spoke about the times they had together, just the two of them. Those who knew love surely regarded all social life as a bit of an interruption? The best bits of life were when it was just the two of you, with shared jokes, and books you both liked, and the silly sort of talk which you could not explain to anyone else? So Bobs had found.

'I have to escape this woman,' whispered Lotte. 'Always she tries to speak German, but she just speaks nonsense.'

'Oliver says he can speak nonsense in four languages,' said Bobs.

'No, no, his German is good, very good. But this Miss Reisz! Darling, you go to the stove and get the sausages, yes, and I take from you that bowl of dip? Yes?'

Lotte was brilliant at parties: did all the work, made all the food, opened the bottles of wine. Granny, by contrast, who said that she loved having people in, never did anything, merely leant against the stove and smoked.

'Fewer than last year, perhaps,' Janet was saying to Michal when Bobs approached. 'But then I don't like a party to be too crowded.'

A few days before, when Michal was sitting with just Bobs and Cuffe, she'd said how sad she found her mother's 'little drinks' these days: all the old crocks and remnants.

'It isn't surprising that Mummy only invites sad old women to her parties – she only knows sad old women.'

'Well,' Cuffe had said, 'why don't I ask a few colleagues from UCL – if you think she'd like that?'

Bobs was not sure that the addition of Cuffe's academics to Granny's crocks had been the perfect recipe for social fizz. Though the dons ate whatever was offered – one man scooping up a whole palmful of peanuts as if he were a chimpanzee – they had shown no signs of wishing to mix. Nor had their arrival done much to improve the balance of the sexes since, apart from the man in specs with a corduroy jacket who had gone quite red after his third glass of wine, they were all women.

Bobs thought parties were very, very sad. She had been to her first school-friends party not long before. There had been about seven of them, asked to stay the night in Amanda's house. They had watched a video, eaten some pizzas which had been delivered to their front door by a young man on a motorscooter, and stayed up quite late talking about various other girls at school. They'd slept in sleeping bags on the floor, and Bobs had missed the warmth and comfort of Oliver's bed. Amanda's party had been boring, but at least it had things to do. Granny would have been better showing her friends a video – a Miss Marple film, perhaps – rather than expecting them to stand in huddles making conversation.

Bobs did not believe that anyone really enjoyed talk which concentrated on politics, the Royal Family, or anything (whether its art, its politico-economic problems or its cuisine) which related to Abroad. It was all right for her age group to talk of holidays, because they did not go on about traffic snarl-ups and restaurants. Madeline, for instance, during Amanda's party, had told them she'd been taken by her father and stepmother on a safari holiday, to soften her up prior to the pair getting married. It sounded fantastic, sleeping in a tent, and seeing some of the wild beasts really close up. Oliver and she would love it – when all this was over. A fondness for the zoo was one of their shared things. Bobs imagined him getting all sunburnt, and her having to rub cream on his nose, as she had done last summer in Cornwall.

Each little group in the room, as Bobs passed by with a wine glass, was murmuring about something boring. One group spoke of cars, another of politics.

'No, really, Bobs, thank you. I'm just fine with mineral water,' said Rosalie Baynes.

'I've been sent over specially to give you this.'

'Well, I'll have it.' A man had arrived at last and, more-over, Granny's face was saved, a man who was on the verge of being celebrated. Claudio Lewis's shock of silver hair, his bow-tie and his mustard-coloured suit marked his belief that he was different from his fellows.

'Why not have an actor?' Rosalie was asking, in that wise-cracking tone of hers. 'They say Reagan's a B-movie actor, but what are most politicians? They're actors who wouldn't even get an audition to advertise cookies.'

'If you read my article last week, you would have seen that I agree entirely; but then, as I realize, there is absolutely no reason why you should have heard of me.'

His slightly agonized tones suggested that there were in fact about a dozen reasons why any reasonably educated person should know his byline in the small political weekly of which he was the editor.

'I'm afraid you'll have to tell me your name again,' said Rosalie. 'Put it down to my being an American idiot.'

As he sipped his wine, his face wrinkled with distaste.

'So, what are your first impressions?'

'Of my future son-in-law? He's perfectly charming.'

'I think we have all known that about Oliver for a very long time,' said Claudio Lewis. 'I really meant, your first impressions of England.'

'I had my first impressions of England when I was a little girl and saw the funeral of King George the Fifth,' said Rosalie. 'And if you want my impression of it now, I'd say it had come down a little since then. Just a little.'

'You must excuse me, I thought . . .'

The sneer on his features, made no better by the wine in his glass, infuriated Rosalie into seriousness.

'I mean, when I first came to England, sure there was poverty, but I don't remember seeing beggars on the streets. There weren't kids sitting out on the sidewalk wrapped in old blankets. There wasn't garbage all over the town. I thought, having a woman Prime Minister, you'd at least clear up the garbage.'

Claudio Lewis held up a finger of admonition. It would have been clear to any observer, though not to Rosalie herself, that the old rogue found her attractive, and he was one of those for whom combat is a form of flirtation.

'I'm going to have to stop you,' he said. 'You're confusing a number of different issues. If you are saying that this country is completely down the drain, I should agree with you. Couldn't agree with you more, as you'd know if you had read my magazine. But it is not because of the beggars.

In fact, the presence of beggars on the streets is one of the few hopeful signs. Have you never read Lamb's Essay on the London Beggars, or Wordsworth's "The Old Cumberland Beggar"?'

'Of course, I read them every night before I go to sleep; but haven't we moved on a little since those days? And there's something else. Little children. Okay, so twenty years ago, you had those kids killed on the Moors. Did you ever read that book about it – *Beyond Belief?* That was what it was. But English children still walked to school, they were still safe to play in the park. The last three or four times I've been to England, I've opened up the paper and there's been a story about someone doing terrible things to children. Either a woman's murdered her baby, or some man's gotten hold of a kid . . .'

'Here you may be on to something,' opined the bow-tied pundit. 'Oh, thank you.'

For Michal was standing there with a bottle and was replenishing his glass. It now seemed as if the contents of his glass were more palatable, since he had dropped the prissy, sneering expression, and was fixing his soft brown eyes on Rosalie with a lecherous leer.

'You are right to say that there is a profound spiritual *malaise* at the very heart of our society – quite largely and simply, I should say, through the decline of religion. Where you are completely wrong, if I may say so, is to imply that your own country is any better off.'

He said *orf.* Rosalie reflected that it was years since she had met an English person who genuinely said *orf*, and that had been a friend of her grandmother's, living in Kensington aged about ninety-six. She wrote Claudio Lewis down as an old fraud. She nevertheless rather liked him, and decided that if he mentioned dinner, she would not have to be asked twice.

'I never said we were better off,' she said. 'You asked me my impressions of England.'

'And I regret to have to tell you this,' he continued, 'but much of the blame for the decline of our society, including all the violence and the child pornography and the like, must be laid at the American door.'

With a grim mouth – it was odd that in anger Michal looked less than half her real age, more like a furious adolescent – Bobs's mother said, 'If we were prepared to tax the rich and spend the money on decent houses, decent flats, decent schools . . .'

'My dear – oh, thank you –' as the glass was refilled – 'there was more decency, as this good lady and I would define those terms, when the poor lived in putrefying slums than –'

'Oh, Claudio, how can you *say* that?'

'My dear Michal,' and he touched her elbow, 'I am sure you do excellent work, and that it is all done with the best intentions, but the fact is that the working class . . .'

Another expression of distaste played about his features, and it was hard to know whether it was the drink or the disadvantaged masses which caused his lips to curl.

213

'You know,' said Michal bleakly, 'I don't do good work. We wouldn't be having this conversation if I did not do rotten work, impossible work. I reckon I've seen fifteen kids in the last week with truancy problems. Not one of them, Claudio, came from a middle-class home. Not one of them had what you would call a home at all. Do you realize, half a mile from here there are tower blocks where the kids live ferally – okay, so they've got a nominal Mum, and a very few know who Dad is or was –'

'My dear, you are missing the point.'

'And those are the kids who are all victims of abuse of one sort or another. And if you are saying there is no connection, no economic connection . . .'

'Sorry . . . peculiar . . . not feeling . . .'

The famous editor's face had assumed an expression of panic and he ran into the hall. A kerfuffle could be heard, since another guest had already occupied the downstairs lavatory. Claudio Lewis could be heard urgently knocking on the door and then making a run for it up the stairs.

'He is an old friend of Mr Hensleigh Rose,' explained the Austrian girl, who had materialized at Rosalie's elbow. 'Each year he comes to see Mrs Rose. But you are drinking water?'

Bobs, who had been unable to resist following Claudio Lewis from the room, returned with a slightly too vivid account of what was going on.

'He is ill,' said Lotte.

'All journalists drink too much,' said Michal.

'I should have known who he was,' said Rosalie. 'Where does he write his stuff?'

Michal, pulling a schoolgirl face, named the weekly periodical of which Claudio was still the editor and to which her late father had contributed reviews.

'If you're looking for a real sign of putrefying decline,' said Michal, 'it would be that little rag he edits. I mean – we've got no real intellectuals in this country.'

'I knew there was some reason why I still liked coming here,' said Rosalie brightly.

Although the room was filling up, Janet, leaning by the stove and smoking again, felt terribly alone. She missed, and hated, and loved Hensleigh all at once, as she surveyed the pathetic remnants of what had been their circle. The party was not the disaster which, in its first grisly half-hour, she had feared. When the room had contained no one but Margot Reisz and those boring college friends of Cuffe's, Janet had told herself, never again. Then some more people had come, and it had seemed a bit more like the old days. Someone (Claudio, bless him for coming) had even run out to be ill.

Ah, their first party, when Philip Toynbee had thrown up on the carpet of that rented flat in Maida Vale and Hensleigh had said, 'A party isn't a party until someone's been sick.' But those had been the days when they had distinguished *regulars* to their little drinks.

'If you use the word regulars, it implies that we keep a

pub,' Hensleigh had corrected her. Well, they very nearly had, a pub for reviewers and poets and dons and the occasional politico. That generation (friends of friends of Philip Toynbee) had all died off. But the younger ones had continued to come, and the parties had all been fun until Hensleigh, darn him, had gone off and left her.

That's what bereavement felt like. Standing in a crowded room, and asking, 'Does anyone here like me? Why are they here?' That was what bereavement felt like, and in Janet's case, long before the little bastard died, it was a familiar feeling, standing in the middle of the room at countless parties, most of them her own, and feeling quite left out by Hensleigh and his friends. Why else rush about so frantically with her dishes of nuts and crisps and dip, telling the waiters (yes, waiters in those days!) to refill the glasses? Something to do, something to banish her loneliness, as the roar of laughter came from the corner of the room where Hensleigh stood, conceited little man with his dark suit and his bow-tie and his suede shoes. He could produce that appreciative roar wherever he went. Sometimes the anguish of envying him his social flair had been worse than the torture of sexual jealousy.

Janet had always been very 'good' about his mistresses, not because she had felt tolerant, but because she shared his snobbish belief that it would be bourgeois to make a fuss. These women came to the parties at 12 Wagner Rise, quite brazenly. In this very room, on this very parquet floor, she had seen Ivy Darwin standing, bold as brass, with her legs apart and her cig alight. God, that hurt, the humiliation of it; the humiliation of that woman's stare. It was knowing that Ivy knew which made it worse. And not knowing how much Ivy knew. (Did Ivy know that nothing went on between Hensleigh and Janet in the bedroom? And if Ivy knew, did that mean that all her guests knew? All her friends? Oh, God.)

If Janet had obeyed her guts, and not her desire to rise above the bourgeois, she'd have torn the bitch's hair out. And yet (tears pricked at the back of her eyes as she leaned against the stove and surveyed her dismal little party today, her widow's party) she would have endured any amount of torment, and any number of evenings with Poison Ivy, just to have Hensleigh back in the room now.

What a bunch of wrecks they all were. Just look at Margot Reisz! It was incredible to think that a reasonably well-known poet had once, in this very kitchen, confided in Hensleigh that he really fancied Margot. It would be a brave man today who approached that pot belly, those pendulous breasts, those whiskery dewlaps. There was no malice in Janet's observation, though some bitterness in the thought that Margot was only a couple of years older than herself. For some psychological reasons of her own, Margot had let herself go, but she was only an extreme embodiment of what was happening to everyone else at the party. There was not a human body in the room, even the supposedly young ones supplied by Cuffe, which was not, by a universal and inexorable process, accumulating its share of varicose veins, quivering fats, withered skin, rheumy, baggy eyes, misshapen or painful spines, brown teeth and, within, God knew what decades-old digestive malfunctionings to produce the blasts of foul breath which alcohol stimulates. The one figure in the kitchen other than Bobs who appeared entirely at ease in her own handsome body was Rosalie Baynes and she, Janet thought (inaccurately), fooled no one.

Hensleigh, ever the selfish bastard, got out before the worst indignities had time to take their effect. A heart attack in his fifties had killed him instantly. It was just like him to get out of things he didn't want to do.

'Darling – would you mind awfully if I didn't?'

That cooing, wheedling tone he could adopt when, just once in a while, she wanted him to come to a dinner given by her friends; wanted him to come with her to the tennis club, or for Sunday lunch with her family. God, he was a snob! He'd have crossed London on bare knees over broken glass for the chance of dinner with someone he esteemed. He could always give the impression that her people and her friends were not worth the bother. Janet had never quite been able to forgive him for cutting her mother's eightieth birthday party because, at two days' notice, he had been asked to a publisher's dinner at the Garrick Club to meet a famous American writer. Could he not see that there was something demeaning in this? He had so obviously been asked at the last minute, to fill a gap in the table when someone else had dropped out.

It was extraordinary, but she had never openly questioned Hensleigh's version of himself. They both knew that, on their marriage, it was she, Janet, who had the little bit of money. It was her family whose wise investments had enabled them to buy 12 Wagner Rise. Her family were respectable professional people, chiefly educated at the better London day schools. His father was a pharmacist in the outer reaches of Surrey. But the difference between you and me, she almost said aloud, is your ruthlessness. When did you ever visit your sister in Kingston? I kept up, with Mum and Dad, and Tony and Rachel and Margot Reisz, and dear God, you were right, she thought as she smoked and looked at them all, what a lot of bloody bores they all are!

'See the conquering hero comes!' exclaimed Margot Reisz, whose great grin revealed nuts and crisps clinging to a brown dental wreckage.

The pair who now entered looked, as bridal couples so often do, stricken. It was as though they had been marked out from humanity for some task or initiation which was not quite of their choosing. Both were nervous, wary.

Oliver, trained like a Pavlovian dog to be polite to old ladies, was the first to fix his features into a delighted grin which was, in the circumstances, almost ghoulish.

'Margot, my dear!' He swept up his old friend, planting kisses on both cheeks. 'How perfectly lovely you look!'

Camilla still looked frozen with shyness, painfully out of

her depth, by the time Bobs advanced with her wine glass, which she thrust into her hand.

'Just water, thank you.'

'Lotte says it will calm your nerves.'

'Oh, really?' Remembering that one was supposed to be kind to children, Camilla switched on a terrified smile, but she could hardly look at Bobs. 'I'll stick to water for now.'

By now Margot Reisz had their wedding journey planned out for them. Where else would they go, but to her own place in the Dordogne?

'Don't let me find anyone trying to persuade you that you can eat a better sausage than ours, in Périgueux! No, well, we're about twenty-five kilometres south, actually.'

'Really, Bobs,' Camilla said with quiet vehemence. 'Okay? Give it to someone else.'

'This dip's the cheesy one,' said Bobs, holding up a bowl full of a yellowish, creamy substance.

'No one could accuse me of turning down Janet's excellent Pouilly-Fumé,' said Miss Reisz. 'No, dear. If you take that empty one . . . Thanks. No, what you do is, you head south through Bergerac, but avoid that treacherous junction where the signs try to lead you to Sainte Foy la Grande. Once you're on the main route heading for Toulouse, it's actually a very short journey and you'll be seeing some of the most heavenly country – we're rather proud of it. But Oliver will have told you of the treats which lie in store . . .'

Camilla had reached the shaken condition in which she

could be sure of nothing. Upstairs, just now, she had been brave enough to ask him, 'Why did you *do* this to me? Why would one human being want to trick another human being – in a matter as important as this? Why, Oliver? *Why?*'

She felt so disconcerted by her discoveries that the previous year could not be seen straight. Just who had she gotten herself mixed up with? Old spectres from childhood, which she had hoped had been locked for ever in the closet, returned to mock and to torture. She had always held herself back from the commitment of sexual relations, aware that when they started to be explored, discoveries would be made, and more discoveries, and yet more, as in a dream when one wandered down half-lit corridors, trying now this door, now that, and finding that some opened to cobwebby interiors while others remained firmly locked. The thing for which she had not been prepared was the sense of being tricked, deliberately deceived. It seemed as if the apparently kind man with whom she had fallen in love, and who now stood beside her, had consciously held back information which it would have been so easy to vouchsafe.

'I usually have supper with Margot on a Thursday,' he had said, in the early days, in reply to some suggestion that he accompany her to a recital of *Lieder* at the Wigmore Hall. 'But I can perfectly easily change it.'

Too frightened to ask who Margot was, lest the reply be something with which she was emotionally unequipped to deal, she had been silent. Was Margot an old friend? Or (this would have been hard to bear) an 'ex' with whom he remained on good terms? Or simply a rival?

And, after that concert at the Wigmore Hall, there had been another allusion to Margot, the confession that he was going to her house in France for a week, in the hope of getting on with some work. Gradually, over the months which elapsed, she stopped being worried by his allusions to Margot. Almost everything he had told her about *La haute latrine* (and she had even fallen for the idea that this was the *gîte*'s actual name) had been to its disadvantage: sleepless nights there had been attributed to a variety of causes: a flimsy straw mattress; the chirruping of cicadas; Margot's having a go at French cuisine, the real thing, none of your Masterchef, but good country dishes; the other guests. The fact that Margot had asked him with uncongenial companions (colleagues of hers from the Ministry of Ag and Fish) had at first set Camilla's heart at rest. So, *La haute latrine* was not a love-nest where he and Margot went to be alone? Then, aflutter once more, she had wondered whether Oliver and Margot had been, of old, such a recognizable item that they could entertain together?

All those early doubts about Margot returned to her memory, jostling with the disturbing knowledge about her man which had now come to destroy all happiness. She was frozen to the spot in Janet's kitchen, unable to respond with any politeness to Margot's friendly invitations to

Merseux-les-Champs. Why had Oliver never set her mind at rest, simply by saying that *Margot was seventy years old*? Could he not see how reassuring this would have been? Or had he wanted to torture her all along, lead her into his snare, string her along with lies? What chance, anyway, had she had against these rivals, these women of Wagner Rise, whom he nicknamed, behind their backs, *la béguinage*? Camilla could not talk philosophy, like Miss Cuffe; or, like Janet, provide him with sophisticated literary companionship. She had sometimes thought, 'Oh, I'd swap a genuine rival for this swarm of female hangers-on!' An affair with another woman, discreetly conducted, something which had fixed perimeters, would have been easier to cope with than the smothering sense that group of women gave, that Oliver was their possession.

At least the kid had been her friend. That was what she had thought.

She could not cope with what she now knew about Oliver. It should have been making her head for the airport, or the police; but she was frozen, entrapped. She still loved him and, though she was now possessed of something which seemed like a reason not to do so, she still believed in him. If she did not believe in him, she was not sure that there was anything left to believe in.

She had been trying to buy him, hadn't she? She realized, even when she'd done it, that the purchase of absurdly lavish presents, such as the Mazda, had been a sign of uncertainty, the demonstration of the very opposite to that assurance which a woman should feel when about to be married.

When she had given him the keys to the car, she had kissed him and said, 'It makes me feel so very privileged, being loved by you.'

He had been so courtly when he responded to her caress. She had always liked the fact that there was such gentleness in his kisses, such an absence of passion.

'I can assure you that I feel privileged too,' he had said.

When his abundant beard had covered her face, she had escaped it as quickly as politeness allowed and, returning from the tiptoe position to her normal height, she had snuggled against his chest like a child. It was then that she had blurted out the central truth of their relationship.

'I need you so much!'

'Dear girl.' And he had kissed the top of her head.

'That's what gives me the sense of privilege: the knowledge that I need you so much, and you don't need me at all.'

'What do you mean? You have no idea how much I need you.'

'You've got Janet and Michal and Catharine and Margot and Bobs.'

He had detached himself from her embrace, and asked in that withering professorial tone, 'Why on earth do you need to make the emotional life into a competition?'

Her happiness – what she had deemed to be their happiness – had dissolved like smoke after this glacial inquiry.

She had so much *not* wanted to spell out her sense of competition, her feeling of being squeezed out by the others. He himself, on many different occasions, had hinted that he found the devotion of *la béguinage* oppressive. The last six months had been a tug of war, this way and that. Sometimes it seemed as if he could not wait to find a job in some American college and come back with her to the United States, to cut loose. At other times he spoke of this situation, this hencoop of admirers clucking around him, as if it were something of which he was no more than the passive recipient, as if he had no responsibility for their possessive adulation, praise and affection. She had come to see, even before she had a more bitter cup to swallow, that this assessment of things would not do. But even now, as she stood there, she needed him. She loved him. And she needed him so much, and she felt so much wounded pride, that she was not sure that she would ever allow the truth to come out. She had not confronted him with what she knew. Let him be the puzzled one for a change! Let him wonder at her frozen unhappiness! This would be better than bearing the pity of *la béguinage*, or being forced to admit to her mother that she had made a mistake.

'*You did not drink your wine?*'

This question was asked in a harsh tone by the au pair, who had come up to Camilla and was so close to her that one was aware of spittle and heat coming from her mouth. In the seconds, maybe milliseconds, which followed,

Camilla read the murderous aggression in Lotte's face. She heard the little girl cry and the other guests gasp. She saw the kitchen knife raised aloft.

'I poison you, I poison you and your bitch mother . . . It makes me laugh to see you shit your pants like a baby, so there is castor oil in your wine, that's why you shit. Why don't you just go away, you bitch? It is me he loves!'

Michal, who now stood closest to Lotte, began to say her name in a slow, calm voice, as if she were trying to tame a wild animal.

'Lotte. Put that knife down, Lotte. Everything's going to be all right. Lotte.'

With the energy of the mad, Lotte showed no sign of releasing her hold on the knife, which she now pointed towards Camilla with jabbing motions.

The effect of the castor oil, combined with fear, now operated on Margot Reisz. An old woman emptying her bowels, as she stood rooted to the spot at one of Janet's 'little drinks', would, in other circumstances, have been monstrous, or farcical; but now it was secondary to the horror of what was happening. Most other guests edged as far away from Lotte as possible, either hiding with Janet near the kitchen stove, or scuttling out into the hall.

'Easy,' said Michal. 'Easy.'

'Make her drop the knife!' said Janet from the other end of the room.

'You think he loves you, bitch? It is me he loves.'

'Someone ring the police!' Janet's voice.

'No, Mum! Lotte, you're okay. Just drop that knife. Lotte!'

'Otherwise, why does he copy out poetry? Bobs, she comes to me, and she says, this paper falls out of a book. Oliver writes down a poem. Is it about Camilla, do you think? She is a little child, she knows nothing –

> *Ich war, o Lamm, als Hirt bestellt,*
> *Zu huten dich auf dieser Welt . . .*

You think he writes this about you, you bitch?'

What happened next was probably compressed into seconds. Lotte started to scream incoherently. Camilla understood none of what she saw. Her optic nerves, however, sent to the brain an indelible photograph. Oliver stood there and let it happen. And what was *it*? So rarely do human emotions show, really show. That was what was so shocking about Lotte, so red in the face, all her veins standing up on her temples, her teeth biting Michal's hand when it was raised to restrain her. You could not make out what she was screaming. Some of it was German, a language which Camilla did not possess.

At football matches you saw supporters yelling like this. It was wild nature, screaming through a human head. In the very moment of seeing, and fearing, what this rival predator intended, Camilla envied its terrible ability to scream for what it wanted.

'No, Mum, really!' said Michal. Janet had reached for the telephone.

'Someone do something,' said Margot Reisz.

'Look, get that woman away from my daughter.'

Rosalie Baynes had stepped forward. Michal was trying to wrest the knife from Lotte but she was not strong enough. Camilla saw the wild thing coming towards her. It was like the bit in a fairy story when the great scaly monster is released from the bottle. She saw the flashing blade. Her eyes of fear met Lotte's eyes of hate, and when she closed her eyes, she just wanted it all to end.

Chapter Fourteen

Perhaps it was the valium, perhaps the shock, or a combination of the two, which had destroyed Lotte's grasp of the English language. For the first ten minutes of her visit, Michal wondered if the girl had been deprived of speech altogether. They sat silently in the bleak day-room, while some of the more able-bodied patients cleared the tables of jigsaw puzzles, tabloid newspapers and the Monopoly board, in order to lay places for lunch.

They sat close together, on two low-slung armchairs of Scandinavian design, upholstered in blue plastic simulated leather. Michal held the hand of the frightened young woman.

Several times, she had said, 'We only want to help, Lotte,' or, 'If it helps to talk', or 'Are they helping you here?'

Crumpled, puffy, tear-stained and seemingly unwashed, Lotte's very appearance belied these optimistic little phrases. She seemed beyond help, or beyond any help which Michal was empowered to offer. She still wore the unbecoming white polo-neck (now grey at throat and cuffs) and the same brown nylon slacks which she had chosen as appropriate costume for Janet's party the previous week.

'What's she been saying?'

It was strange that, before he went away, Oliver had asked this so often. Presumably the philosopher needed an explanation of a situation which was on one level self-explanatory, on another beyond explanation. What was there to analyse? What did it matter what this poor young woman had been saying?

Presumably, she had been in love with Oliver for months, years, and things had simply come to a head. From Michal's viewpoint, it was galling not to have noticed it developing; she had allowed this situation to grow up under her mother's roof without considering the effect of Oliver's engagement on Lotte. They had all been so selfishly absorbed in their own reactions. Michal had been frightened of the effect it would have on her relationship with Cuffe. She had also been worried that certain new practical difficulties in her own life would have to be faced if Oliver were to leave. Who, from now on, would fetch Bobs from school on Thursdays and Fridays, or accompany her to orchestral practice on Monday evenings? Who would help her clear out the flipping rabbit hutch, and the rat's cage? Not Cuffe, for sure, if the last few days had been an indication.

None of them had even thought about Lotte. When she

had arrived, during the second year of Bobs's life, it had seemed as though she was just one in a series of nannies. All the predecessors had been unsatisfactory, and when they realized how unusually reliable she was, they began to take her for granted. Lotte had made it possible for Michal to begin her affair with Cuffe, who had, from the start, shown less interest in her lover's child than any man would have done. Although she had larded the girl with formulaic expressions of gratitude, 'What would I do without you?' had never been a question to which Michal had sought a realistic answer.

On the contrary, by the time Michal was separated from Terence, and had moved back to 12 Wagner Rise, and fallen in love with Cuffe, she had held in her mind two quite contradictory assumptions which had never been put to the test. On the one hand, she took Lotte for granted; on the other hand, she assumed that one of these fine days, Lotte would want to return to Austria. The particular fine day she had in mind was placed, it was true, in an infinitely extensible future. At first, it was when Bobs was potty-trained that Michal imagined herself paying for an air ticket to Vienna. Then it was once Bobs got started at school. Until the incident at the party, it was 'once Bobs can travel on her own'.

Nannies in England were no longer like their predecessors of the pre-war generation. They were young women, usually non-English, who looked after babies *faute de mieux*, as a way of getting free accommodation and spending-money for London life. They had no wish to attach themselves to families in perpetuity, as Helene Demuth had attached herself to the household of Karl Marx, out-living Karl, her erstwhile lover, and poor Jenny, and eventually being bundled off, with the unpublished volumes of *Das Kapital*, as a legacy to Engels, where she lived as the boozy lodger-cum-housekeeper in his house at the bottom of Primrose Hill. Such figures belonged to the past. In spite of the stolid, virginal qualities which made Lotte such a good nanny, she would surely decide at some juncture to have a life of her own.

Lotte was a good-looking woman. Michal had never made a pass at her, but she had sometimes sat on the sofa with her arm round her, an intimacy which Lotte permitted and seemed to enjoy. Michal liked the Austrian's firm swimmer's thighs, her breasts, still in her thirties unpendulous, and her blank oval face framed with blonde hair. Cuffe and Michal, a little unkindly perhaps, had sometimes imagined asking her to share their bed; but this was only the smalltalk of lovers and it had not been meant seriously; Lotte was too good to frighten away.

That Lotte was 'moody' was a fact which coloured the whole of life at 12 Wagner Rise. Janet, no stranger to moods herself, had often complained about these squally passages. The last such minor storm which Michal remembered, was when she had thoughtlessly rearranged a pile of bedlinen in the airing cupboard, not realizing that each sheet and pillowcase had its place in Lotte's system. She had been so cross about it, slamming the kitchen and bedroom doors, that it was left to Bobs to be the intermediary.

'Lotte would prefer it if we left the tidying of the airing cupboard to her.'

'Fine by me.'

'She says it undermines her, having us putting sheets and duvet covers all in the same pile.'

Janet used to say, in the early days, that life in the house was impossible, coping with all their moods.

'When Lotte's happy, you two are having a row, and when you two are getting on well, Bobs is sickening for something.'

But that had been said long ago, before Oliver came and soothed them all. The worst such squall had been when Janet, not remotely suggesting that she wanted Lotte to leave, had asked the girl if she had any plans. The question had come out clumsily. It took some such form as, 'I sometimes think we're exploiting you. We don't pay you very much, and the sad fact is that I can't afford to pay you any more. You look after us all so well, Lotte. It's not just Bobs you nanny. But goodness knows, it can't last for ever.'

There had been tears after this, and this time Oliver had been elected Lotte's mouthpiece. She had been to his room and told him, in German, that Mrs Rose was trying to get her to leave. She had wept and implored him to intercede. Any such intercession was entirely unnecessary, as a moment's inquiry had made plain. Janet had gone up to

Lotte's room to reassure her and to offer her an extra two pounds a week to stay as long as she liked.

Now they understood. Lotte's willingness to stay in the house on slave wages was completely explicable. She too was of the tribe who worshipped Oliver. Her love had reduced her to this. All her beauty, all the aspects of Lotte which inspired the lewd fantasies of Cuffe and Michal, had been snatched away. She seemed merely heavy, sweaty. She had not cleaned her teeth, and her breath was bad.

In this she was not unique. One of the things which made this ward so depressing was the fact that none of the patients had made any effort with their appearance. They had all stopped thinking of themselves as lovable beings. Michal watched the two men who were laying the table, with those wholly unbreakable tumblers which she remembered from schooldays. One was a young man with a pale, spotty face and hair that was so greasy that it looked as if it had been rubbed with margarine. Another was twenty years older, bald, semi-shaven, with food and other stains on his baggy trousers. It would surely have helped everyone if the place could be kept a bit tidier? The squalor of magazines lying around, cigarette packets and magazines everywhere, and the television relentlessly blabbing in the background would all have been intolerable to Lotte in the days of her health.

'You probably won't want to talk now. We just wanted you to understand, and –' it was a little difficult to say this without callousness to poor Camilla – 'we do all love you.'

'Never can I come back, I am so ashamed,' said Lotte at last. 'I am so *awful*, so awful.'

Her English had slipped to the almost incomprehensible level which Michal could remember on Lotte's first arrival.

'He never no more.'

Tears rolled down her cheeks, and her pink eyes quickly reddened. When Michal squeezed her hand, the tears came more copiously.

'No one's sending you away,' she said. 'No one is blaming you.'

'I think he is loving me and then he is marrying the new, he is marrying. And my heart is broken, and what happens to me I do not know. He goes now to America?'

'He's gone away for a few days. Just for a little. He's taken . . .'

'He takes her? Have I not killed her?'

'Lotte, I told you, you haven't killed anyone.'

'I'm so awful. So ashamed. I do not know, I am just feel-ing so angry, you see. It is like a child again, so angry. I see this new car, so rich, she is, yes, well, good little Bobs tell you? *Ja*? There is something within me, and I cannot con-trol it. I have played the tricks. So she pays for the car, I spoil the tyres, *ja*? And if I put holly in the old lady's bed, maybe she is thinking England is not so good, and they are both going to America, they are leaving us all, and Oliver too? I pray, if they only are going to America, I pray, I pray.'

And a great gulp, heaving her chest, turned into another flood of sobbing.

Chapter Fifteen

Perhaps it was the valium, perhaps the shock, or a combination of the two, which made Camilla so uncommunicative. If it were not for the occasional, quietly murmured response to a nurse's inquiry, about the positioning of drips or the comfort of pillows, her mother might have supposed that the girl had lost the power of speech. For the first time Rosalie Baynes felt glad of the company of Janet. A third party, during the hospital visit, consoled her for the dreadful loneliness she felt at the side of her daughter's bed.

This whole trip, planned in order to build bridges, to open up a sympathetic line which had never quite been present between mother and daughter, had only emphasized the gulf. Now that the crisis was over, Rosalie felt as if she was sitting beside the bed of a stranger. A life, with all its consciousness and mystery, had been brought back to them, by the care of the medics; but it was a life of which the mother knew nothing. She had dutifully felt all the right emotions during the crisis itself: fear when the crazed young Austrian *au pair* had lunged at Camilla with a Sabatier knife; longing for her daughter to live; terror when the doctor took her into intensive care; gushes of relief when it had been discovered that the lung had not been perforated. Sure, she loved her daughter – 'whatever love is', as the Prince of Wales had once said in a memorable television interview. In the hours of sitting beside the tiny, pale, etiolated young woman who was the fruit of her womb, Rosalie had gone back thirty-six years and remembered the days before her daughter was born. She'd been laid up with high blood pressure, and she had been haunted – more, even, than when pregnant with her son – by the thought of that mysterious life inside her. She was not a particularly religious woman, but she had turned the pages of the Bible which lay on her bedside locker.

For my reins are thine: thou hast covered me in my mother's womb . . . My bones are not hid from thee: though I be made secretly and fashioned beneath in the earth. Thine eyes did see my substance, yet being imperfect: and in thy book were all my members written; Which day by day were fashioned: when as yet there was none of them . . .

It was her favourite psalm, and she had found herself repeating it again, as she prayed for her grown-up daughter's safety.

'I wonder what you are going to be like, little stranger,' she had said to the baby in her womb. And now, after her childhood and her college years, and her year in England, Camilla remained the same impenetrable mystery. Only once, when they'd sobbed together in the Basil Street hotel, had Rosalie felt the veil lifting. Then she had seen another human being who herself longed to be a mother. It was difficult to think of any comparable moment in all the previous thirty-six years. She knew that Camilla was not deliberately unfriendly. She probably wanted to be kind to her mother. But Rosalie felt dreadfully shut out by the absence of sympathy. She was a warm, friendly person. Her friends confided in her, joked with her, gave her some inkling of what was going on inside their heads. She had felt closer to her two daughters-in-law than she ever had to poor little Camilla.

And now a tiredness with the whole thing overcame her. She did not like to admit to herself that she felt the restlessness of one who had been in a foreign country for long enough, and who now pined for home.

Janet's party had been planned as the finale. The young were to have taken their bow. Oliver, for his own impenetrable reasons, and Camilla, for hers, were to marry later in the summer. Rosalie and Howard would come over for the small celebration. The couple would live, in the first instance, in the Knightsbridge apartment, flying out to Connecticut for the honeymoon, where they would negotiate a building plot for a vacation-residence. Ultimately, who knew, they might live in the United States. But as far as that little part of the drama was concerned, the last act had been finished, the last movement in a complicated symphony had been played. Once the kid was out of danger in the hospital, Rosalie had been beset by that heaving disappointment which assails an unwilling member of a concert audience who has patiently held out to what felt like the end, only to discover that what had been reached was no more than the interval.

'But I must be able to speak with him,' murmured poor Camilla. With her short hair spiky against the pillow, she looked like a sick child. Her eyes were wide but unfocused in their anxious stare.

'Oliver has been simply marvellous,' said Janet.

'But I want him here. *Here*. I must speak with him. Please.'

'He sat with you the first day, when you were unconscious,' explained Janet.

'He must come – get him – can't you just get him round here? *Please*.'

'Janet's just explained, honey. He's taken Bobs off to the seaside.'

'I don't understand.' It was an expression of something like terror from the pillows.

'I don't suppose there is a man in a thousand who would have had the imagination to do what Oliver has done,' said Janet. 'We've all been worried sick about you, my dear. Michal has been an absolute brick, visiting poor Lotte.'

'That woman needs locking up for a very long time,' opined Rosalie.

'We're trying to find out if there were any warnings in her medical records,' said Janet. 'You see, she's been living with us for nearly ten years, and there was never the small-est sign of abnormality. Unless you think wanting to live at Wagner Rise is abnormal. I'm sorry to joke, but it's the only safety-valve I know. We can only assume that she has been driven mad by love. There was poor Ollie in the attic, writing his book and completely oblivious –'

'Please. Janet. His book . . . Please, let me see him. Let me talk. You see, I *understand*. That's what I want him to know. He doesn't need to run away. I understand.'

'It will be the drugs,' said Janet, addressing the mother across the bedclothes. 'She's been murmuring lots of strange things, apparently. The doctors' advice – very sensi-ble – is not to take too much notice.'

'I must see Oliver alone. Please. Mom.'

'Then, you see,' continued Janet, with her analysis of the Austrian's love-trials, 'he went out and got himself engaged to Camilla. Well, something snapped inside Lotte. She couldn't *stand* it.'

'Please. You don't understand. I understand . . .'

'You see, Lotte always was a very childish person. It seems an awful thing to admit, but when someone vandal-ized Oliver's lovely car, I really believed it was Bobs who had done it!'

'It crossed my mind, too,' said Rosalie. 'And all the other little tricks.'

'My dear, why didn't you mention them at the time? You

must have thought you'd stepped into an absolute mad-house – apple-pie beds, stink bombs, the word DIE written in lipstick on your bedroom mirror. No wonder you moved into a hotel!'

'I guess I didn't want to get Bobs into trouble; I didn't want to be in the position of accusing anyone. That always makes you look dumb. "You made me an apple-pie." "I didn't." "You did." I mean, that's dumb. Besides, if the truth is told, it hurt a little. I wanted you all to like me – I guess.'

'And we do, we do. I wish you were staying with me now.'

'I'm comfortable in Camilla's apartment. Besides, you don't want me in your hair. You've all been very kind, but this has been a difficult time for all of you.'

'You see, that's where Oliver is such a saint. So imaginative. Of course, our first worry has been about Camilla's safety. And then we've had to worry about poor Lotte, who is our responsibility. She's no family here at all. And in the middle of a crisis like this, we'd all somehow stopped noticing Bobs. None of us asked how all this was affecting her.'

'Very little, I'd guess,' said Rosalie. 'Children are marvel-lously resilient. Partly because, although they are intensely conservative, they have no sense of the normal. Look at the way British children got parcelled up and sent off to the United States during World War Two. Some of my best friends in Boston, where I was raised, were a couple of teenage kids who'd been sent over from Beckenham. They had a six-year-old sister. They all grew up happy. Just think of what that might have done for your psyche.'

'Perhaps you're right,' said Janet. 'Maybe we fuss about children too much these days.'

'Fuss? I don't know. We don't seem to fuss when we want to get a divorce. We send 'em to and fro, weekends, like they were packets of groceries. But you don't see any more nervous breakdowns among those kids than the ones who are raised normally, like our two. That's what I mean, children adapt. They're resilient.'

'Well, the other thing, of course,' said Janet, 'was that someone had to cope with Bobs, regardless of how she was feeling. Someone had to get her packed lunches ready, fetch her from school, and on top of everything else, Michal couldn't cope.'

'I never saw a kid who was more self-sufficient,' said Rosalie. 'If you ask me, it is Oliver who needed her company, not the other way about.'

A light whimper from the bed was ignored by the two women who had found their stride. Rosalie asked, as politely as possible, whether this was a hospital for *poor* people, and wondered whether there was any possibility of getting her daughter moved to a place where the elevator wasn't full of garbage, and where you got a room to yourself. Janet, defensive, explained that the National Health Service had its problems, but if the Bayneses wanted a private hospital, it would cost several times more than the Basil Street hotel. They fell to talking of their own childhoods, in London and in Boston. Rosalie professed a continued loyalty, despite enforced residence in other US cities, to the Red Sox, which Janet thought must be a reference to some sport.

'Anyway,' said the grandmother, darting back to the subject of their hero, 'he took her off for some sea air. Walks on the cliffs. They are going to fly a kite. Isn't he an *angel*?'

'Please, you must . . .'

'Honey?'

'Just, get him back, will you?'

'He'll come, dear. You'll see.'

Chapter Sixteen

Advancing towards the back of a truck at eighty, the nose of the sports car avoided a hit by inches. They were so close to the back of the lorry, all they saw was its billows of brown exhaust, its mud-smeared yellow number-plates. Then, by a jerky swerve of the driver's wrist, the Mazda edged into the middle of the road and faced an oncoming car.

Lights flashed. A horn sounded. A quick lurch, and they were safe again, in front of the lorry and just behind a large estate dawdling at fifty, whose back window carried the legends I LOVE JESUS and BABY ON BOARD.

'Come on, come *on*,' said Oliver, as his front bumper almost entered this rear window. He flashed headlights on, off, on, and swerved out for another blind overtake.

The brow of a little hill made the next stretch of road all but invisible. To take it on the right-hand side of the road was Russian roulette.

Bobs, in the left-hand seat, was in no position to judge quite how dangerous this was; but she had begun to sense the game was becoming reckless. It was like being on the big dipper at the fair, only without any of the fairground sense that this was fun, or that it would soon be over.

Whizzing along the motorway at a hundred in a straight line had been great. Only since they'd come on to country roads did the adventure start to feel nasty. Sixty felt fast here, and as the needle veered between seventy and ninety, there were many moments when the car scarcely held the road. This shooting to within inches of rear bumpers, this jumping of lights, this hurtling through hamlets at a speed which made it difficult to read the signs – PLEASE DRIVE CAREFULLY THROUGH THE VILLAGE – this succession of near misses at junctions and bends made her feel truly sick.

She was determined not to be sick. It was more than a desire not to disgrace herself, as poor Margot Reisz had done at the party. It was something to do with the balance of power between them; and if this was a phrase which had not formed itself in Bobs's brain, it was certainly a concept there. If I'm sick, he'll be the one who is sorry for me, he'll be the strong one. Since she was about three years old, she had known that she exercised control over this man. The insouciant refusal to panic when he had first announced his engagement had been her way of establishing her superiority in the pecking order. While Mum and Granny and Cuffe had squawked and flapped, Bobs's calmness spoke of an intimacy with Oliver which could survive, if necessary, his marriage, even his emigration.

She had had her plans, though. And a resolute refusal not

to allow all her feelings to show had been an essential strategy. She was frightened to show anyone, Oliver or the others, precisely what feelings had been awoken by the arrival of Camilla in their lives.

The concentration to avoid nausea was so specific that she could not restrain other spontaneous expressions of fear. Since babyhood, she had never been much of a weeper, but now the tears streamed from her eyes, not at the prospect of his willingness to go off with another, but at the fear of destruction itself. Powerless in the cramped, whizzing little machine, her most basic and most animal desire to survive could only confront the last enemy writhingly.

And besides, they had left Wagner Rise in such a hurry that she had barely had time to say goodbye to Hector, Cuthbert or Josh. She thought of Hector's sensitive and intelligent face as he lolloped about the house, missing her. She had dreaded his death almost as soon as she got him. The knowledge that a rabbit's life was shorter than a human being's had given their friendship a dreadful poignancy. The bereavement was written into the deal from the beginning. When she first started to be aware of this, it had seemed as if there was nothing worse; but the prospect of her own death *was* worse. She could explain the sadness to herself, if Hector died. No one would be able to explain it to him, if she was the one who went first. She thought of his wet, pink nose sniffing round her room in search of her. The rabbit. That was how the Cuffe, and Granny, always referred to Hector.

'Have you fed the rabbit?'

That's what they'd be saying now, that is, if they so much as remembered him. They would probably have locked him in the hutch. Cuthbert would certainly be in the run. He would be missing her bedclothes, which smelt of himself, and the jokes of Josh, the rat, which no one else could hear, but which Bobs had persuaded herself were called out from time to time by this skittish, smooth little friend.

It was so irresponsible to have gone away and left them all like this. She remembered the mess in the cages, and the reproachful sad expressions of the animals when they had been left behind during holidays. At least, then, they had Lotte to talk to.

Bobs felt frightened by what had happened to Lotte; frightened by the knowledge that it had been, in part, her responsibility. She needed to explain the nature of this responsibility to Oliver, and that was another reason why she must not seem vulnerable. If she could but maintain her steely inner strength, an act of willpower might prevent her from being sick; might even prevent the car from flying off the road. She was gradually weakening, though, as the tears streamed.

When the car at last jolted to a halt, with such violence that she was thrown forward against the seat-belt, it was as much as she could do to hold back for those few seconds which it took to unclip the belt and open the door.

It was horrid, throwing up, especially when the semi-digested bits, rather than making a clean cascade through the gullet, spattered. Smelly lumps got stuck, not just at the back of the throat, but in her nose. She had avoided damage to her jumper, but the left sandal and a white sock had suffered hits.

Oliver's hand held her neck, stroked her back. As she spluttered and coughed the contents of her stomach on to the grass, he murmured something.

Perhaps it was, 'It's all right, it's all right.' He was thinking of a time years before. It had been a critical moment of love, he saw that now. He had been alone at 12 Wagner Rise one evening – alone but for Lotte, who was watching television in her room. The women were out. Before they left, they had joked about leaving their philosopher to 'babysit'. Quite late (perhaps Lotte had by then gone to bed) he had heard Bobs, then aged about four, crying. He had run to her and found that she had woken herself up vomiting.

It had gone everywhere; and just as he had persuaded her to get out of the soiled bedding, another projectile burst had occurred, coating carpets, chair, books, toys. Oliver, who was more than usually fastidious about the bodily functions, had feared that he would be sick himself. But Bobs, poor, tear-stained little Bobs, had been so vulnerable, so frightened by what was happening, so dependent, that his threatened retching had subsided. She had run to him, with the instinct to be protected, and he had hugged her, messy and stinking as she was.

He had picked her up and taken her to the bathroom

and stripped off her sodden pyjamas. In the bath, she had calmed down and stopped weeping. The process of cleaning up, first Bobs, then her room, had taken over an hour. After the bath, when she had been powdered and dressed in clean warm pyjamas from the airing cupboard, he had put her to sleep in his own bed, with a plastic bowl beside her, against the recurrence of nausea. But she had slept, calm and undisturbed, for the next six hours.

While slaving in her room, with rags and disinfectant, taking bedding downstairs to the washing machine, sponging teddy bears, removing sick from the crevices of a Fisher-Price truck, he had realized that this was an act which he had performed for no other human being. In the present instance, he could have alerted Lotte and asked for her help, but he took particular satisfaction in not doing so. It had seemed like eternity, that sponging and scrubbing and wiping, that eventual restoration, with clean sheets and almost clean air (how that vomit smell had lingered); but once through that eternity, when he had changed his own pyjamas and snuggled beside the sleeping form in his own bed, he had known that he loved Bobs; that he would be prepared to do anything for her, putting his own life in jeopardy for hers, should that be necessary.

Now, as he watched the child retching on the grass, he was shaken by remorse. At the wheel of the car, he had been a creature possessed. His love for Bobs, which was the centre of his life, had been overpowered by a mingling of panic and a need to save face. He had not cared if he was

frightening her by driving so fast. Death in a motor accident would have provided the end of a nightmare.

Half an hour before the party, Camilla had come to his
room. A volume of Victorian photographs had been open
on his table. His trousers were around his ankles. The
embarrassment of that was bad enough. But then she had
confronted him. She *knew*. Camilla did not tell him how
she had been made privy to his secret. Only after Lotte had
gone mad at the party did he draw his own conclusions –
the maid had somehow stolen his notebook and shown it to
Camilla? Was that what had happened?

The words – so painfully few – which Camilla and
Oliver had exchanged before the party both had, and had
not, been the showdown he had been dreading ever since
the notebooks had disappeared. He had assumed that,
when she knew his true nature, when she had found out
about himself and Bobs, she would want to bring disgrace
on them all, to trumpet the unmentionable secret. But she
had not. Her few, terrible words had made plain that she
intended to keep it a secret. It would be their secret.

'Does Bobs have any idea that you know?' he had asked
Camilla. And she had replied, so cryptically, 'Oliver, you
and I are together now. And I am not going to pass up my
only chance of having a baby because of this. When the
baby's born . . .'

'But *does* Bobs know? . . .'

Did the child know? Through the whole ghastly period
since the party, he had been unable to make up his mind.

When Lotte had lunged towards Camilla with a knife, everyone's attention had been diverted. Even he could not be indifferent to the fact that his fiancée had just been stabbed. And yet it was an irrelevance to his chief concern – whether the child *knew*? And whether, now that Camilla knew, it was possible for either of them, him or Bobs, to go on living? Oh, it would be so much easier if they were both dead! And yet, as he looked at Bobs now, at her pale unhappy face, shaken with the immediate shame of sickness, he was overcome with an intolerable tenderness, which made him wish he had not driven so fast, and which made the idea of killing her unendurable.

'I was driving too fast,' he said. 'Here. Have some water.'

She accepted the plastic bottle. She was still crying.

'Can't we go home?' she whimpered.

'Look at that!'

The car had all but reached its destination, a stretch of the coast where they'd all spent a recent holiday. Some fifty yards from the roadside, the tufty, velvety grass grew to the edge of the cliff. An afternoon sun, high in a blue sky, shone on calm sea. There were one or two boats, small as ants, bobbing towards the horizon.

'It's lovely.'

There was something apologetic in her tone, as if she were being offered a beautiful present which she was churlish enough to refuse.

'I'm sorry I drove so recklessly.'

She half smiled through her tears.

'Boy racer,' she said. But when he tried to hug her, he felt himself being frozen off. She was stiff and unwilling.

'A few days will do us good, eh? Away from London? Away from all that?'

She did not reply to his words. She walked off, to the very edge of the cliff, and stared truculently out to sea. All he could see was the back of her, that dark bob, that curved gentle neck, those bony shoulder blades which projected like breasts from her blue jumper. As she walked away, she kicked off her sandals and, with one index finger, eased off her white socks, so that she walked barefoot in her shorts.

Only last summer, in this very place, there had been a marvellous holiday. He thought of her, lithe and giggling in her all-in-one black bathing dress, taking his hand and insisting that he come into the sea. How he had howled with protest! How she had laughed, as they splashed into the breakers. And then she had fallen backwards, willingly, into the icy water. Emerging from the waves, she had cried out, 'It's lovely when you're in!' And he had done the same, fallen into the water. And she had been right. The initial feeling of cold was nothing. If only they had both died then, on that holiday, in a genuine accident! If only death had come, without premeditation or thought, before this hell had started.

He could do it now. He could run at her from behind, and push her in the small of the back. And as he pushed, he could jump.

She laughed, when he came towards her.

'Careful!' she said, 'you'll fall.'

It was later, when they were booked into a twin-bedded room at the Seaview, that she took the plunge.

'You guessed, didn't you? Are you really eggy with me?'

'Why should I be cross?'

'I only did it for the best. I knew you did not really want to marry Camilla – you somehow thought you ought to. Isn't that right? But I should never have shown Lotte that bit of poetry. That was all I showed her – I didn't show her the notebooks.'

'*You?*'

'You see, it was in German, and I don't understand German. It's something about being a shepherd, looking after me? And poor Lotte thought you'd written it all about her.'

'I didn't write it. I copied it out. Someone else wrote it – someone called Heine. But that hardly matters.'

'It would if you were going in for a competition.'

'But it wasn't meant for you to see, or Lotte, or anyone.'

There was a long pause.

'So you are eggy.'

On his bed, he groaned. He began the process, which would take until the end of a long life, reinterpreting the events of the previous week. Camilla had not said, because she had not quite had the chance to say, that she had learnt the truth directly from Bobs herself. When he had asked her if Bobs knew anything, she had replied with what was, for Camilla herself, the primary truth: that she wanted a child herself, and was prepared to accept one even in these painfully grotesque circumstances. It was, he supposed, Camilla's only line of defence, to ignore the written evidence which the child had placed before her.

They were lying on separate beds, looking at the ceiling.

'They are a bit soppy, aren't they? What you wrote. Or did you copy the notebooks from Heine too?'

'No. They're what I wrote.'

'Indiscreet.'

'It was indiscreet to read them, not necessarily to write them.'

'Oh, Oliver, I'm sorry. I just didn't want you to go. I couldn't bear you going. And the others were all being so silly, and so unkind to Camilla. And I just thought, if Camilla really knows how Oliver feels about me – if she could see one of those exercise books . . .'

'*You* didn't . . .'

'Was it an awful thing to do – to show Camilla what you'd written?'

In the midst of the groan which was his reply was the word, 'When?'

'It was the only way I could think of telling her kindly. It was unfair, in a way. I see that. But if I'd just told her that you loved me, she wouldn't have believed me. And you did say you'd marry me.'

It was a very long pause before he managed to say, 'You

are saying that it was you who showed her my private . . .
my book . . . when, when? When did you show her?'

'About a week ago.'

'But why didn't she say you'd . . . oh, God!'

'Perhaps she didn't know what to say. It was a tiny bit
embarrassing.'

Chapter Seventeen

'I am sorry,' said Cuffe, 'to keep coming back to my old friend William James, but it is an important point. *"No concrete test of what is really true has ever been agreed upon."'*

'You're meant to be a woman,' said one of her more talkative students, a slightly obstreperous, frizzy-haired young woman called Elaine Burra. 'Whose side are you on?'

'Are we talking empiricism here, or are we just discussing Baynes versus Baynes?' Cuffe asked. Again, she quoted from the great man. '*"Objective evidence and certitude are doubtless very fine ideals to play with, but where on this moonlit and dream-visited planet are they found?"'*

Her class on James and Pragmatism was always heavily subscribed. There were about sixty people in the room. On good days, she felt that she was beginning to teach them how to think. Many weeks went past, however, in which she felt that most of her class were sitting there waiting to be told *what* to think, and to tap the more memorable of her sentences on to their laptops.

'You are taking the side of a man who ruined his daughter's life? Who made it impossible for her to have relationships? Who raped a little girl of six, for Christ's sakes?'

Elaine's obsession with the case was widely shared, not least by Cuffe herself – though Cuffe had told none of them that she actually knew Camilla Baynes. Perhaps it was perverse to be invoking William James in this murky tale of childhood sexuality, which was more the territory of his brother. But the topic, however it was viewed, would not go away. Everyone she knew in Philadelphia was rushing home to watch Court TV at all available hours. That little courtroom in Detroit had become the focus of national interest. There were probably fifty million people who had sat watching while Rosalie Baynes, in a calm, steady voice, had defended her husband Howard against the daughter's wild claims. When Mr Braithwaite had asked her why her son had gone abroad and was unavailable to give evidence about his childhood, the nation had divided. Some took it that he knew something which he was not prepared to say on the witness stand. Everyone thought it peculiar that Frank Baynes had not been able to fly home from Singapore to defend his father on so serious a charge.

Another member of the class, a huge boy in size fourteen trainers, was taking issue with Elaine Burra.

'Take the pornography,' he said.

'I'd rather not,' said Cuffe, which made everyone laugh.

'Well, right, so Camilla's come up with all this stuff

about her father reading, like, really strange child pornography, like, you know, Victoriana, what's the name of the guy, like, he wrote *Alice in Wonderland*, and she's saying, her Dad jerked off over these old photographs of little girls, right, that this old pervert took, like a hundred years ago?'

'That's what we should be discussing here,' said Elaine, 'that men have been exploiting female sexuality since the beginning. And we're all brought up to think *Alice in Wonderland*'s so cute, you know, like this little girl following her rabbit down into dark cavernous places? Like, she's trying to make sense of all the crazy behaviour of the grown-ups? And like she's up for trial, in a courtroom, and they're all saying, "*Off with her head!*" which is a paradigm of exploitative paedophile gender-orientated sexuality. Those pictures which Lewis Carroll took, of young girls with no clothes on, are the illustrations for his beautiful little fairy story, they are the true template off of which we should be reading these texts, which are texts about enslavement . . .'

'Okay,' said the size fourteen trainers boy, who came from Oregon. He did not look okay, he looked completely baffled, but he wanted his say. 'And you have the testimony of the man's wife, okay, his goddamned wife, who's been sharing his bed and cooking his meals, that her husband never in his life saw these Victorian pornographies. Right?'

'That woman's brainwashed –'

'Look, here, what Professor Cuffe is saying, is that no

one's established any grounds for saying – what's evidence?'
This from a young black law student.

Cuffe allowed the class to pursue its own jabbering life.
Very occasionally issues pertinent to the notions of pragmatism surfaced as they discussed this televised trial. There
was no point in trying to stop them. Like everyone else in
America, they had to have their say. And, however distressing the nature of the material, perhaps William James
himself, the greatest of all American philosophers and psychologists, would have liked their technique, their attempts
to use empirical examination of data as a means of illus-
trating generalized notions.

Cuffe missed her parents (now advancing in years), and
she managed to visit them at Christmas or in the summer,
most years. Aside from this, there was nothing she missed
about England. All that she cherished about the place she
had brought with her, when she accepted the post of professor of philosophy at the University of Pennsylvania.
Margot still wrote occasionally, so that Cuffe was vaguely
au fait with the news of 12 Wagner Rise, but in practical
terms it had as much reality, and rather less interest, than
Alice's Adventures in Wonderland. Michal was doing well in
her job, had received promotion. The sprog was doing A-
levels and had a 'conditional offer' to go to York. (Cuffe had
almost forgotten what a conditional offer was, so little had
she bothered to keep polished her modern English usage.)
Margot Reisz still gamely had them all to stay in the South
of France.

It was as if the one drama in their lives had not really been central. Cuffe remembered each detail of the incidents involved – the sprog telling them of Oliver's engagement, the meetings with Camilla and Rosalie Baynes, the unfortunate incident in which Lotte had attacked Camilla with the kitchen knife. Now that seven years had passed since the incident, Cuffe's perspective had altered. It amazed her that anyone had considered it remotely possible that Oliver should marry Camilla Baynes. The whole episode was peripheral, and she would almost have forgotten it, were it not for this moonlit and dream-visited planet's capacity for replaying its dramas; or, like a down-at-heel theatrical company, using old actors, however inappropriately, merely because they happened to be on the payroll, rather than because they were suitable to the task.

The idea of Camilla Baynes as the voice of wronged American childhood, or of her mother as a television presence in millions of living-rooms, as familiar as Lucille Ball, was one of the more bizarre twists of fate.

Rosalie, by now a heroine to half the population, did not seem to have aged in the least. Her clothes were simple, elegant and unshowy – blue skirts, check jackets, a variety of turtle-necks, usually pink or pale blue, and discreet costume jewels. She had the same silver-blonde hair, cut slightly shorter than when Cuffe had last seen her, the same restrained make-up, the same ironical tones which suggested wisecracks even when none came. Contact lenses had replaced specs. On TV, she was an embodiment of a certain kind of decency, willing to stand not only by her man but by her sanity. Her rebuttals of her daughter's painfully disgusting claims were made with dignity, so that even those who thought she was lying believed that she represented common sense. (And there was a strong body of opinion which took the view that, even if Howard Baynes *had* done these dreadful things, what was the good of raking them all out of the closet *now*? And, even if it was worth raking them out now in a therapist's consulting-room, what good was served by doing it in a court of law?)

Such strange areas of psychosexual behaviour were beyond Cuffe's experience, hence beyond her understanding. She could not imagine her own decent, good-humoured and adored Dad indulging in the behaviour of which Howard Baynes stood indicted. Therefore it was beyond her comprehension that a daughter could so hate her daddy that she would be prepared to humiliate him in front of fifty million Americans.

Like many of her fellow-Americans – for this is what Cuffe now was; she had no ambitions to return to England – she did not know how the jury would find. Her acquaintance with Camilla Baynes had been in tense, difficult circumstances; it had only lasted a matter of weeks; and Cuffe now found it a challenge to make any connection between the shy young woman she had known, though so slightly, in England nearly eight years before, and the extraordinary figure who had now become so familiar on the television screen. The extent to which one could ever know another mind was a familiar old problem within her profession. On the ordinary social level, of course, what was meant by familiarity with another temperament was a series of impressions gathered slowly, usually based on areas considerably less bizarre than those disclosed in Court Number Seven to Judge Chang and the jurymen and jurywomen of Detroit.

Cuffe had known an awkward, diminutive young woman, expert at dating a piece of china, incompetent in clothes sense, religious (which Cuffe herself wasn't particularly), and possessed of a disconcerting mixture of determination to win her man and social diffidence. Even setting aside the essential awkwardness of the situation – the fact that Camilla Baynes came to 12 Wagner Rise as the woman ambitious to steal Oliver from his adorers – Cuffe sensed that she would have been a difficult nut to crack. There had always been an air of truculence about her which had seemed odd in the hour of her romantic triumph. After the accident, during the long hours in hospital when Janet Rose had befriended Camilla's mother, it had emerged that this diffident ill humour was not solely brought on by the embarrassment of visits to Wagner Rise. Rosalie, who by the time she left had won the affection of all, had confided in Janet that she had never been able to understand Camilla. There were hints of a mystery, of a certain frigidity.

All this was compatible with the strange testimony given

in court. That Camilla had been in some senses of the word mad, however, made it rather hard to conclude that one set of strange antics explained, still less proved, another. Everyone agreed that the bravest hour of Rosalie's occupation of the stand had been the examination, and cross-examination, involving the daughter's anatomical memories of her father. Mr Braithwaite had allowed his client to describe the tumescent manhood of Howard Baynes, and if anyone had a view on this matter, it was presumably Howard's wife who could be relied upon to set them right.

Certainly, the vignettes which Camilla had so unforgettably painted for the television-viewing public, enforced fellatio, masturbation, fingerings, foul language, would have been extraordinary things to invent. It was Miss de Bono's skill which suggested, not that Camilla was telling deliberate untruths, but rather that the mere fact that these terrible images had arrived in Camilla's mind did not compel the conclusion that they did so as a result of memory. Dreams, after all, can seem as real to the waking mind as the humdrum events of last week. After a nervous breakdown as severe as Camilla's had been, it was hardly surprising that all manner of strange flotsam and jetsam had floated to the surface. The difficulty was in knowing what to make of them or, indeed, whether it was sensible to make anything of them at all. One of the psychologists called as a witness by Miss de Bono had pointed out the commonplace that the most blameless individuals – nuns,

headmasters, rabbis – had been known to scream obsceni-
ties in the sleep induced by anaesthetics. Did this entitle us
to suppose that these distasteful outbursts came from a
bank of memory? Or would it be more rational to conclude
that there was in the murky deeps of the subconscious
something like the sludge at the bottom of a pond, which
could, when disturbed, provide rank smells and clouding of
waters, but which did not constitute, in less disturbed
moments, the tranquil life of the pond, its weeds, its insects,
its reedy banks and their mammalian inhabitants?

It was the plaintiff's submission that she was incapaci-
tated for a fulfilled life by childhood abuse; that she was, for
example, unable to consummate regular heterosexual
attachments. Cuffe had been worried, given the thorough-
ness with which the lawyers were choosing to explore the
life experiences and psyche of Camilla Baynes, that her
former fiancé would be sub-poena'd to give evidence. It
was Oliver's good luck that, after the engagement was
broken and Camilla had returned to New York, she had
formed another attachment, this time to a dentist in
Brooklyn. This engagement had been even shorter-lasting
than that to the English philosopher, but it had the advantage, from the lawyers' viewpoint, of having been on home
soil, and by the time it had broken down, so had poor Miss
Baynes. Her emotional collapse, and her subsequent intern-
ment at a psychiatric clinic near her parental home, had led
to the painful series of impressions or recollections which
caused her to denounce Howard Baynes as a sexual preda-

tor. The dentist's testimony to the court had been of the briefest, and it would seem as though there was little dispute about the adult Camilla's neurotic distaste for sex. Camilla's lawyers clearly did not want to have a string of men testifying that their client was unbalanced, in this or any other area, and chose to concentrate their fire on the area of Camilla the child. Infant-school teachers, nurse-maids, childhood friends, and the family doctor (who recalled no physical blemishes of any kind on her seven-year-old person when he had attended it) were of more use to the judge and jury.

So Oliver, to Cuffe's intense relief, escaped questioning, and her loquacious philosophy class, and her colleagues, and her neighbours, had absolutely no inkling that she had any connection with the case.

Philly wasn't such a bad place as a setting for her slow adaptation to bland middle age. She liked her job. She had an affectionate relationship with her lover, Anne Neroni, a pixy-headed, dark-haired Ph.D. student who was working on Lacan. They had no desire to live together, but a couple of times a week they'd eat some pasta, or see a movie, or go back to Anne's tiny apartment at Grad 'B' Towers, on Chestnut Street. Anne reminded Cuffe of herself when young, pale, pencil thin and intense. Intensity had diminished for Cuffe when she passed the age of forty. Anne would have no place in the suburban set-up which Cuffe had made for herself – the large living-room scattered with children's toys, the au pair, the giant fridge full of snacks, the kids themselves, the husband.

More than she had realized at first, the house in Larchwood Avenue had been an attempt to re-create something of 12 Wagner Rise and its comforting routines, its washer whirring in the utility room, its mindless telly, watched not merely by the kids, but by her husband.

Ol taught two days a week at Drexel University, an easy bus ride down Chestnut. The teaching was routine stuff, Plato to Popper in twenty-five spoon-sized portions, and he had by his own confession lost his desire to fly high, to say anything new. He had turned into a bit of a couch potato, watching television for an average of five hours a day. He seemed to be addicted to all of it – the baseball games, the religious programmes, *Larry King Live*, soaps, ads. He said that it was all useful material for his column, a fortnightly 'Letter from America' which he wrote for a leftish English weekly, which did not pay much, but which he described as his bread and butter money.

When her class was over, Cuffe went to the lot for her substantial crimson Buick, one of her most treasured possessions. The one thing which wasn't bland about Larchwood Avenue was the crime rate. People in her department told her, before she bought the house, that once you went in streets higher than the forties, you were into the badlands; but she had not listened. The leafy street, with its substantial family villas, had looked to her like Philly's answer to North Oxford or Grange Road,

Cambridge. When she heard of the third neighbourhood stabbing in one month, she had given up walking to work, and propelled herself from door to door in the heavy old American car. (She was the only person she knew who drove an American car, all her colleagues preferring Volvos or Japanese makes.)

Purring up Walnut Street on the way home, she thought about the things the kids in her class had been saying about the Baynes trial. It was odd, her instinct that Oliver should want to watch it, but not to discuss it. They'd turned off the gamier bits of the televised trial when one of the kids was in the room, but otherwise, like all their neighbours, they'd been gripped. But they had said nothing about it; and that, Cuffe knew, was the way things would stay.

Sometimes it made her sad to think of the dullness of Oliver's life, the dullness of Oliver. She did not know whether she herself had lost faith in his genius, or whether he had really changed and become a dull American house-husband, with a brindled beard and a check shirt. Had something switched off inside him or inside her? When they had left England, seven years before, she had still believed that he was in the Russell and Wittgenstein league, a true original, a great mind, a life-changing presence in the intellectual scene. All he had needed, she believed, had been space, calm, time, and his masterpiece would be acclaimed by all the world.

His decision to sell his few remaining books, and to destroy all his notebooks and manuscripts before they left

England, had not diminished her belief in his genius. Such grand, clean sweeps took place in the lives of the truly great. His luggage, when he left England, had consisted of a few clothes and a copy, which the sprog had rather tiresomely given to him, of *Alice's Adventures in Wonderland*. It was a book the pair of them, Oliver and the sprog, had almost by heart. In her neat little hand, Bobs had written on the flyleaf:

> *Either the well was very deep, or she fell very slowly, for she had plenty of time as she went down to look about her, and to wonder what was going to happen next.*

The book was still lying round the house somewhere. And now, a short journey from the campus to Larchwood, there was that house, coming into view. And there was Oliver, standing at the window with a peanut-butter cookie in one hand and a baby in another.

Chapter Eighteen

There was quite enough to occupy Roberta O'Hara, during a month-long visit to Manhattan, without her feeling obliged to fill the vacant hours with old friends. The merchant bank for which she worked had sent her over to review their American portfolio, and for the first week breakfasts, luncheons and dinners were all occupied, together with the hours between. It was a useful exercise, putting faces, as they termed it, to such holdings as Potash Corp Sask, Travelers Aetna Prop or Quintiles Transnational. In the midst of so much business, it was less timidity which prompted the twinges of regret at having written to Oliver, suggesting a meeting, than it was a selfish need for solitude in a comfortable hotel room. Nevertheless, Saturday had dawned, the first day on which no eager young person in a suit was scheduled to persuade her, in some smoke-free office or restaurant, of the desirability of investing in this equity or that. Oliver's voice on the answering machine, heard for the first time in seventeen years, proposed an encounter at noon.

She had not envisaged a meeting with him so early in her American month. To meet at the end of the first week would allow for the possibility of further meetings – Philadelphia was only a couple of hours away on the train – and she had not quite reckoned on a renewal of ties. She was an orderly person, who liked to plan. All that she had intended, by her brief letter to Larchwood Avenue, was the possibility of seeing him just once more. Curiosity impelled her, and a desire to put the past to rest. There would have been no chance, in a single meeting, of filling in seventeen years' worth of news. It would suffice to exchange the haziest of sketches of lives which had grown so very far apart.

Roberta lived with her mother, and with Lotte, and with Peter, in a large garden flat in Belsize Park. This much Oliver would have learnt from Margot Reisz, who still kept in touch, and who passed the chief items of news between the two families. Margot probably did not realize quite how poor Janet had been when she died. The sale of 12 Wagner Rise had been a necessity. (Roberta had been a student at the time.) It had been shocking to discover the extent of her grandmother's improvidence, and this fact had determined Roberta's choice of a potentially lucrative career. Michal had been shocked by her child going into the City, but mother and daughter got on well enough to over-come this disappointment, and the money which had started to accumulate, once Roberta's skills as an investment manager developed, were able to quiet Michal's left-wing conscience. Margot, still tireless at eighty-seven, in her voluntary addressing of envelopes for the Labour Party, ribbed Roberta for having sold out to Capital.

From Margot, presumably, Oliver had an impression of Roberta's life, the death of her grandmother, the first-class degree at York University, the job in the bank, the arrival of Peter. (Would Margot have mentioned Peter?) Similarly, from Margot were conveyed to the three women of Belsize Park snapshots, figurative or actual, of Oliver's life, the arrival of children (Jonothon and Cal), the holidays in Florida and Cape Cod, the unaccountable failure of the English newspaper to renew his contract for the 'Letter from America'.

Michal, whom Roberta had grown to like as well as to love, had taken Cuffe's suicide hard. It was this, rather than painful memories further back in time, which made Roberta decide not to tell her mother that she had written to Oliver or suggested meeting him. Cuffe's abandonment of her lover had been cruel enough. What Michal could not understand or forgive was that she should have chosen to take her own life when the marriage had failed to work. Why had she simply not come back to England? Why not, even after all that had happened, come back to her?

Cuffe had killed herself when Roberta was in her first year at York. With the unimaginativeness of the young, Roberta had received the news coldly. She had never liked the woman, and she had never forgiven her for marrying Oliver. Their emigration to the United States had been a kind of death, so that to read in a letter from Michal that Cuffe had poisoned herself with vodka and sleeping pills had aroused no grief in Roberta. When she came back home for the vacation, she found that Michal was completely distraught. Her mother had died of cancer only six months earlier, but this bereavement was much worse. All the sorrows caused by Cuffe's original desertion were reawakened and multiplied by death's terrible finality.

'Why did we let her go? Why? Why didn't she come back? . . . Oh, that bloody man, I could kill him . . . Oh God, oh God . . .'

Roberta could not reach Michal in her abyss of misery, but she could stay beside her. This she did, watching with horrified fascination a human being's seemingly limitless capacity for sorrow. Hitherto, the most harrowing experience of Roberta's life had been watching Hector die of meningitis: thirty-six hours of seeing a beloved creature suffer, with no language to explain to himself or to herself what was happening. He had hidden in corners whimpering, run round in circles, and evinced such agony that she had wished she had the courage to kill him with a brick. Instead, they had taken him to the vet for an injection. It had been terrible to lose him but it had been worse to know his pain, to feel that beneath the natural surface of things there always lurked this capacity of life to hurt us beyond bearing.

Her mother's affliction was like this, and in that long summer of whimpering and hugging, of tears and rages, Roberta had time to reassess the whole strange story. To her mother's *Why, why, why?* there were some uncomfortable answers, but there would have been small gain in providing them. She had tortured herself, in her late teens, with the unanswerable question of how far she had been to blame for Camilla's mental undoing. She presumed and hoped that she would never know whether Cuffe had lately discovered something about Oliver which changed her whole perception of the man. It was not merely the desire to protect herself which made Roberta keep silent. If the whole Baynes versus Baynes trial had taught them anything, it was surely the fact that only misery and confusion result from digging up the past? Howard had been acquitted. Everyone except the lawyers had lost a great deal of money. Rosalie had divorced him six months after the trial: they had read that in a newspaper article.

Had Oliver really been unkind enough to tell Cuffe the truth about himself? Roberta would have done much to satisfy her curiosity on this point, but not so much that she would stir up a hornets' nest and make yet more people miserable. Suppose Cuffe had known all along? Or suppose her suicide had nothing to do with Oliver's past? It was better not to know. Not knowing, however, made it so much more difficult to touch Michal with kindness. She could not leave the subject alone, of Oliver's decision to break off his engagement to Camilla, of Cuffe's immediate

agreement to marry him, of their emigration, of their failure to talk it through or to explain.

'What were they running away from?'

It would have felt so vain for Roberta to answer, 'Me',
even though that was what she believed. Love. Love was
the trouble. She had only felt it for a human being in this
one instance, and she knew that on that level of intensity it
was an unrepeatable experience. Her mother thought she
had felt it several times – perhaps she was right. Roberta
felt strengthened by her knowledge. It was as clear as a
raincloud before a deluge, slate grey, when the definitions in
the light make every object so much more distinct than
their normal impressionist fuzz. She saw that she was specially placed to be kind. She was never going to be
interrupted in this duty by 'falling in love'. She would
always be there for her mother, a kind friend and companion. You did not need large numbers of people in order to
exercise this particular virtue; nor did they have to be dramatically poor, or afflicted, or interesting. As far as human
energy was concerned, she would devote her life to making
her mother feel loved, to being a kind friend to Lotte, to listening to Margot Reisz's interminable anecdotes. It was
almost as if she had decided to become a nurse, and home
was her Scutari, her field of battle-scarred warriors.

Michal had recovered, slowly. Her protests that Roberta
could not possibly wish to live with her and Lotte, that she
must find a flat of her own where she could mix with her
own age group, had all been formulaic flannel. For five or

six years, it had all worked, and Roberta saw no reason why she should not live in this way for the rest of her days.

This was the twenty-seven-year-old woman who now prepared herself for meeting the one man she had ever loved. While she dressed in her hotel room, and surveyed the long, sallow, beaky face in the glass, and brushed the thick, slightly oily hair which she kept neatly bobbed, Roberta indulged the fantasy that he wanted to see her in order to start again where they had left off. It was shocking, when this little daydream flitted into the mind, to discover how seriously she took it. She surely wouldn't let herself fall for that one, would she?

Thank God for Peter, and the fact that she missed him so much! When falling asleep this last week, she had thought of him; when waking, she had reached out for him. Early mornings were the time she missed him most. On her second morning in New York, she had woken early and walked in Central Park, near her hotel. It was an hour when she would normally have been with Peter. Consciousness of him, and a painful yearning to see his sharp intelligent features, had possessed her as she walked along in the early-morning sunlight. The phenomenon of 'seeing' those we love when they have just died, or when we are unwillingly parted from them, is well attested. Looking down the path on that day, she had seen Peter coming towards her. Her brain knew that he was in Belsize Park, where it was lunchtime. Her eyes and her heart saw him, and she had broken into a run at his approach. He had come towards

275

her, too, ears sharp, nose wet, eyes bright. Of course, it had been another German Shepherd, out with a jogger, and not Peter at all.

Lotte was good with him: he would not be lacking for exercise or food in Roberta's absence. He and the stout Austrian (who looked about sixty these days, though she was ten years younger) would twice a day be seen stomping on Hampstead Heath. But he would be feeling numb and bleak. Quite possibly, he would be feeling what Roberta had felt, aged ten, when Oliver, with no warning to herself, had run away with Cuffe.

If she had one question to ask him on this noonday meeting in Manhattan, it would be this: *Why couldn't you say?* She understood well enough, with the perspective of time and age, that Oliver would have felt great embarrassment to continue living with Roberta as she grew up. She knew too much, and too much of which the others all knew nothing. She just wished, and sometimes she had wished it to the point of heartbreak, that he could have attempted, however embarrassing it was, to have come to the menagerie and made a little farewell speech.

Vanity, she had decided, plays a bigger part in the male than in the female psyche. She sometimes thought that if she had been more impressed by those notebooks, he would not have been so anxious to run away. But they *were* soppy. It had been true, but not necessarily right to say so.

There was one intimate fact which continued to interest

her. Camilla had talked about rapes. It had been the submission of the defence that none had taken place. Roberta knew by instinct that Camilla was telling the truth. She knew that Camilla's case and her own were different; that though certain things had passed between her and Oliver which a lawyer would have deemed unsavoury, she had never lost her virginity, and therefore never lost her power. He'd run away from her because she was calling the shots, and her callow refusal to be impressed by the *magnum opus* was worse than it would have been, in other circumstances, to impugn a man's virility. She knew this was the Ladybird Book of psychology, and that nothing was simple, or not so simple as that. But it did fascinate her, this knowledge. She wondered if Oliver had made it clear to Cuffe what the intimacies had been like. Had he told her about bananas and cream, and was that what made her reach for the nembutal and Smirnoff cocktail? Or had he, as Roberta always suspected, tried to tell the truth, and fudged the issue, leaving, by his vagueness about the actual physical details, a much worse impression than she would have received if he had come clean?

Would he recognize this figure who looked back at her now from the glass – black jacket, black trousers, white shirt, Gucci loafers? When did he last see a photograph of her? Margot Reisz had taken a few snaps in the garden at Belsize Park. Perhaps she had sent one of those to Larchwood Avenue? It wasn't a very good likeness of her or Lotte, but it was lovely of Peter, who sat between them, bless him, with his tongue out and his head on one side in that marvellous Jack London pose.

Oh, hell. Why had she written to Oliver Gold and suggested this meeting? She did not want to go through with it now. Anything would be better than this crashing embarrassment. Life went on. It was its only lesson, as far as Roberta had been able to discover. There was no progress in the Darwinian sense of improvement, but there was temporal progression. Her childhood self had gone, like her childhood skin. She was a different person, so was he.

If she just cut the meeting, no one would be the wiser. He would not telephone her again, nor would he come round to the hotel to bother her. It would be kinder to Michal, in many ways, to stand him up.

She took a mackintosh over one arm, and a tiny, fold-up umbrella. They'd forecast rain. There was a light drizzle falling on Madison Avenue as she stepped out of the hotel lobby. The zoo, at the southern end of Central Park, was a ten-minute walk. At this rate she would be bang on time, or even, as was her wont, a little early.

The zoo was so small that there was no danger of their missing one another. They had agreed to meet at the little kiosk where one paid for tickets. It gave her some satisfaction to have got there before him. A small queue had formed, divorced dads, mainly, and their young children. One such was standing there with a goofy grin on his face, a bald, paunchy old duffer with a white moustache and a very pretty ten-year-old child in tow. She had the china-doll neatness of appearance which had always made Roberta feel, if she were to adopt a child, that she would like one from the Far East. She guessed (rightly as it turned out) that this little girl was Vietnamese in parentage. Her jet-black bob framed a round, pale intelligent face with black currants for eyes. She wore a flimsy cotton skirt, rather short for a day of such uncertain temperature, and dark-blue jersey.

The truth dawned slightly before Roberta saw that the paunchy old duffer was holding up a copy of *Alice's Adventures in Wonderland*.

'Hi, Bobs,' he said. 'Meet Cal.'

Abacus now offers an exciting range of quality titles by both established and new authors. All of the books in this series are available from:

Little, Brown and Company (UK),
P.O. Box 11,
Falmouth,
Cornwall TR10 9EN.

Fax No: 01326 317444.
Telephone No: 01326 372400
E-mail: books@barni.avel.co.uk

Payments can be made as follows: cheque, postal order (payable to Little, Brown and Company) or by credit cards, Visa/Access. Do not send cash or currency. UK customers and B.F.P.O. please allow £1.00 for postage and packing for the first book, plus 50p for the second book, plus 30p for each additional book up to a maximum charge of £3.00 (7 books plus).

Overseas customers including Ireland, please allow £2.00 for the first book plus £1.00 for the second book, plus 50p for each additional book.

NAME (Block Letters) ....

....

ADDRESS ....

....

....

☐ I enclose my remittance for ....

☐ I wish to pay by Access/Visa Card

Number

Card Expiry Date